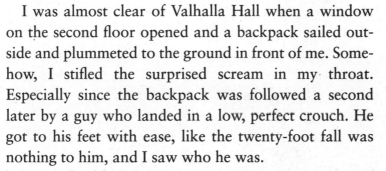

I was almost clear of Valhalla Hall when a window on the second floor opened and a backpack sailed outside and plummeted to the ground in front of me. Somehow, I stifled the surprised scream in my throat. Especially since the backpack was followed a second later by a guy who landed in a low, perfect crouch. He got to his feet with ease, like the twenty-foot fall was nothing to him, and I saw who he was.

Logan freaking Quinn.

It was more dark than light now, and the Spartan looked even more dangerous in the blackening shadows. The pale, milky moon brought out the blue highlights in his thick, wavy black hair. Logan dusted a few leaves off his designer jeans, then glanced up to find me staring at him. His eyes narrowed in his chiseled face.

"Well, well, if it isn't the Gypsy girl out here in the dark all by herself. . . ."

TOUCH OF FROST

A Mythos Academy Novel

Jennifer Estep

KENSINGTON PUBLISHING CORP.

www.kensingtonbooks.com

K TEEN BOOKS are published by

Kensington Publishing Corp.
119 West 40th Street
New York, NY 10018

ISBN-13: 978-0-7582-6692-7
ISBN-10: 0-7582-6692-8

First Kensington Trade Paperback Printing: August 2011
10 9 8 7 6 5 4

Printed in the United States of America

To my mom, my grandma, and Andre—
just for being themselves

Acknowledgments

Any author will tell you that her book would not be possible without the help and hard work of many, many people. Here are thanks for some of the folks who helped bring Gwen Frost and the world of Mythos Academy to life:

Thanks to my agent, Annelise Robey, for encouraging me to try writing a young adult book.

Thanks to my editor, Alicia Condon, for taking time out of her busy conference schedule to meet with me in the first place and for all her editorial suggestions. They really helped make the book so much better.

And, finally, thanks to all the readers out there. Entertaining you is why I write books, and it's always an honor and a privilege. I hope you have as much fun reading about Gwen's adventures as I do writing them.

Happy reading!

Chapter 1

"I know your secret."

Daphne Cruz leaned closer to the mirror over the sink and put another coat of pale pink gloss onto her lips, pointedly ignoring me the way all the pretty, popular girls did.

The way everyone did at Mythos Academy.

"I know your secret," I repeated in a louder voice.

I pushed away from the statue of a sea nymph that I'd been leaning against, strolled over to the door that led out of the girls' bathroom, and locked it. I might not care who knew Daphne's dirty little secret, but I was willing to bet that she would before we were through. That's why I'd made sure that all of the white marble stalls were empty and waited for the rest of Daphne's friends to leave their spots on the cushioned settee in the corner before I'd approached her.

Once Daphne was satisfied that her lips were glossed to a high sheen, she dropped the tube into the depths of her oversize pink Dooney & Bourke purse. Next, she drew out a hairbrush and went to work on her smooth, golden locks. Still ignoring me.

I crossed my arms over my chest, leaned against the door, and waited. The intricate raised figures of warriors and monsters carved into the heavy wooden door pressed against my back, but I ignored the odd lumps and bumps. The two hundred bucks I was getting for this job meant that I could afford to be patient.

After another two minutes, when her hair had been brushed a dozen times and she realized that I wasn't actually, you know, *leaving,* Daphne finally deigned to turn and look at me. Her black eyes flicked over my jeans, graphic T-shirt, and purple zip-up hoodie, and she let out a little snort of disgust, obviously offended that I wasn't wearing the latest designer threads like she was. That I didn't have the matchy-match look down pat that she and her friends had going on.

Apparently, today's theme had been argyle, because the pattern was on everything that Daphne wore, from her pink cashmere sweater to her black pleated skirt to the printed black and pink tights that showed off her legs. The contrast of light and dark colors made her perfect, amber skin look that much more luminous. So did the shiny lip gloss.

"You know my secret?" Daphne repeated, a sneer creeping into her voice. "And what secret would that be?"

So the Valkyrie wanted to be snotty. Not a problem.

I smiled. "I know you took the charm bracelet. The one that Carson Callahan was going to give to Leta

Gaston as a *will-you-go-to-the-homecoming-dance-with-me* present. You snatched it off the desk in his dorm room yesterday when he was helping you with your English lit paper."

For the first time, doubt flickered in Daphne's eyes, and disbelief filled her pretty face before she was able to hide it. Now, she was looking at me—*really* looking at me—trying to figure out who I was and what I wanted. After a moment, her eyes narrowed.

"You're that Gypsy girl," Daphne muttered. "The one who sees things."

That Gypsy girl. That's what everyone at Mythos Academy called me. Mainly because I was the only Gypsy trapped here in this school for magical warrior freaks. The middle-class girl whose strange ability had landed her here among the rich, popular, and undeniably powerful. Like Daphne Cruz, a spoiled, pampered wannabe princess who also happened to be a Valkyrie.

"What's your name?" Daphne asked. "Gail? Gretchen?"

Wow. I was impressed that she even knew it started with a G.

"Gwen," I told her. "Gwen Frost."

"Well, Gwen Frost," Daphne said, turning her attention back to her purse. "I have no idea what you're talking about."

Her voice and face were both just as smooth as the gilded silver mirror in front of her. I might have even believed her, if her hands hadn't clenched the tiniest bit as she put her hairbrush back into her purse. If I hadn't known just how good girls like her could lie.

Just how good everyone could lie.

I reached into my gray messenger bag and drew out a clear plastic bag. A small silver charm shaped like a rose glinted inside. I might as well have shown her a bag full of pot from the way Daphne visibly recoiled.

"Where—where did you get that?" she whispered.

"Carson hadn't finished putting all the charms on Leta's bracelet when he showed it to you during your tutoring session yesterday afternoon," I said. "I found this one way, way back behind his desk in his dorm room. It fell down there when you grabbed the bracelet and stuffed it into your purse."

Daphne let out a laugh, still keeping up the act. "And why would I do something like that?"

"Because you're crazy about Carson. You don't want him to ask out Leta. You want him for yourself."

Daphne slumped over, her hands dropping to one of the sinks that lined the wall below the mirror. Her fingers curled around the silver faucets, which were shaped like Hydra heads, before sliding down to the basin. Her French-manicured nails scraped across the white marble, and pale pink sparks of magic shot out of her fingertips. Daphne might only be seventeen like me, but Valkyries were incredibly strong. I knew that if she wanted to, Daphne Cruz could rip that sink out of the wall easier than the Hulk could.

Maybe I should have been scared of the Valkyrie, of the weird princess pink sparks, and especially of her strength and what she could do to me with it. But I wasn't. I'd already lost one of the people I cared about most. Everything else dulled in comparison to that.

"How do you know all that?" Daphne asked, her voice barely above a whisper.

I shrugged. "Because, as you put it, I see things. And as soon as I found this charm, I knew that you were the one who took the bracelet."

I didn't tell Daphne anything else about my Gypsy gift, about my ability to know an object's history just by touching it, and she didn't ask.

Instead, the Valkyrie kept staring at me with her black eyes. After about thirty seconds of silence, she came to some sort of decision. Daphne straightened, reached into her bag once more, and drew out her wallet. It matched her designer purse.

"All right," she said. "How much will it take for you to give me that charm and forget about this whole thing? A hundred dollars? Two?"

This time, my hands were the ones that clenched into fists. She was trying to buy me off. I'd expected nothing less, but the gesture still made me angry. Like everyone else at Mythos Academy, Daphne Cruz could afford the very best of everything. A few hundred dollars was nothing to her. She'd spent that much on her freaking *purse*.

But a few hundred dollars wasn't nothing to me. It was clothes and comic books and a cell phone and a dozen other things that girls like Daphne never had to worry about.

"Carson's already paid me," I said.

"So?" she said. "I'll pay you more. However much you want."

"Sorry. Once I give my word to somebody, I keep it. And I told Carson that I would find the charm bracelet for him."

Daphne tilted her head to the side like I was some strange creature that she'd never seen before, some mythological monster masquerading as a teenage girl. Maybe it was stupid of me, not taking her up on the cash that she was so willing to give me. But my mom wouldn't have taken Daphne's money, not if she'd already made a promise to someone else. My mom, Grace, had been a Gypsy, just like me. With a gift, just like me.

For a moment, my heart ached with guilt and longing. My mom was gone, and I missed her *so much*. I shook my head, more to push the pain aside than anything else.

"Look, just give me the bracelet. That's all I want. That's all Carson wants."

Daphne's lips tightened. "He—he knows? That I took the bracelet? And why?"

"Not yet. But he's going to if you don't give it to me. Right *now*."

I opened the top of the plastic bag and held it out to her. Daphne stared at the rose charm glinting inside. She bit her pink lip, smearing her gloss on her teeth, and looked away.

"Fine," she muttered. "I don't know why I even took it in the first place."

I did because I'd flashed on Daphne when I'd touched the charm. As soon as my fingers had brushed the silver rose, an image of the blond Valkyrie had popped into my head. I'd seen Daphne sitting at Carson's desk, staring at the bracelet, her fingers tightening around the metal links like she wanted to rip them in two.

And I'd felt the other girl's emotions, too, the way that I always did whenever I touched an object or even another person. I'd felt Daphne's hot, pulsing jealousy that Carson was thinking about asking out Leta. The warm, soft, fizzy crush that Daphne had on Carson herself, despite the fact that he was a total band geek and she was part of the popular crowd. Her cold, aching despair that she didn't like someone the rest of her snobby friends would approve of.

But I didn't tell Daphne any of that. The less people knew about my gift and the things I saw and felt, the better.

Daphne yanked the bracelet out of her bag. Carson Callahan might be a band geek, but he had money, too, which was why the bracelet was a heavy, expensive thing loaded down with a dozen charms that jingled together. Daphne's nails scraped against one of the charms, a small heart, and more pink sparks of magic fluttered like fireflies in the air.

I held out the bag again, and Daphne dropped the bracelet inside. I closed the top and tied off the plastic, careful not to touch the jewelry itself. I didn't want another slide show into Daphne Cruz's psyche. The first one had almost made me feel sorry for her.

But any sympathy I might have had for Daphne vanished when the Valkyrie gave me the cold, haughty stare that so many mean girls before her had perfected.

"You tell anyone about this, Gwen Frost, and I'll strangle you with that ugly purple hoodie you're wearing. Understand me?"

"Sure," I said in a pleasant tone. "But you might want to pull yourself together before you go to your next class, Daphne. Your lip gloss is smeared."

The Valkyrie's eyes narrowed, but I ignored her venomous dirty look, unlocked the bathroom door, and left.

Chapter 2

I stepped out of the bathroom and into the hallway. Somewhere deeper in the building, a bell chimed, warning me that I had five minutes to get to my next class, so I fell in with the flow of students walking toward the west wing of the English-history building.

From the outside, Mythos Academy looked like an elite Ivy League prep school, even though it was located in Cypress Mountain, just outside of Asheville, up in the high country of western North Carolina. Everything about the academy whispered of money, power, and snobbery, from the ivy-covered stone buildings to the perfectly manicured grassy quads to the dining hall that was more like a five-star restaurant than a school cafeteria. Yeah, from the outside, the academy looked *exactly* like the kind of place rich people would send their spoiled trust fund babies to in preparation for them going on to Yale, Harvard, Duke, or some other acceptably expensive college.

Inside, though, it was a different story.

At first glance, everything looked normal, if a bit stuffy and totally old-fashioned. You know, suits of polished armor lining the halls, each one clutching a sharp, pointed weapon. Stone carvings and expensive oil paintings of mythological battles covering the walls. White marble statues of gods and goddesses standing in the corners, their faces turned toward each other and hands held up over their mouths, as if they were gossiping about everyone who passed by their perches.

And then, there were the students. Ages sixteen to twenty-one, first-year students all the way up to sixth-years, all shapes, sizes, and ethnicities, with books and bags in one hand and their cell phones in the other, texting, talking, and walking all at the same time. Each one wearing the most expensive clothes their parents could afford, including Prada, Gucci, and, of course, Jimmy Choos.

But if you looked past the designer duds and flashy electronics, you'd notice other things. Strange things. Like the fact that so many of the students carried weapons. Swords, bows, and staffs mostly, all stuffed into what looked like fancy leather tennis bags. Color-coordinated to match the day's outfit, of course.

The weapons were just accessories at Mythos. Status symbols of who you were, what you could do, and how much money your parents had. Just like the colorful sparks and flashes of magic that crackled in the air like static electricity. Even the lowliest geek here knew how to chop off somebody's head with a sword or could turn your insides to mush just by muttering a spell or two.

It was like going to school in an episode of *Xena: Warrior Princess.*

That's what all the kids at Mythos Academy were—warriors. Real, live mythological warriors. Or at least the great-great-whatever descendants of them. The girls were Amazons and Valkyries, for the most part, while the boys tended to be Romans or Vikings. But there were other warrior types mixed in as well—Spartans, Persians, Trojans, Celts, Samurais, Ninjas, and everything in between, from every ancient culture, myth, or fairy tale that you'd ever heard of and lots that you hadn't. Each one with their own special abilities and magic, and the egos to match.

As a general rule, though, everyone was rich, beautiful, and dangerous.

Everyone except for me.

Nobody looked at me and nobody spoke to me as I trudged toward my sixth-period myth-history class. I was just *that Gypsy girl,* and not rich, powerful, popular, pretty, or important enough to register on anyone's social radar. It was late October now, almost two months into the fall term, and I had yet to make a friend. I didn't even have a casual someone I could sit with at lunch in the dining hall. But my friendless state didn't bother me.

Not much had, since my mom's death six months ago.

I slid into my seat in Professor Metis's myth-history class just before the bell chimed again, indicating that everyone should be where they were supposed to be by now.

Carson Callahan turned around in his seat, which was in front of mine. "Did you find it yet?" he whispered.

Carson was a tall guy, six feet even with a bony, lanky frame. He always reminded me of a triangle, because he was all sharp angles, from his ankles to his knees to his elbows. Even his nose was straight and pointed. His hair and skin were a dusky brown, and the square frames of his black glasses made his eyes look like malted milk balls set into his face.

I could see why Daphne liked him, though. Carson was sweet and cute, in that shy, quiet way that geeks so often are. But Carson Callahan wasn't just any kind of geek—he was a hard-core band geek and the drum major of the Mythos Academy Marching Band, even though he was only seventeen and a second-year student like me. Carson was a Celt and supposedly had some sort of magical talent for music, like a warrior bard or something. I didn't know what exactly. For the most part, I tried not to notice such things. I tried not to notice a lot of things at Mythos—especially the fact of how very much I didn't belong here.

I handed Carson the bagged bracelet, careful not to let my fingers touch his so I wouldn't flash on the band geek. Because in addition to feeling Daphne's emotions, I'd also gotten a glimpse of Carson's when I'd fished the rose charm out from behind his desk yesterday. I didn't just see the person who had touched something last—I could flash on everyone who'd ever handled an object. *Ever.*

Which meant that I knew who Carson really wanted to give the silver bracelet to and that it wasn't Leta Gaston like he claimed.

"As promised," I said. "Now, it's your turn."

"Thanks, Gwen."

He put a hundred-dollar bill, the back end of my finder's fee, onto my desk. I took the money and slid it into my jeans pocket.

As a general rule, I ignored all the other Mythos students, and they ignored me—at least until they needed something found. It was the same gig that I'd done back at my old public high school to earn extra cash. For the right price, I found things that were lost, stolen, or otherwise unavailable. Keys, wallets, cell phones, pets, abandoned bras, and crumpled boxers.

I'd overheard an Amazon in my calculus class complaining that she'd lost her cell phone, so I'd offered to find it for her, for a small fee. She'd thought I was nuts—until I fished the phone out of the back of her closet. Turned out that she'd left it in another purse. After that, word had spread around campus about what I did. Business wasn't exactly booming yet, but it was picking up.

Since my Gypsy gift let me touch an object and immediately know, see, and feel its history, it wasn't too hard for me to find or figure things out. Sure, if something was lost, I couldn't actually, you know, touch *it*—otherwise, the item wouldn't be missing in the first place. But people left vibes everywhere—about all sorts of things. What they had for lunch, what movie they wanted to see tonight, what they really thought of their so-called best friends.

Usually, all I had to do was skim my fingers across a guy's desk or rummage through a girl's purse to get a pretty good idea about where he'd last left his wallet or where she'd put down her cell phone. And if I didn't immediately see the exact location of the missing item, then I kept touching stuff until I did—or got an image of who might have swiped it. Like Daphne Cruz snatching the charm bracelet off Carson's desk. Sometimes, I felt like Nancy Drew or maybe Gretel, following a trail of psychic bread crumbs until I found what I was looking for.

There was even a name for what I could do—psychometry. A fancy, froufrou way of saying that I saw pictures in my head and got flashes of other people's feelings—whether I wanted to see them or not.

Still, part of me enjoyed knowing other people's secrets, seeing all the things big and small that they so desperately tried to hide from everyone, including themselves sometimes. It made me feel smart and strong and powerful—and determined not to do totally stupid things, like let a guy take pictures of me in my underwear.

Tracking down lost cell phones might not be the most

glamorous job in the world, but it was way better than slinging greasy fries at Mickey D's. And it certainly paid much more here at Mythos than it had at my old public high school. Back there, I would have been lucky to get twenty bucks for a lost bracelet, instead of the cool two hundred that Carson had given me. The bonus cash flow was the only thing I liked about the stupid academy.

"Where was it?" Carson asked. "The bracelet?"

For a moment, I thought about ratting out Daphne and telling Carson about her massive crush on him. But since the Valkyrie hadn't been overtly mean to me in the bathroom, just vaguely threatening, I decided to save that bit of information for a time when I might really need it. Since I didn't have money, strength, or great magical power like the other kids at the academy, information was the only real leverage that I had, and I saw no reason not to stock up.

"Oh, I found it behind your desk in your dorm room." The rose charm anyway. It had been wedged deep down between the desk and the wall.

Carson frowned. "But I looked there. I know I did. I looked everywhere for it."

"I guess you just didn't look hard enough," I said in a vague tone, and pulled my myth-history book out of my bag.

Carson opened his mouth to ask me something else when Professor Metis rapped on her podium with the old-fashioned slender silver scepter that she also used as a pointer. Metis was of Greek descent, like so many of the profs and kids at Mythos were. She was a short woman with a thick, stocky body, bronze skin, and black hair that was always pulled back into a high, tight bun. She wore a green pantsuit, and silver glasses covered her face.

She looked all stern and serious, but Metis was one of the better professors at Mythos. She at least tried to make her myth-history class interesting by sometimes letting us play games and do puzzles and stuff, rather than just memorizing boring facts.

"Open your books to page one thirty-nine," Professor Metis said, her soft green gaze flicking from student to student. "Today, we're going to talk some more about the Pantheon as its warriors battled to defeat Loki and his Reapers of Chaos."

But today wasn't going to be a fun day. I rolled my eyes and did as she asked.

In addition to going to school with all the mythological warrior kids, I also had to learn about their whole stupid history. And, of course, there was a group of good magic guys who had banded together and called themselves the Pantheon whose sole purpose was to fight a group of bad magic guys called Reapers who wanted to, well, bring about the Chaos.

So far, Professor Metis had been pretty vague about what exactly *the Chaos* was, and I hadn't exactly been paying rapt attention to all the mumbo-jumbo magic stuff. But I was guessing it involved death, destruction, and blah, blah, blah. I'd much rather read the comic books that I had stashed in the bottom of my messenger bag. At least they had some basis in reality. Genetic mutations could *totally* happen.

But gods and goddesses duking it out? Using warrior whiz kids to fight some ancient battle today in modern times? With mythological monsters thrown in just for fun? I wasn't sure I believed all *that*. But everyone here at Mythos did. To them, myths weren't just stories— they were *history, facts* even, and they were all very, very *real*.

While Professor Metis droned on once again about how absolutely evil the Reapers were, I stared out the window, looking at my reflection in the glass. Wavy brown hair, a smattering of freckles on my winter white skin, and eyes that were a curious shade of purple, made more so by the hoodie I was wearing.

Violet eyes are smiling eyes, my mom had always said in a teasing voice. Her eyes had been the same color as mine, although I'd always thought they'd made her look beautiful and me just like a freak.

A dull ache flooded my heart. Not for the first time, I wished that I could rewind time and go back to the way things had been before I'd come to Mythos Academy.

Six months ago, I'd been a normal teenager. Well, as normal as a girl with a strange ability could ever be. But the Gypsy gift ran in the Frost family. My grandma, Geraldine, could see the future. My mom, Grace, had been able to tell whether or not people were lying just by listening to their words. And I had the ability to know, see, and feel things just by touching a person or an object. But our Gypsy gifts had always been just that—gifts, small things that we could do—and I hadn't thought too much about them, where they had come from, or if other people had magic like ours.

Until the day that I picked up Paige Forrest's hairbrush after gym class.

We'd been in the locker room changing after playing basketball, which I hated because I totally sucked at it. Seriously, sucked *out loud* at it. Like, sucked so bad that I'd managed to hit myself in the head with the ball when I was trying to shoot a free throw.

After class, I'd been hot and sweaty and had wanted to pull my hair back into a ponytail. Paige's brush had been lying on the bench between us. Paige wasn't one of my close friends, but we were in the same semipopular circle of smart girls. Sometimes, we hung out when our group got together, so I'd asked her if I could use her hairbrush.

Paige had stared at me a second, a strange emotion flashing in her eyes. "Sure."

I picked it up, never dreaming that I'd feel anything. Despite my psychometry, I usually didn't get much of a vibe off common, everyday objects like pens, computers, dishes, or phones. Things in public places that lots of people used or that had a simple, specific function. I only got the biggies, the deep, vivid, high-def flashes, when I touched objects that people had some personal connection to, like a favorite photograph or a cherished piece of jewelry.

But as soon as my hand had closed around the hairbrush, I'd seen an image of Paige sitting on her bed with an older man. He'd brushed her long black hair exactly one hundred times, just like everyone claims you're supposed to. Then, when he was finished with her hair, the man had unfastened Paige's robe, made her lie back on the bed, and started touching her before he took off his pants.

I'd started screaming then, and I didn't stop.

After about five minutes, I passed out. My friend Bethany had told me that I'd kept right on screaming, even when the paramedics came to take me to the hospital. Everyone thought I was having an epileptic seizure or something.

I think Paige knew, though. About my Gypsy gift and what I could do. Two weeks before, she'd asked me to find her missing phone. I'd walked around Paige's room, touched her desk, her nightstand, her purse, and her bookcases, and eventually seen an image of her little sister swiping the phone so she could snoop through Paige's text messages. Sometimes, I wondered if Paige had put her hairbrush there on the bench just for me to pick up. Just so someone would *know,* just so someone would *feel* exactly what she was going through.

I'd woken up in the hospital later that day. My mom, Grace, was there, and I told her what I'd seen. That's what you did when something terrible was happening to one of your friends. And because my mom was a police detective who'd spent her whole life helping people. I wanted to be just like her.

That night, my mom had arrested Paige's stepdad for abusing her. My mom had called when she was at the police station and told me that Paige was safe now. She'd promised to be home in another hour, just as soon as she finished the paperwork.

She never made it.

My mom had been hit by a drunk driver after she'd left the police station that night. Grandma Frost had told me that she'd died instantly. That she'd never even seen the other car swerving toward her or felt the horrible, horrible pain of the crash. I hoped that was how it had happened, because my mom had been so torn up in the wreck that the casket had been closed at her funeral. What I could remember of it, anyway.

I hadn't gone back to my old school after that. My friends had been supernice about everything, especially Bethany, but I hadn't wanted to see anyone. I hadn't wanted to do anything but lie on my bed and cry.

But one day three weeks after my mom's funeral, Professor Metis had shown up at my Grandma Frost's house. I didn't know exactly what Metis had said to her, but Grandma had announced that it was finally time for me to go to Mythos Academy so I could learn how to fully use my Gypsy gift. I thought that I could control my psychometry just fine already, and I'd never really understood what my grandma had meant when she'd said *finally,* as if I should have been going to Mythos all along or something—

"...Gwen?"

The sound of my name snapped me out of my memories. "What?"

Metis peered over the rims of her silver glasses at me. "I asked you which goddess was responsible for the Pantheon's victory over Loki and his Reapers?"

"Nike, the Greek goddess of victory," I said automatically.

Professor Metis frowned. "And how do you know that, Gwen? I haven't mentioned Nike yet. Have you read ahead to the next chapter already? That's very industrious of you."

I'd done that very thing last night, mainly because I was bored out of my mind and there hadn't been anything good on TV. Given my lack of friends at Mythos, it wasn't like I had anything else to do to occupy my time here.

I don't think Metis meant it as a jibe, but snickers rippled through the room at her words. My cheeks flamed red, and I sank a little lower into my seat. Great. Now, everyone would think that I was *that nerdy Gypsy girl* who had nothing better to do than study. It might be true, and I might be insanely proud of my 4.0 GPA, but I didn't want the other kids to know that.

It occurred to me that I wasn't quite sure how I knew the answer to Metis's question. I didn't think Nike had even been mentioned in the chapter that I'd read. But since it wasn't the strangest thing that I'd encountered at Mythos, I pushed it out of my mind.

Professor Metis speared one of the louder snickerers with a dirty look before asking him an even more obscure question about Reapers.

When I was sure Metis wasn't going to call on me again, I went back to staring out the window and brooding about how I'd caused my own mom's death just by picking up the wrong girl's hairbrush.

Chapter 3

Myth-history was my last class of the day. As soon as the bell rang, I stuffed my textbook into my bag.

"See ya, Gwen."

Carson Callahan called out a cheery good-bye and slid the plastic bag with the charm bracelet into one of the pockets on his designer khaki cargo pants. I nodded at him, shouldered my bag, and left.

I walked down the crowded hallway, pushed through the first door I came to, and stepped outside. Five main buildings made up the heart of Mythos Academy— math-science, English-history, the gym, the dining hall, and the library—all grouped together in a loose cluster, like the five points of a star. Even though I'd been going here for two months now, the buildings all looked the same to me—dark gray stone covered with thick, heavy vines of glossy ivy. Large, creepy Gothic structures, with towers and parapets and balconies. Statues of various mythological monsters like gryphons and Gorgons perched on all the buildings, their mouths open in silent, angry snarls.

An enormous open quad and a series of curving walkways connected the five buildings to each other before the ash gray cobblestones snaked down a hill and farther out to the student dorms and the other structures that made up the rest of the lush academy grounds. Green grass still rolled over the smooth lawns, despite the October chill. Here and there, tall maples and oaks spread their limbs wide, their leaves holding on to the last bright blazes of bloody crimson and pumpkin orange.

I zipped up my hoodie, stuck my hands in my pockets, and headed across the quad, skirting around the groups of students who'd stopped to talk, pull out their cell phones, and check their messages. I'd made it about halfway when high, trilling laughter caught my ear.

I turned my head and saw Jasmine Ashton holding court underneath the towering maple tree that stood in the center of the quad.

Jasmine Ashton was the most popular girl in my class, which was made up of the seventeen-year-old, second-year students. Jasmine was also a Valkyrie with a mane of strawberry-blond hair, bright blue eyes, and the most expensive designer clothes that money could buy. She was the kind of girl who made everyone else look plain— even her thin, gorgeous, similarly dressed friends. Jasmine sat on an iron bench underneath the maple tree, looking at something on her laptop and giggling, along with Morgan McDougall, her best friend.

With her black hair, hazel eyes, curvy body, and super-short skirts, Morgan was only slightly less beautiful and popular than Jasmine, which made her the number-two diva in our class. Morgan's reputation for being a raging slut who'd sleep with almost anyone made her number one with the guys, though. Naturally.

Two more girls sat on either side of Jasmine and Morgan, while Daphne Cruz perched on a fleece blanket on the grass in front of the bench. All the popular Valkyrie princesses tended to stick together.

The girls weren't alone. Samson Sorensen stood behind Jasmine, rubbing her shoulders with the rapt devotion of a slave. No wonder, since the Viking was Jasmine's boyfriend and one of the cutest guys in school. Sandy brown hair, hazel eyes, dimples. Samson could have easily passed for a Calvin Klein model. He also happened to be the captain of the swim team. No football here. All the kids at Mythos did fancy, froufrou sports like swimming, tennis, archery, and fencing. Seriously, fencing. What was the point of that?

Seeing Jasmine and Samson together was like staring at a life-size version of Ken and Barbie. They just looked that perfect together, like they'd been made for each other.

The other students at Mythos might not pay much attention to me, but I was still able to hear plenty of juicy gossip on my own. Rumor had it that there was Big Trouble in paradise between the happy couple. Evidently, Samson was ready to go All the Way, since he and Jasmine had been dating since last year, but she wasn't ready to cash in her V Card just yet—

I was so busy staring at them that I slammed into a guy walking the opposite way across the quad. And, of course, my messenger bag slid off my shoulder and hit the ground, spilling my books everywhere. Because that's just what happened to girls like me.

"Sorry," I muttered, falling to my knees and attempting to scoop everything back into my bag before anyone got a good look at anything, especially the now-empty tin of chocolate-chip cookies that Grandma Frost had baked for me and the comic books that had slid out. The colorful pages flapped and fluttered like dragonflies in the breeze.

Instead of walking around me like I'd expected him to, the guy I'd hit decided to crouch down next to me instead. My eyes flicked up to his face. It took me a second to recognize him, but when I did, I froze. Because Logan Quinn was the guy I'd just rammed into.

Uh-oh.

Even among the rich warrior kids at Mythos, Logan Quinn was the kind of guy who scared *everyone*. He did whatever he wanted, whenever he wanted to. And a lot of what he liked to do involved hurting people.

Everything about Logan screamed *bad boy,* from his thick, silky, ink-black hair to his intense ice blue eyes to the black leather jacket that highlighted his broad shoulders. Oh yeah, he was sexy, in a rough, rumpled, *I-just-climbed-out-of-some-girl's-bed* kind of way. Apparently, Logan lived up to the hype and was well on his way to sleeping with most, if not all, of the hottest girls at Mythos. Supposedly, he signed the mattresses of the girls that he scored with just to keep track of all of them. Something that the other guys had taken to doing, although not with as much success as Logan. Except maybe in Morgan McDougall's room.

Logan Quinn was also descended from a long line of Spartans. Yeah, *those* Spartans, the warriors who held off thousands of bad guys before most of them kicked it at the ancient battle of Thermopylae. All of which had been brought to life by Gerard Butler and his chiseled man abs in *300*. Professor Metis had let us watch the movie in class three weeks ago, before she proceeded to lecture us about the historical importance of the battle. But Gerard's abs had been impressive enough for me to daydream about them and tune out Metis.

There were only a handful of Spartans here at Mythos, but all the other students tread carefully around them. Even the richest, snobbiest kid knew better than to piss off a Spartan. At least, to his face anyway. That's because Spartans were hands-down the best fighters at the academy. Spartans were born warriors. That's all they knew how to do, and that's all they ever did.

Unlike the other kids, Logan Quinn didn't carry a weapon with him. Neither did the rest of the Spartans I'd seen. They didn't need to. One of the things that Spartans were known for was their ability to pick up any weapon—or any *thing*—and automatically know how to use and even kill someone with it. Seriously. Logan Quinn was the kind of guy who could stab me in the eye with a freaking Twizzler.

Sometimes, I didn't know if I really believed all the

crazy stuff around me. Like Spartans and Valkyries and Reapers. Sometimes, I wondered if I was stuck in an insane asylum somewhere, just dreaming all this. Like Buffy. But if that was the case, you'd think that I would be having a better time, that I'd at least imagine myself to be one of the popular Valkyrie princesses or something—

Logan reached for one of the Wonder Woman comics that had been in my bag. The motion snapped me out of my daze.

"Give me that!"

I snatched the comic book up off the grass. I didn't want Logan Quinn contaminating my things with his scary, Spartan, psycho-killer vibes, which could happen if he touched them. That's how objects got emotions attached to them in the first place—by people touching and handling and using them over time. I stuffed the Wonder Woman issue deep into my bag, along with all the others and the empty cookie tin, which was shaped like the chocolate-chip treats it had once held.

Logan raised an eyebrow but didn't say anything at my obvious freak-out.

"Sorry I ran into you," I muttered again, getting to my feet. "Don't kill me, okay?"

Logan also stood, and this time his mouth lifted up into something that almost looked like a smile. "I don't know," he murmured. "Gypsy girls make for awful easy killing. Wouldn't take but just a second."

His voice was deeper than I'd thought it would be, with a rich, throaty timbre. Startled, I looked up and stared into his face—and spotted the amusement sparkling in his icy gaze.

My own eyes narrowed. I didn't like being made fun of, not even by a dangerous bad boy like Logan Quinn. "Yeah, well, this Gypsy girl happens to have a grandma who can curse you so bad that your dick will turn black and fall off, so watch your step, Spartan."

That wasn't true, of course. My Grandma Frost saw the future. She didn't curse people—at least, not that I knew of. It was hard to tell with Grandma sometimes. But there was no reason for Logan Quinn to know that I was bluffing.

Instead of being intimidated, his mouth made that smiling motion again. "I think I'd rather watch you walk away, Gypsy girl."

I frowned. Was he—was he actually *flirting* with me? I couldn't tell, and I didn't want to stick around to find out. Keeping one eye on Logan Quinn, I carefully skirted around him and hurried on my way.

But for some reason, his soft laughter followed me all the way across the quad.

I left the smooth, grassy quad behind, strolled by the dorms and other smaller outbuildings, and walked to the edge of campus, where a twelve-foot-high stone wall separated Mythos Academy from the outside world. Two sphinxes perched on top of the wall on either side of the entrance, staring down at the black iron gate that lay between them.

Supposedly, the wall and the gate were enchanted,

imbued with spells and other magic mumbo jumbo so that only people who were supposed to be at the academy—students, teachers, and the like—could pass through. When I'd come to Mythos, at the beginning of the fall semester, Professor Metis had made me stand in the entrance right between the two sphinxes while she'd said a few words in a low voice. The statues hadn't moved, hadn't blinked, hadn't done anything but sit on their high perches, but I'd still felt like there was something inside the stone figures—some old, ancient, violent force that would rip me to pieces if I so much as breathed wrong. That had been the first creepy thing that I'd experienced at Mythos. Too bad it hadn't been the last.

After Metis had finished her chant, spell, or whatever it had been, she'd told me that I was now free to enter the academy grounds, like I'd been given the password to the supersecret Fearless Five superhero lair or something. I didn't know exactly what would happen if someone who wasn't supposed to be at the academy—like, say, a Reaper bad guy—tried to slip through the gate or climb the wall, but surely those sphinxes and their long, curved claws weren't just for decoration.

I wondered about a lot of things that I would have been better off forgetting about entirely.

Metis had also told me that the sphinxes were only designed to keep people out—not trap students inside—and that I shouldn't be afraid of them. It was kind of hard to be afraid of something that you didn't really believe in. At least, that's what I kept telling myself every time I snuck off campus.

I glanced around to make sure no one else was in sight, then jogged up to the gate, turned sideways, sucked in my stomach, and slipped through one of the gaps in the bars. I didn't look up at the sphinxes, but I could almost feel their watchful eyes on me. *They're just statues,* I told myself. *Just statues. Ugly ones at that. They can't hurt me. Not really.*

A second later, I slid free of the bars to the other side. I let out a breath and kept walking. I didn't turn around and look back at the statues to see if they were really watching me or not. Whether I believed in the sphinxes' magic or not, I knew better than to tempt fate.

Students weren't supposed to leave the academy during weekdays, which was why the gate was shut. Professor Metis and the other Powers That Were at the school liked all the warrior whiz kids to stay close by so they could keep an eye on them, at least during school nights.

But I'd been sneaking out ever since I'd gotten here two months ago, and I'd seen other kids do the same, usually on beer or cigarette runs. What was the worst they could do to me? Kick me out? After all the freaky stuff that I'd seen here, I'd be *thrilled* to go back to public high school. I wouldn't even complain about the crappy cafeteria food—much.

Mythos might be its own little world, but what lay beyond the wall was surprisingly normal, since Cypress

Mountain was a charming little suburb in its own right. A two-lane road curved around in front of the school, and a variety of shops clustered on the other side, directly across from the imposing spiked iron gate. A bookstore, some coffee shops, several high-end clothing and jewelry boutiques, even a car lot full of Aston Martins and Cadillac Escalades. And, of course, a couple of upscale wine stores that helped the academy kids party hard, despite the supposed campus ban on alcohol.

The shops were all located here to take advantage of the limitless credit cards and enormous trust funds of the Mythos students. Apparently, the gods and goddesses had all rewarded their mythological warriors with sacks full of gold, silver, and jewels back in the day and the various descendants of those warriors had kept the gravy train of wealth going, adding to their bank balances over the years, which was why all the kids at the academy were so loaded today.

I waited for a lull in the traffic, crossed the street, and walked down to the bus stop at the end of the block. I only had to wait five minutes before the bus rumbled by on its midafternoon route, taking tourists and everyone else who wanted to ride from Cypress Mountain down into the city. Twenty minutes and several miles later, I got off in a neighborhood that was a couple of streets removed from the artsy downtown Asheville shops and restaurants.

If Cypress Mountain was some whacked-out version of Mount Olympus with its population of rich warrior whiz kids, then Asheville was definitely where the poor mere mortals lived. Older, well-worn homes lined either side of the street, mostly two- and three-story houses that had been cut up into apartments. I knew the area well. My Grandma Frost had lived in the same house all her life, and my mom and I had only been a few miles away in one of Asheville's modest middle-class subdivisions. At least when I'd started going to Mythos I hadn't had to move across the country or anything. I don't think I could have survived being that far away from Grandma Frost. She was the only family I had left now that my mom was gone. My dad, Tyr, had died from cancer when I was two, and the only memories I had of him were the faded photos my mom had shown me.

I walked to the end of the block and skipped up the gray concrete steps of a three-story house painted a soft shade of lavender. A small sign beside the front door read: *Psychic Readings Here.*

I opened the screen door, then used my key to let myself inside. A heavy black lacquered door off to my right was closed, although the murmur of soft voices drifted out from behind it. Grandma Frost must be giving one of her readings. Grandma used her Gypsy gift to make extra cash, just like I did.

I walked through the hallway that ran through the middle of the house and veered left, going into the kitchen. Unlike the rest of the house, which featured dark paneling and somber gray carpet, the kitchen had a bright white tile floor and sky blue walls. I slung my messenger bag onto the table and dug the hundred that Carson Callahan had given me out of my jeans pocket. I stuffed the money into a jar that looked like a giant chocolate-chip cookie. It matched the empty tin in my messenger bag.

Ever since I'd started going to Mythos, I always gave half of whatever money I made to Grandma Frost. Yeah, my grandma had plenty of money of her own, more than enough to take care of us both. But I liked helping out, especially since my mom was gone. Besides, giving Grandma the money made me feel like I was doing something useful with my Gypsy gift, besides just finding some girl's lost bra that she should have known better than to take off in the first place.

My eyes flicked over the other bills inside the cookie jar. Grandma had had a good week giving her readings. I spotted two more hundreds in there, along with a couple of fifties and a few twenties.

The voices kept murmuring in the other room, so I raided the fridge. I fixed myself a tomato sandwich sprinkled with salt, pepper, and just a dash of dill weed. A thick slice of sharp cheddar cheese and a layer of creamy mayonnaise completed the sandwich, along with my favorite, yeasty sourdough bread. For dessert, I sliced off a piece of the sweet, spongy pumpkin roll that Grandma had stashed in the fridge. I licked a stray bit of cream cheese frosting off the knife. Yum. So good.

In addition to our Gypsy gifts, all of the Frost women had raging sweet tooths. Seriously, if it had sugar or chocolate (or preferably both) in it, Grandma and I would totally eat it. My mom had been the same way, too. Grandma also happened to be an awesome cook and an even better baker, so there was always something gooey and sinful in her kitchen, usually fresh out of the oven.

I ate my dinner, scraping every last one of the pumpkin roll crumbs up off my plate with a fork, then cleaned up. Once that was done, I pulled out one of my Wonder Woman comic books and settled myself at the kitchen table, waiting for Grandma Frost to finish with her client.

Yeah, maybe liking superheroes made me even more of a geek than I already was, but I enjoyed reading comics. The art was cool, the characters were interesting, and the heroine always won in the end, no matter what bad stuff happened along the way. I only wished real life was like that—and that my mom had somehow walked away from her car accident the way that I'd read about so many heroes doing over the years.

The old, familiar pain pricked my heart, but I pushed away my sad thoughts and dove into the story, losing myself in the adventure until I almost forgot about how much my own life sucked—almost.

I'd just finished reading the last page when my grandma stepped into the kitchen.

Geraldine Frost wore a gauzy silk purple blouse, along with a pair of loose black pants and slippers with curled pointed toes that made her look like a genie. Not that you could really see what Grandma was wearing, since scarves covered her from head to toe. Purple, gray, emerald green. All those colors and more flowed through the thin layers of fabric, while fake silver coins jingled together on the long, fringed edges.

Rings studded with gems stacked up on her gnarled fingers, while a thin silver chain flashed around her right ankle. Her iron gray hair fell to her shoulders, pushed back by another scarf that she was using as a headband. Her eyes were a bright violet in her tan, wrinkled face.

Grandma Frost looked like what I'd always thought a real Gypsy should—and exactly like what her clients expected when they came to get their fortunes told. Grandma always claimed that people paid her as much for her appearance as for what she revealed to them. She said that looking the part of the wise old mysterious Gypsy always made for better tips.

I didn't know exactly what made us Gypsies. We didn't act like any Gypsies I'd ever read about. We didn't live in wagons or wander from town to town or cheat people out of their money. But I'd been called a Gypsy ever since I could remember, and that's how I'd always thought of myself.

Maybe it was the fact that I was a Frost. Grandma had told me that it was a tradition for all the women in our family to keep that name, since our Gypsy gifts, our powers, were passed down from mother to daughter. So even though my parents had been married, I'd inherited my mom, Grace's, last name of Frost, instead of my dad, Tyr's, last name of Forseti.

Or maybe it was the gifts themselves that made us Gypsies, the strange things that we could do and see. I didn't know, and I'd never gotten a real answer from my mom or grandma about it. Then again, I'd never even thought to ask until I'd started going to Mythos, where everyone knew exactly who they were, what they could do, where they came from, and how big their parents' bank balances were.

Sometimes, I wondered just how much Grandma Frost knew about the academy, the warrior kids, Reapers, and the rest of it. After all, she hadn't exactly protested when Professor Metis had come to the house and announced my change in schools. Grandma had been more resigned than anything else, like she'd known that Metis was going to show up sooner or later. Of course, I'd told my grandma all about the weird things that went on at Mythos, but she never blinked an eye at any of them. And every time I asked Grandma about the academy and why I really had to go there, all she said was for me to give it a chance, that things would eventually get better for me.

Sometimes, I wondered why she was lying to me— when she never had before.

"Hey there, pumpkin," Grandma Frost said, dropping a kiss on top of my head and brushing my cheek with her knuckles. "How was school today?"

I closed my eyes, enjoying the soft warmth of her skin against mine. Because of my Gypsy gift, because of my psychometry magic, I had to be careful about touching other people or letting them touch me. While I got vivid enough vibes from objects, I could get major flashes, major whammies of feeling, from actually coming into contact with someone's skin. Seriously. I could see everything that they'd ever done, every dirty little secret that they'd ever tried to hide—the good, the bad, and the seriously ugly.

Oh, I wasn't like a complete leper when it came to other people. I was usually okay when it came to small, brief, casual touches, like passing a pen to someone in class or letting a girl's fingers brush mine when we both reached for the same piece of cheesecake in the lunch line.

Plus, a lot of what I saw depended on the other person and what he was thinking about at the time. I was pretty safe in class, at lunch, or in the library, since mostly the other kids were thinking about how totally boring a certain lecture was or wondering why the dining hall was serving lasagna for like the hundredth time that month.

But I was still cautious, still careful, around other people, just the way that my mom had taught me to be. Despite the fact that part of me really liked my gift and the power it gave me to know other people's secrets. Yeah, I was a little dark and twisted that way. But I'd learned a long time ago that even the nicest-seeming person could have the blackest, ugliest heart—like Paige Forrest's stepdad. It was better to know what people were really like than to put your trust in someone who just wanted to hurt you in the end.

But there was nothing to be afraid of with Grandma Frost. She loved me, and I loved her. That's what I felt every time she touched me—the softness of her love, like a fleece blanket wrapping around me and warming me from head to toe. My mom had felt the same way to me, before she'd died.

I opened my eyes and shrugged, answering Grandma's question. "The same, more or less. I did make two hundred bucks by finding a bracelet. I put a hundred of it in the cookie jar, just like usual."

Grandma hadn't wanted to take my money when I'd started giving it to her, but I'd insisted. Of course, she wasn't actually spending any of it, like I wanted her to. Instead, Grandma put all the money that I gave her into a savings account for me—one that I wasn't supposed to know about. But I'd touched her checkbook one day when I'd been looking through her purse for some gum and had flashed on her setting up the account. I hadn't said anything to Grandma about it, though. I loved her too much to ruin her secret.

Grandma nodded, reached into her pocket, and pulled out a crisp hundred of her own. "I made a little money, too, today."

I raised my eyebrows. "You must have told her something good."

"Him," Grandma corrected. "I told him that he and his wife are going to be the proud parents of a baby girl by this time next year. They've been trying to have a baby for two years now, and he was starting to give up hope."

I nodded. It wasn't as weird as it sounded. People came to Grandma Frost and asked her all sorts of things. If they should get married, if they were ever going to have kids, if their spouses were cheating on them, which numbers they should pick to win the lottery. Grandma never lied to anyone who came to her for a reading, no matter how hard the truth was to hear.

Sometimes, she was even able to help people—like *really* help them. Just last month, she'd told a woman not to go home after work but to spend the night with a friend instead. Turned out that the woman's house had been broken into that night by a guy who was wanted for rape, among other things. The police had caught the man just as he was leaving her house, a knife in his hand. The woman had been so grateful that she'd brought all her friends over to get psychic readings.

Grandma Frost sat down in the chair opposite me and began pulling off some of her scarves. The fabric fluttered down to the table in colorful waves, the coins on the edges tinkling together. "You want me to make you something to eat, pumpkin? I've got an hour before my next appointment shows up."

"Nah, I had a sandwich. I've got to go back to the academy anyway," I said, getting to my feet, grabbing my bag, and looping it around my shoulder. "I've got to work my shift at the library tonight, and I have a report on the Greek gods that's due next week."

The tuition was just as astronomically expensive as everything else was at Mythos, and we just weren't rich enough to afford it—unless Grandma was holding out on me and hiding secret stacks of cash somewhere. She might be, given how vague and mysterious she'd been about me going to the academy in the first place. Either way, I had to work several hours in the library each week to help offset the cost of my stellar education and expensive room and board. At least, that's what Nick-amedes, the head librarian, claimed. I just thought he liked the free slave labor and bossing me around.

Grandma Frost stared at me, her violet eyes taking on an empty, glassy look. Something seemed to stir in the air around her, something old and watchful, something that I was familiar with.

"Well, you be careful," Grandma Frost murmured in the absent way that she always did whenever she was looking at something that only she could see.

I waited a few seconds, wondering if she'd tell me to look out for something specific, like a crack in the side-walk that I might trip over or some books that might topple off a shelf at the library and brain me in the head. But Grandma didn't say anything else, and, after a mo-ment, her eyes focused once more. Sometimes her visions weren't crystal clear but more like a general feel-ing that something good or bad was going to happen. Plus, it was hard for her to even have visions concerning family in the first place. The closer Grandma was to someone, the less objective about the person she was, and the more her feelings clouded her visions. Even if she had seen something, she'd only tell me the broad outlines, just in case her emotions were screwing up her psychic reception or making her see what she wanted to see—and not what might actually happen.

Besides, Grandma always said that she wanted me to make my own choices, my own decisions, and not be influenced by some nebulous thing that she saw, since sometimes her visions didn't come true. People often zigged when Grandma had seen them zag in her visions.

This must have been one of those times, because she gave me a smile, patted my hand, and moved over to the fridge.

"Well, at least let me wrap you up some pumpkin roll to take back to the academy," she said.

I stood there and watched Grandma Frost bustle around the kitchen. I wasn't psychic, not like she was. I couldn't see things without touching them, and I never got a glimpse of the future or anything.

But for some reason, a shiver crawled up my spine all the same.

Chapter 4

By the time I rode the bus back up to Cypress Mountain, avoided looking at the silent, staring sphinxes, slipped through the iron gate, and walked to the library, it was almost six and twilight had started to fall over campus. Soft shades of purple and gray streaked the sky, even as black shadows crept up the sides of the buildings, looking like blood sliding up the stone. I shook my head to banish the weird thought and walked on.

The Library of Antiquities was the largest structure at Mythos Academy and sat at the top of the cluster of the five main buildings that formed the loose points of the star. Supposedly, the library was only seven stories tall, but it always seemed to me like its towers just kept reaching up and up and up, until they finally pierced the sky with their sharp, swordlike points.

But what made the library supercreepy were the stone statues that covered it. Gryphons, gargoyles, dragons, even something that looked like a giant Minotaur. The figures were everywhere you looked, from the wide, flat steps that led up to the front entrance to the crenellated balcony on the fourth floor to the corners of the sloping roof. And they were all so detailed and lifelike that it seemed like they'd actually been real at one time—real monsters crawling all over the building until something or someone had frozen them in place.

I eyed the gryphons perched on either side of the gray stone steps. The statues loomed over me, and both gryphons sat at attention, eagle heads high, their wings folded behind them, and their thick lions' tails curled around the sharp, curved claws on their front paws.

Maybe it was my Gypsy gift, my psychometry, but I always felt like the two gryphons were watching me, tracking my movements with their lidless eyes. That all I had to do was touch them and they'd come to life, spring out of the stone, and tear me apart. It was the same feeling I had whenever I had to walk by the sphinxes down at the front gate and all the other statues on campus. I shivered again, tucked my hands into the pockets on my hoodie, hurried up the steps, and headed inside the library.

I walked through a hallway and a pair of open double doors that led into the main space. Like everything else at Mythos, the Library of Antiquities was old, stuffy, and pretentious. But even I had to admit that it was something to see.

The main part of the library was shaped like an enormous dome, and the curved ceiling was cut out all the way to the top. Supposedly, frescoes adorned the top arch of the dome, paintings of mythological battles accented with gold, silver, and sparkling jewels. But I'd never been able to spy any of them through the perpetual darkness that shrouded the upper levels.

What I could see were all the gods and goddesses. They ringed the second floor of the library like sentinels watching over the students studying below. The statues stood at the edge of the curved balcony, separated by slender, fluted columns. There were Greek gods like Nike, Athena, and Zeus. Norse gods like Odin and Thor. Native American deities like the Coyote Trickster and Rabbit. All thirty feet tall and carved out of thick white marble. If you climbed up the stairs to the second floor, you could walk in a circle past them all, something that I'd never wanted to do. Like the gryphons outside, the statues seemed a little too lifelike to me.

My eyes roamed over the gods and goddesses, staring at them one by one, until I reached the lone empty spot in the circular Pantheon—the place where Loki should have stood. There was no statue of Loki in the library or anywhere else at Mythos. I imagined it had something to do with him being such a bad guy and trying to destroy the world with his Reapers of Chaos. Not exactly the kind of god you wanted to build a shrine to.

I pulled my eyes away from the empty spot and walked on.

Bookshelves lined either side of the main aisle before it opened up into an area filled with long tables. A freestanding cart off to the right sold coffee, energy drinks, muffins, and other snacks so students wouldn't have to leave the library to get something to eat while they were studying. The rich, roasted smell of coffee filled the air, overpowering the dry, musty odor of the thousands of books.

I didn't stop walking until I reached the long checkout counter that stood in the center of the library. Several glassed-in offices lay behind the counter, separating one half of the domed room from the other. I stepped around behind the counter, plopped down on the stool next to the checkout computer, and slung my bag off my shoulder. I didn't even have time to pull out my myth-history book and start on my report before a door in the glass wall behind me squeaked open and Nickamedes stepped outside.

Nickamedes was the head guy at the Library of Antiquities. A tall, thin man with black hair, piercing blue eyes, and long, pale fingers. He wasn't that old, maybe forty or so, but he was one giant pain in my ass. Nickamedes loved the library and all the books inside, loved them with a passion that bordered on serial killer creepy. What he didn't really care for were all the students who tromped through his little kingdom on a daily basis—especially me. For whatever reason, the librarian had disliked me on sight, and his attitude hadn't improved during the two months that I'd been working here.

"Well," Nickamedes huffed, crossing his arms over his chest. "It's about time you got here, Gwendolyn."

I rolled my eyes. The uptight librarian was the only one who called me by my full name, something that I'd asked him not to do, with zero success so far. I think he did it just to annoy me.

"You're ten minutes late for your shift—*again,*" Nickamedes said. "That's the third time it's happened in the last two weeks. Where were you?"

I couldn't exactly tell him that I'd slipped off the academy grounds to go see Grandma Frost, since, you know, students weren't supposed to leave campus during the week. It was one of the Big Rules, after all. I didn't want to get Grandma in trouble—or worse, not be able to go see her anymore. I'd already learned that it was better to sneak around Nickamedes and the other Powers That Were at Mythos than it was to confront them head-on. So I just shrugged.

"Sorry," I said. "I was busy doing stuff."

Nickamedes's blue eyes narrowed at my vague, smart-ass answer, and his lips pressed into a thin line. "Well, let me tell you about the newest piece that I pulled out of storage this morning. Several classes have been assigned to study it this semester, so I'm sure you'll be getting a lot of questions about it."

The library was full of glass cases filled with dusty pieces of junk that had supposedly belonged to some god, goddess, mythological hero, or even monster. You couldn't walk down the aisles without tripping over them. Every other week, Nickamedes pulled something else out of storage and put it on display. Part of my job was to know enough about whatever it was to help the other kids find reference books and more information on it.

I sighed. "What is it this time?"

Nickamedes crooked his finger, telling me to follow him. We walked to the left past several tables full of students. A large glass case sat in an open space in the middle of the library floor. Resting inside was a simple bowl that looked like it was made out of dull, brown clay. *Boring.* At least some of the swords looked cool. This? A total snooze.

"Do you know what this is?" Nickamedes said in a hushed tone, his eyes bright.

I shrugged. "It looks like a bowl to me."

Nickamedes's face scrunched up, and he muttered something under his breath. Probably cursing my lack of enthusiasm again. "It's not just any *bowl,* Gwendolyn. This is the Bowl of Tears."

He looked at me like I should have known what that was. I shrugged again.

"The Bowl of Tears is what the Norse goddess Sigyn used to collect the snake venom that dripped onto her husband, Loki, the first time that he was imprisoned by the other gods, long before the Chaos War. Whenever Sigyn emptied the Bowl, the venom would drip onto Loki's face and burn him, making him cry out. His screams of pain were so great that the earth shook for miles around him. That's why it's called the Bowl of Tears. It's a very important artifact, one of the Thirteen Artifacts that the

Pantheon and the Reapers fought over and with during the last great battle of the Chaos War. . . ."

It was all very blah, blah, blah, and my eyes immediately glazed over. More stupid gods and goddesses. I didn't see how Nickamedes kept them all straight. I was having a hard enough time just trying to pick one for my report that was due for Professor Metis's myth-history class.

Finally, after five long, *long* minutes of spouting non-stop facts, Nickamedes wound down. A professor who'd been sitting at a nearby table came up and asked him a question, and the librarian moved off to answer the other man. I shook my head, trying to banish the drowsiness that I felt, and went back to my spot behind the counter.

For the next three hours I checked out books, answered questions, and did other menial tasks. The library was the one place where the other Mythos students were actually forced to notice and speak to me, if only so they could get their homework done.

Since students weren't supposed to go off campus during the week, the library was also a place to Hang Out and Be Seen, and lots of kids liked to sneak off and hook up in the stacks. I'd found more than one used condom when I'd shelved books. Yucko. Doing it against a case full of musty books wasn't exactly the way that I wanted to lose my virginity, but it was all the rage at Mythos. This month, at least.

Jasmine Ashton, Morgan McDougall, and Daphne

Cruz were among those who came into the library during my shift. The three Valkyries grabbed some iced mochas and raspberry muffins, then plopped themselves at the table closest to the coffee cart so everyone coming and going would see them. Samson Sorensen was with them, too, although he seemed to be more interested in the sports magazine he was thumbing through than anything else.

After a few minutes, Jasmine moved off to circulate through the crowd and talk to the other popular kids who'd come to the library tonight. Morgan and Samson put their heads together and started talking, but evidently Daphne had actually come here to study, because she moved down the table a little away from the others.

Daphne saw me sitting behind the checkout counter. The Valkyrie gave me a dirty look, dragged her laptop out of her bag, and opened and started typing on it. I resisted the urge to stick my tongue out at her. It wasn't my fault that Daphne had a monster crush on a band geek and that her mean-girl friends would make fun of her if she ever told them that she liked him, much less actually tried to date him.

Finally, around nine o'clock, the library emptied out as the kids packed up their books and headed back to their dorm rooms for the night and the ten o'clock curfew. Nickamedes said he had to go over to the math-science building and run an errand before he closed the library. Instead of letting me go ahead and leave, the librarian pushed a cart full of books in my direction and told me to have them shelved by the time he got back. Like I said, he was a giant pain in my ass.

But there was nothing I could do. If I left without putting the books away, they'd just be waiting here for me the next time I had to work. Nickamedes was kind of a dick that way. So I pushed the metal cart into the stacks, grabbed the books, and started putting them back where they belonged. Almost all the titles were old reference books that had been handled by hundreds and hundreds of students over the years, so I didn't get any big vibes or flashes by touching them. Just a general sense of kids flipping through the pages and hunting for whatever obscure information they needed to finish their latest essay.

I supposed that I could have worn gloves to cut out the flashes entirely, both here in the library and everywhere else. You know, the old-fashioned white silk kind that crawled all the way up to a girl's elbows. But that would have definitely branded me as a freak at Mythos— the Gypsy girl with the glove fetish. I might not fit in at the academy, but I didn't want to advertise how different I was either.

I did keep my eyes and ears open for any students who might not have finished their nightly hookup in the stacks. Last week, I'd rounded a corner and had seen two guys from my English lit class going at it like rabbits.

But I didn't hear anything and I didn't see anyone as I roamed through the library and slid the books back into their appropriate places. The whole thing would have gone a lot faster if the cart that I was using hadn't been old and rickety, with a loose wheel that pulled to the right. Every time I tried to turn a corner with the stupid cart, it inevitably slid into whatever antiques case happened to be nearby.

There were hundreds of them in the library, just like the one that Nickamedes had dragged me over to earlier. Shiny glass cases that contained all kinds of stuff. A dagger that had belonged to Alexander the Great. A necklace that the warrior queen Boudicca had worn. A jeweled comb that Marc Anthony had given Cleopatra to show his undying love for her before they'd both kicked it.

Some of the items were kind of cool, though, and I'd take a quick look at the silver plaque on the front or the ID card inside to see exactly what it was. I'd never tried to actually open any of the cases, as they all had some kind of magic mumbo jumbo attached to them to prevent people from stealing the stuff inside. But I always wondered how much some of the items would go for on eBay, if they were real. Probably enough to tempt even Jasmine Ashton, the richest girl at Mythos, into walking off with them in her designer purse.

Ten minutes later, I put away the last book, grabbed the cart, and tried to steer it back to the checkout counter. But, of course, the metal contraption had a life of its own and zoomed toward yet another case. I managed to stop the cart just before it slammed into the glass.

"Stupid wheel," I muttered.

I walked around the cart and was trying to shove it back from the other side when a wink of silver caught my eye. Curious, I looked down into the case that I was standing next to.

A sword lay inside it, one of hundreds in the library. My eyes skimmed over the glass, looking for the plaque that would tell me whose sword it was and what she'd done with it that was so freaking special. But there wasn't a plaque on the case. No silver plate on the outside, no little white card on the inside, nothing. Weird. Every other case that I'd seen had had some sort of ID on or in it. Maybe Nickamedes had forgotten about this one, since it was way back here in the stacks in no-man's-land.

I should have shoved the cart into the aisle, gone back to the checkout counter, and packed up my messenger bag so I could leave the very *second* that Nickamedes came back. But for some reason, I found myself stopping and looking down at the sword once more.

It was a simple enough sword—a long blade made out of a dull silver metal with a hilt that was just a little bit bigger than my hand. A small weapon, compared to some of the enormous crowbars that I'd seen in the library.

Still, something about the shape of the sword seemed . . . familiar to me. Like I'd seen it before. Maybe there had been an illustration of it in my myth-history book. Maybe some bad guy had used it in the Chaos War, if it had ever even really taken place. I snorted. Probably not.

I cocked my head to the side, trying to figure out why the sword was so interesting. And I realized that the hilt almost looked like . . . a face. Like half of a man's face had somehow been inlaid into the metal. There was a slash of a mouth, a groove of a nose, the curve of an ear, even a round bulge that looked like an eye. Weird. But it wasn't ugly. It looked almost . . . *alive.*

There were some words on it, too. I could just see them glinting on the blade right above the hilt, like they'd been carved into the metal there. I squinted, but I couldn't quite make out what they were. *V-i-c—Vic* something, I thought, leaning close enough to leave a nose print on the smooth glass—

CRASH!

Startled by the sudden noise, I jumped back and pressed myself against the bookshelf. Eyes wide, heart in my throat, blood pounding in my ears. What the hell was that?

I didn't consider myself to be a scaredy-cat, and I certainly wasn't some wimpy girly-girl who was afraid of her own shadow. But my mom had been a police detective. She'd told me lots of horror stories about people getting mugged and worse. And the Library of Antiquities wasn't exactly as warm and friendly as a park on a summer day. Nothing was at Mythos.

Now that I thought about it, I hadn't heard anything while I'd been shelving books. No sounds, no rustles of clothes, nothing to indicate there was anyone left but me in the entire library—

Something cold and hard dug into my palm. I looked

down and found that I'd wrapped my hand around the glass case, my fingers curled around the metal clasp, a second away from opening it and grabbing the weapon inside.

But the really strange thing was that the sword was staring at me.

The cover on the bulge on the hilt had slid up, revealing a pale eye that regarded me with a cold, steady stare. It was an odd color, too, not quite purple and not quite gray either—

Then, my brain kicked in and reminded me that this was all super, super *creepy*. I shrieked and stumbled away from the glass. My shoulder hit the edge of one of the bookcases, and I hissed as the sting of it flooded my body.

But the small pain lessened some of my panic. Deep down, I knew that my imagination was totally playing tricks on me. Swords didn't have eyes, not even in a place as crazy as Mythos Academy. And they certainly didn't *stare* at people. Especially not someone like me, that unimportant, nerdy Gypsy girl who saw things.

And the noise? That was probably just books that some kid had stacked up crooked on a shelf, finally toppling over. Probably done on purpose just to scare whoever was in the library this late. It had happened before, usually to me.

I stood there a second more to calm my racing heart, then pushed away from the bookcase. I thought about just grabbing the cart and forcing it back to the main library desk, loose wheel and all. But I had to look at the sword first. I had to convince myself that I wasn't going crazy. That I wasn't actually starting to *believe* all the stuff that Professor Metis kept spouting at us in myth-history class about evil gods and ancient warriors and Chaos and the end of the world and blah, blah, blah.

So I risked a quick glance over my shoulder. The bulge that I'd thought had been an eye before was nothing more than a bump on the hilt. Completely covered, completely silver, completely normal. Nothing more. It certainly wasn't *staring* at me.

I let out a sigh of relief. Okay. Gwen wasn't losing her mind just yet. Good to know.

I grabbed the cart and pushed it back toward the counter. Screw Nickamedes and his pissy attitude. Creepy swords and weird noises were enough for me. I was leaving. Now.

I broke free of the stacks and rounded the end of the aisle. I was halfway back toward the counter when I saw something move out of the corner of my eye. I glanced over to my left.

And that's when I saw her.

Jasmine Ashton.

The blond Valkyrie lay on her back in front of the case that Nickamedes had shown me earlier tonight, the one with Loki's supposed Bowl of Tears in it.

Except all the glass on the case had been shattered and there was no Bowl inside of it anymore.

And someone or something had slit Jasmine's throat from ear to ear.

I froze, not sure what was going on. I blinked a few

times, but the scene didn't change. Broken case. Stolen Bowl. A girl with a big, bloody slash across her pale throat.

I stood there another moment, shocked and dumbstruck, before my brain kicked in and started working once more. I pushed the cart out of the way and ran over to Jasmine. My foot slipped out from under me, and I put my hand down to brace myself. Something wet and cold and sticky covered my fingers, making me flinch. I raised up my hand to find it coated with blood—Jasmine's blood.

It was *everywhere*. Under the smashed case. Beside it. Splashed up onto the wooden tables. Puddles of the Valkyrie's blood covered the floor like crimson water that hadn't been mopped up.

"Oh, shit!"

I was almost hyperventilating, so I made myself take deep breaths the way that my mom had always told me to whenever I got panicked. Whenever I was in a bad, bad situation. After several seconds, I felt better. At least, good enough to pick my way through the pools of blood over to where Jasmine lay.

Strawberry-blond hair. Blue eyes. Beautiful face. Designer clothes. The Valkyrie looked the same as she always did—except for the slash in her throat and the knife on the floor next to her. A long curved gold dagger with an enormous ruby set into the hilt. The lights made the gem glint and gleam, like a giant red eye watching me. For some reason, the dagger was the only thing here that wasn't covered with blood. Bizarre.

I crouched down beside Jasmine, trying not to stare at the horrible wound on her throat. I couldn't tell if she was still breathing or not, and there was only one way to find out.

I had to touch her.

And I really, really didn't want to.

As much as I liked learning people's secrets, I knew that my Gypsy gift would kick in the second that I put my fingers on the Valkyrie's skin. Then, I would see and feel and experience exactly what Jasmine had when her throat had been cut. It would be *horrible,* just as horrible as seeing all the awful things that Paige's stepdad had been doing to her. Maybe even worse.

But there was no getting around it. I had to find out if Jasmine was still alive. I'd taken CPR in health class at my old school last year, so maybe I could help her—or at least run and find someone who could. I had to try, anyway. I just couldn't stand here and do nothing, not when Jasmine looked so—so *broken.*

So I crouched down and stretched out my trembling hand toward her neck. My fingers loomed closer to her pale skin, before finally jerking forward and making contact.

I closed my eyes and bit my lip, expecting to be overwhelmed with emotions and feelings. Expecting to feel all the pain and terror and fear that Jasmine just had. Expecting to be overcome with all those horrible emotions and just start screaming—

I felt nothing.

Not fear, not terror, and especially not pain. Nothing.

I didn't even get the faintest flicker of feeling off Jasmine's body. No vibes, no flashes, nothing. I frowned and pushed my fingers deeper into her neck, placing my whole hand on her skin just above the cut on her throat.

Still nothing.

Weird. Really weird. I always saw something, always felt *something,* especially when I was actually touching someone, in this case someone who'd just had her throat brutally sliced open—

Out of the corner of my eye, I saw a quick, furtive movement. But before I could turn and see what it was, something cold and heavy slammed into my temple. A bright, white flash of pain exploded in front of my eyes, before the darkness swallowed me.

Chapter 5

The first thing I was aware of was the voices. Low, steady voices that seemed to bore into my skull like a dentist's whiny drill. They kept on talking, one after another. Each one sent another spike of pain through my head.

"...obviously after the Bowl; Jasmine just got in the way...."

"...but why kill her? It doesn't make sense...."

"...Reapers don't have to make sense...."

"Shut up," I mumbled.

The voices stopped, and I started to sink back down into the quiet blackness—

"Gwen?" a familiar voice murmured.

"Mom?" I mumbled again.

A hand smoothed back my hair. "No, Gwen. Not your mom. Can you open your eyes for me, please?"

Then I remembered. My mom was dead. Killed by some drunk driver. And I was stuck here at Warrior

Freaks R Us. My heart squeezed in on itself, aching even more than my head did, and a hot tear trickled out of the corner of my eye before I could stop it. I missed my mom so much. I missed everything so much. My old school, my old friends, and everything else that I'd lost just because I'd wanted to know another girl's secret—

"Gwen?" the voice asked again, more insistent this time. "Come on. Open your eyes for me, please."

My head still hurt, but after a few seconds of concentrating I managed to crack open my eyes, letting the light trickle in.

Black hair, bronze skin, green eyes, silver glasses. Professor Metis's hazy face swam before me, and I had to blink several times before she came into focus.

"Professor Metis? What's going on?" I asked, struggling to sit up.

Metis put her hand under my back and helped me up into a sitting position. My brain swam around inside my skull for a few seconds before it snapped back into place and the world stopped spinning.

To my surprise, I was still in the Library of Antiquities, although I was now lying on top of one of the tables instead of in the middle of the cold marble floor.

Other people were in here now, too. Like Coach Ajax, the big, burly, biker-looking, tattooed guy who oversaw the athletic programs and trained all the kids. Ajax stood a few feet away talking to Nickamedes. The coach's onyx skin glistened under the library's golden lights, and his chiseled muscles twitched and jumped with every move he made. He looked like the kind of guy who could break concrete blocks with his bare hands.

As if sensing my stare, the two men turned and walked over to us. They both nodded to Professor Metis, who nodded back.

"Gwen," Metis said, putting her hand on my shoulder. "I'm glad to see you're feeling better."

"Professor? What are you doing here?" I asked, still confused.

Metis gestured at the two men. "Ajax, Nickamedes, and I make up the academy's security council. We're responsible for the safety of everyone at Mythos, for protecting students and staff from Reapers of Chaos and other threats. So we really need to know what happened here tonight. Do you think you can tell me what you saw? It's very important, Gwen. We don't want anyone else to get . . . hurt."

Hurt. Well, I supposed that was a polite way of saying what had happened to Jasmine, instead of the ugly truth—the fact that she'd been brutally attacked.

Their eyes fixed on my face. Metis's gaze green and understanding, Coach Ajax's black and hard, Nickamedes's blue and suspicious.

I drew in a breath and told the three of them about working in the library. How I'd been shelving the last of the books when I'd heard a crashing sound. How I'd thought it was just some books falling over, only to come out of the stacks and find Jasmine sprawled underneath the smashed glass case with her throat cut and blood everywhere.

"I went over to try to help her," I said in a shaky voice. "I was feeling her throat for a pulse when some-body . . . somebody hit me."

I looked over at the case, expecting to see nothing but broken glass. But Jasmine was still there, still lying in thick puddles of her own crimson blood, her sightless blue eyes staring up at the ceiling.

My throat closed in on itself. "Is she—"

"Dead," Coach Ajax rumbled in his deep voice. "Bled out."

Nobody said anything.

"Are you sure there's nothing else you remember?" Professor Metis asked. "Even the smallest detail might be helpful, might help us catch the person who did this."

I thought back, trying to remember, but nothing came to mind. My head still hurt too much for that. I reached up and touched my left temple. A lump the size of a robin's egg thumped under my fingers, and I winced at the sharp pain that stabbed through my skull.

I dropped my hand into my lap, looked down, and re-alized that I was covered in blood—Jasmine's blood. It was on my sneakers, on my jeans, and all over the front of my T-shirt and hoodie. And worst of all, dull brown bloodstains covered my hands like a coat of dried paint.

I sucked in a breath, waiting for my pyschometry to kick in and show me Jasmine's murder, to let me feel all the horrible pain that she must have experienced. Any second now, it would start. It always did.

But the seconds slid by and turned into a minute, then another one. And still, nothing happened. I didn't get any flashes or vibes from Jasmine's blood. Not a single one. Just like I hadn't gotten any from touching her body. Strange. Even for me. Maybe my psychometry was on the fritz or something because of the massive migraine that I had. For once, I was happy that I didn't see anything. Even though I wasn't getting any vibes from it, the sight of Jasmine's blood on my skin and clothes still made me want to vomit. I curled my stained hands into fists and looked away from them.

"I'm sorry. I don't remember anything else," I said in a low voice.

"Well, I think it's rather obvious what happened," Nickamedes said. "A Reaper slipped into the library and stole the Bowl of Tears. Jasmine, unfortunately, got in the way and was killed as a result."

Despite everything that had happened and the fact that my head was still pounding, I frowned. That didn't seem right to me—not right at all. Mainly because Jasmine had already been in the library earlier. Why would she come back so late? And especially without her friends? Jasmine never went anywhere without her doting entourage of Valkyrie princesses. They were always stacked on top of her like LEGOs.

But the one thought that kept beating through my brain right along with the pain was: *Why? Why her and not me? Why had she died and I hadn't? Why had I been spared again? Why was I always the one left be-hind to pick up the bloody, broken pieces?*

"I told you that you were taking a risk putting it on display," Coach Ajax said. "The Bowl of Tears is exactly the kind of thing that the Reapers would love to get their hands on. It's one of the Thirteen Artifacts, after all."

Nickamedes shrugged. "There are dozens of things here that the Reapers would love to get their hands on, and there are security spells on all of them to keep them from being taken out of the library. I just don't understand how the Reaper could have gotten the Bowl out of the library without sounding the alarm—much less slipped onto campus to start with. None of the alarms were tripped on the outer wall, at the main gate, or here in the library. I thought that the perimeter security spells were strong enough, and I double-checked the ones on the Bowl myself this morning."

"Obviously not," Ajax muttered.

The two men glared at each other, and Professor Metis stepped in between them.

"Enough," she said. "I'll call the cleanup crew and alert the others. I'm sure the academy board will want to increase campus security, magical and otherwise, at least for a few days, until we're sure that whoever did this isn't coming back for more artifacts."

Coach Ajax and Nickamedes glared at each other a few more seconds before they both nodded. Then, the two of them, along with Metis, moved off a few feet and started talking about what to do and who to notify.

They weren't as upset by this as I'd thought they'd be. It almost seemed . . . *normal* to them. Like something that had happened before. At my old school, the teachers would have *freaked out* if a girl had been murdered in the library. But here, it didn't seem that shocking. More like . . . an inconvenience. With paperwork to do, calls to make, and blood to clean up. Or something like that.

Well, it wasn't normal to me, not at all, and all I could do was stare down at Jasmine. So pretty, so popular, so rich, and what had it gotten her? Nothing but an early death. I thought about Paige Forrest and how she'd been the same way. Pretty and popular, but with this horrible secret, with this horrible thing that had been happening to her that nobody knew about.

I wondered if Jasmine was the same way. If she'd had some secret reason for coming back to the library tonight. If there was something more to this than just some mysterious anonymous bad guy stealing a magical, mythological bowl—

"Gwen?" Professor Metis's voice made me jump. "I'll take you back to your dorm room now, if you like."

I stared down a final time at Jasmine's lifeless body and the sticky crimson puddles all around her. It almost looked like the Valkyrie was resting on a giant red pillow, instead of being cold, bloody, and dead. I shuddered and looked away.

"Yeah," I said. "I'd like that a lot right now."

*   *   *

Metis said something else to Coach Ajax and Nickamedes; then the two of us left the library. It was after ten now, and the quad was deserted. Moonlight frosted everything a bright, glittering silver, even the two gryphons that sat at the base of the library steps. My breath steamed in the cool night air, and I put my bloody hands into my pockets, trying to protect them from the chill. But no matter what I did, I just couldn't get warm.

We didn't speak until we were halfway across the quad.

"I know this must be difficult for you, Gwen. Finding Jasmine the way that you did," Professor Metis said. "But this isn't the first time something like this has happened at Mythos."

My eyes widened. "You mean students have been murdered before? Here at the academy?"

She nodded. "A few."

"How? Why?"

"By Reapers mostly. The students had something that they wanted or got in their way, just like Jasmine did tonight. Or the students were working for the Reapers and did something wrong, something that got them killed. In a few cases, students have actually been Reapers themselves."

Kids my age? Working for the bad guys? Being Reapers themselves? I didn't know what to make of that.

Metis stared at me. "I know that the academy, this

world, is new to you, that you don't really believe in any of this. In the gods, the warriors, the myths, the Chaos War, any of it. I can tell by the way you're always staring out the window during my class. You recite the facts to me, but your mind's not really there."

Her voice was gentle, but I still winced. I thought that I'd hid my disbelief a little better than that. Since my mom had died, I'd gotten pretty good at faking things. Like telling Grandma Frost that everything was fine at my new school. Or convincing myself that I didn't really care that I didn't have any friends. That it didn't bother me that no one would talk to me. That I was as tough and strong and brave as my mom had been, when all I really wanted to do was curl up on my bed and cry myself to sleep every night. I might be able to see other people's secrets, but I had some of my own, too—ones that I desperately wanted to keep hidden.

"But it's real, Gwen. All of it. Whether you believe it or not," Metis continued. "Reapers of Chaos are everywhere, even here at Mythos. They can be anyone—parents, teachers, your fellow students. And they will do whatever it takes to get what they want."

"What is it that they want, exactly?" I asked. "Why are they the bad guys?"

Metis sighed. "You really haven't been paying attention in class, have you?"

I winced again.

"The Reapers want one thing—to free Loki from the prison realm that the other gods have placed him in. And we, the students and teachers here, the members of the Pantheon, are at war with them, trying to prevent that from happening. That's what all the students here are being trained for. To learn how to fight with whatever skills and magic that they have to keep Loki from escaping from his prison. That's why losing the Bowl of Tears is such a big blow. It's an old artifact with a lot of magic, with a lot of power, and it can help the Reapers get closer to freeing Loki."

I frowned. "So what happens if Loki gets free? What would be so bad about that?"

"Because the last time Loki was free, he raised an army to try to kill the other gods, to enslave mortals, and to bend everyone to his will. Hundreds of thousands of people died, Gwen. And hundreds of thousands more will die if Loki is freed once more. The world as we know it will be utterly destroyed."

So the Chaos was death, destruction, and blah, blah, blah, just like I'd thought. Another war, just like the one that had been fought before. Except when Professor Metis talked about it this time, a shiver swept up my spine. Like it was actually *real*. Like it could actually *happen*.

We left the main quad behind and stepped onto one of the walkways that led out to the dorms. The student dorms were smaller versions of the main academy buildings—lots of gray stone, lots of thick, green ivy, lots of creepy statues everywhere.

Somehow, Metis knew that I roomed in Styx Hall, without me even telling her. She walked me all the way up to the front door. Since the student curfew was ten o'clock on weeknights and the dorms automatically locked down after that, Metis had to swipe her professor ID badge through the scanner to get the door to open for me.

I could have told her not to bother. That there was a sturdy persimmon tree that reached up to a second-floor window on the back of the building. The window had a busted lock, and whatever magic was on it to keep students in or bad guys out had dissolved or disappeared a long time ago. Now, all the girls used it and the tree to slip out at night and see their boyfriends. Everyone except me, of course. I didn't have a boyfriend, much less just another girlfriend to hang out with after curfew.

"Now, don't worry," Metis said. "Ajax and Nickamedes have already started increasing the security at the library and over the whole campus. Nickamedes is out casting more spells right now. The dorms themselves are already quite secure. They all have wards on them to ensure the students' protection, but Nickamedes is going to increase the power and complexity of those as well."

Her voice was so calm and matter-of-fact that it reminded me of the teachers at my old school and how they'd all tell us to patiently file outside when we were having the yearly fire drill. They'd been so calm because they'd all known that there was no real fire and they didn't even think there was a problem to start with.

I thought of how easily I'd been able to walk down to the main gate, slip past the sphinxes, and leave campus earlier today. Apparently, just as easily someone had been able to come into the library and kill Jasmine tonight. Nickamedes's spells and the rest of the academy's magical security hadn't stopped either one of those things from happening. Just like all the academy's rules and threats of punishment didn't stop kids from drinking, smoking, or having sex in their dorm rooms. But I didn't say anything.

"Now," Metis said, taking my silence for some kind of agreement. "Would you like me to take a look at that bump on your head? I can heal you, if you wish. You'll never even know you were hit."

I blinked. "You can heal me? How?"

Metis held out her hands, palms up. They looked as smooth as polished bronze underneath the streetlight burning over the dorm. "I have a magical talent for healing injuries. All I have to do is place my hands on someone, picture them getting well, and they do."

Now that was a pretty cool power, and I'd heard of a few other kids on campus having that kind of ability. All the students at Mythos had something going for them, the magic that classified them as a particular type of warrior. Valkyries and Vikings were incredibly strong; Amazons and Romans were superfast; Spartans could kill you with whatever happened to be handy. As if that wasn't enough, the students had other magic as well, bonus powers as it were, everything from enhanced senses to the ability to shoot lightning out of their fingertips or create fire with their bare hands.

I wondered what the healing power made Metis, if she was a Valkyrie or an Amazon or something else, instead of just my myth-history professor. I might have even taken a chance and let Metis heal me, if it hadn't been for the whole *touching-my-head* part. I didn't want to touch anyone or anything else strange tonight. I'd seen enough horrible things in the last two hours. I didn't want to see any more.

"No, thank you," I said. "I'll just go . . . sleep it off or something."

Understanding flashed in Metis's eyes, and she nodded. "Very well. I examined you at the library before you woke up. The wound isn't that severe. You should be fine with a good night's sleep. But if you have any problems, blurred vision or anything like that, come see me immediately."

I doubted that I'd get a good night's sleep after finding a murdered girl, but I didn't say anything. Instead, I just nodded.

Professor Metis started to go, but she hesitated and turned to look at me once more. "I don't know if I said this before, but that was very brave of you, Gwen, trying to help Jasmine like you did. Most people would have just screamed and run away."

I shrugged. I hadn't thought it was brave. It had just been instinct more than anything else. A foolish one, since I'd gotten knocked out and Jasmine had died anyway.

"It was just like something your mother would have done," Metis said in a low voice.

I stared at her, wondering at the familiar tone in her voice. It almost sounded like she knew my mom. But how could she? As far as I knew, Grace Frost had never even set foot in the academy—

"She was a police detective, right?" Metis added.

"Yeah," I said, wondering how the professor knew that. I'd never told anyone at Mythos anything about my mom. "She was a cop. A good one."

But now she's gone, and it's all my fault. Tears filled my eyes, my throat closed up, and I couldn't finish my thought. The usual stab of loss and guilt pierced my heart, overpowering everything else.

Deep down, I knew that I didn't have anything to do with the drunk driver who'd T-boned my mom's car and then driven off, leaving her to die in the wreck. It had been an accident, a stupid, stupid accident, and nothing more.

Still, I wondered what my life would have been like right now, right this very *second,* if I hadn't seen the awful things that Paige's stepdad had been doing to her.

I couldn't help but think that my mom, Grace, would still be alive. That I'd be across town in our old house, in my old bed. That tomorrow I would have gotten up and gone to my old school with all of my old friends. Instead of being stuck here at Mythos Academy, where a girl had just been murdered and danger and bad guys lurked around every corner, according to Metis.

I couldn't help but think that my life would be so much better. So much simpler. So much closer to *normal* than this freak-show world that I was trapped in.

Metis opened her mouth like she wanted to say something else, but I turned around so she wouldn't see the hot tears that burned my eyes.

"Well, go in and try to get some rest now," she said in a soft voice. "And feel free to call me, if you need to talk about anything, anything at all."

"Yeah," I said. "Sure. Thanks, Professor."

Instead of looking back at her, I opened the door and stepped inside the dorm, shutting Metis and everything else out for the night.

Chapter 6

Jasmine Ashton's murder was the talk of Mythos Academy the next day.

But not in the way that I expected.

All the professors announced the news in their first-period classes. My finding Jasmine's body wasn't mentioned. The official story was that Nickamedes had been the one to discover her in the library, along with the smashed case and the fact that someone had stolen the Bowl of Tears. The professors assured all the students that Jasmine had apparently been in the wrong place at the wrong time and that since the Bowl was gone, whoever had killed her was probably long gone along with it. But, just to be on the safe side, students should stick together in groups and find a professor immediately if they saw anything suspicious.

After that, there was a campuswide moment of silence for Jasmine, so we could all pray for her soul or whatever they did at Mythos.

Two of the Valkyries Jasmine had been friends with

were in my first-period English lit class, and I thought that they might ask to be excused, to go back to their dorm rooms for the rest of the day and just process what had happened to their friend—to just feel sad and grieve and cry for her. But the two girls opened up their textbooks, got out their laptops, and started working on the latest critical thinking essay like the rest of us. Like everything was *normal*. Like nothing out of the ordinary had taken place. If it hadn't been for the faint headache that I still had, I would have thought that I'd imagined everything that had happened last night.

My eyes went from face to face, but everyone was just as calm and collected as the two Valkyries were. Nobody cried. Nobody looked upset. Nobody seemed scared at all that one of their classmates had been murdered last night.

Last year at my old school, David Jordan, a popular football player, had been working his after-school job at a convenience store when he'd been shot to death during an armed robbery. The next day at school, people had been *hysterical*. Crying, weeping, screaming, wondering why David had been shot, why he'd had to die, what he'd ever done to deserve something like that, something so violent and awful and random. The school had brought in grief counselors to talk to all of David's friends and everyone else who'd been shaken up by his death.

Jasmine Ashton had been the most popular girl in my second-year class. Yeah, she wasn't the first student at Mythos to die, according to Professor Metis, but Jasmine's death had to be one of the most unexpected, the most shocking. But everyone was so calm about it.

It was *creepy.*

And it was the same everywhere that I went all day long. Oh, the kids talked about Jasmine and her gruesome murder, but not in the way that I expected.

"So who do you think will be homecoming queen now that Jasmine's gone?" the girl sitting in front of me whispered in my fourth-period chemistry class. "Because the dance is on Friday and we already voted for all the kings and queens last week."

The petite Amazon sitting across from her shrugged. "Oh, the profs will just give it to the runner-up, which has to be Morgan McDougall. She was Jasmine's number two. Besides, you know how Morgan is. She'll be more than happy to wear that tacky crown, even if it wasn't really hers to start with."

The two girls giggled at their cattiness.

Then, the one in front of me leaned closer to her friend. "Speaking of something else that wasn't hers to start with, I heard that Morgan and Samson Sorensen were getting *very* cozy at lunch today. Really *comforting* each other, if you know what I mean."

That caught the Amazon's interest. "Really? That's quick work, even for a total slut like Morgan. Tell me more...."

The talk was the same all day long. Who would be homecoming queen, if Morgan and Samson were hooking up, even who was going to get to move into Jasmine's primo dorm room whenever her parents cleared out her stuff. Apparently, the Ashtons were vacationing on some remote island off the coast of Greece and the school higher-ups hadn't been able to reach them yet to tell them about their daughter's death. But everyone had a cell phone these days, even parents. It sounded to me like the Ashtons just didn't want to be bothered with Jasmine's murder. They probably didn't want to cut their sweet vacation short to come deal with everything.

Finally, in myth-history class, I couldn't stand it any longer. I tapped Carson Callahan on the shoulder and asked him about it.

"What is wrong with people here?" I muttered. "The girl was *murdered*. In the *library*, where we all have to go practically every single day. And nobody even talks about it, except to wonder who's going to be the stupid homecoming queen now and which Valkyrie's going to sink her claws into Samson Sorensen next. Nobody *cares*. Not about Jasmine anyway or who might have killed her or the fact that maybe he's still here on campus hiding out somewhere."

Carson gave me a sad look, like he and everyone else knew a secret that I didn't. "Do you know how many kids I've grown up with who have died, Gwen? Lots of them. So many that I've lost count. We go to Mythos for a reason. We're warriors, and warriors die. That's just how things are. Sure, some of the kids have car accidents or get drunk at the beach and drown or whatever. And sometimes, they're in the wrong place at the wrong time and get ripped to shreds by Nemean prowlers or murdered by Reapers. Sometimes, they're even Reapers themselves, and you have to kill them before they kill you."

I'd never thought that a band geek like Carson could be so blasé about something like this. That he could talk about kids dying and killing other kids like it was all okay. Like it was the way that things were *supposed* to be.

I just looked at him. "But doesn't it bother you? What happened to Jasmine? Or at least the fact that it happened here?"

He shrugged. "Sure it does. But nobody ever said that Mythos was a hundred percent safe. Kids sneak out past the sphinxes all the time. It's not that much of a stretch to think that a Reaper could sneak in if he really wanted to. Besides, Jasmine wasn't exactly the nicest girl around. She was kind of a bitch, if you really want to know, always being mean to and putting other people down just to make herself look cool. But nobody ever said or did anything about it because her parents are so loaded and so powerful."

"But—"

Carson sighed. "Look, I know you're new, Gwen, but pretty much everybody here has lost someone that they love, someone that they care about a whole lot more than a spoiled bitch like Jasmine Ashton."

There was a harshness in his voice now, a tightness in his face, and a strained sadness in his brown eyes that I recognized.

"Who have you lost?"

"My uncle," he said. "He was killed fighting a group

of Reapers last year. He was out having dinner with his girlfriend when it happened."

"But why? What did he do to them? Did he have an artifact or something they wanted?" I asked, thinking of the stolen Bowl of Tears.

"Nothing," Carson said in a cold voice. "He didn't have a thing that they wanted. They just saw him and killed him because they're Reapers and they like hurting people, especially warriors like us. They kill us before we can kill them because they know that we're a threat to them, that we're all here learning how we can stop them and Loki for good—forever. But not everyone gets to live to see that day, whenever it comes."

The raw pain in his face made me wince.

"Carson, I'm sorry. I didn't know."

"Now you do," he said in a quiet voice, and turned back around.

Carson didn't speak to or look at me during the rest of class. I couldn't blame him. I'd been trying to understand, trying to figure out why things were so different here, and I'd put my foot right in my mouth.

After myth-history, I walked over to the Library of Antiquities. As I crossed the quad, I realized that the other kids had felt something over Jasmine's murder after all. I could see it in the way that they huddled together in tight groups, in the strain on so many of their faces, in the way they talked just a little too fast and laughed just a little too loud. Yeah, they'd felt Jasmine's death just as much as I had and were trying to deal with it—even if it wasn't in the way that I'd expected.

I didn't know if that made me feel better or worse.

Apparently, I wasn't the only one who was curious, freaked out, or whatever, because there was a much, much larger crowd in the library than usual. Almost every table was full, and almost every student was sneaking glances at the spot where I'd found Jasmine's body.

There wasn't anything to see. The broken case and the shattered glass had been cleaned up, along with Jasmine's blood. And, of course, her body was gone, too. There was nothing there, not even some flowers, teddy bears, or a few lit candles to remember the dead Valkyrie. After David Jordan's murder, people had turned his locker into a shrine, with photos and cards and stuff. But not here at Mythos.

Eventually, the crowd cleared out and I found an open spot at the end of one of the long library tables. I pulled out my books and tried to study, tried to focus on the report that I had to write for Professor Metis's myth-history class, but I couldn't concentrate. It didn't help that all the kids around me were still talking about Jasmine.

"... got what she deserved, if you ask me," one girl whispered. "Jasmine always thought that she was better than everyone else."

"Oh yeah," another guy agreed. "It's a terrible thing, but at least I won't have to put up with her in Ancient Languages anymore. She always made fun of me."

"Me too, but what really freaks me out is the fact that there was a Reaper in the library." The girl shuddered. "They're not supposed to be able to even get on campus, much less steal something from the library. That bothers me a lot more than Jasmine ever did."

I knew the other kids were grieving, venting, or whatever in their own way. And yeah, maybe Jasmine had been a spoiled bitch, like Carson had said. But still, somebody should care that she was dead. I mean *really* care. Somebody should be sad that she was gone. Somebody should want to know exactly what happened to her and why. Somebody should try to make sure that it didn't happen again to some other kid.

Paige Forrest's face flashed through my mind, and I remembered the way that she'd looked at me that day. There had been a . . . *desperation* in her eyes. In that moment, in the second before I'd touched her hairbrush, part of me, some small part of me, had realized that Paige was hiding something—something *big,* something *huge.* And I'd wanted to know what her secret was, the way that I always did, so I'd picked up her hairbrush. I'd just never imagined how truly terrible Paige's secret was.

Thinking so much about Paige triggered a rush of images and feelings, and I saw it all again in my head. Paige's stepdad brushing her hair, then making her lie back on the bed so he could touch her. I felt it all again, too—all of Paige's shame and fear and helplessness. Once I saw something, once I flashed on an object or a person, those feelings, those memories, were a part of me forever and I always remembered them, could always see and feel them. I supposed it was a Gypsy version of a photographic memory. I could call up specific memories and focus in on them, examining every little thing that I'd seen, felt, or heard. But other times, they just hit me like Paige's were doing right now, whether I wanted them to or not. In a way, I supposed that it was a punishment for me being so damn nosy sometimes.

I dug my nails into my palms, willing Paige's memories away before I started screaming again. I drew in slow, deep breaths and focused on another image—my mom. Remembering her face, her voice, her smile, her laugh, trying to pull every single detail into supersharp focus. A trick that she'd taught me to deal with the unwanted memories. Think about something good and forget the bad as much as you could.

It didn't always work, but this time it did. Paige's ugly memories faded from my mind and got locked away in a dark, distant corner of my brain, right alongside all the other bad stuff that I'd seen and felt over the years.

Still, the flashes of feeling made me think about what I'd done to help Paige. Yeah, I'd wanted to know her secret, but I'd also told my mom what was going on. And, in some small way, I'd helped my mom stop Paige's stepdad from hurting her. I thought about what Professor Metis had said last night—about how proud my mom would have been that I'd tried to help Jasmine when most people would have just run away.

And, in that moment, I made my decision.

Maybe it was crazy. Maybe it was this nagging feeling

I had that there was something more to all this than just stealing a magical bowl. Maybe it was stupid or silly or just plain wrong.

But I wanted to know more about Jasmine. Specifically why she'd been in the library so late last night. What had really happened to her and who was responsible for it.

Maybe . . . maybe I *needed* to do it for myself, to know why it had happened, to know why whoever had stolen the Bowl of Tears had killed Jasmine but had left me alive. Maybe it was some kind of weird survivor's guilt or something.

But somehow, someway, I was going to find out the answers to my questions. After all, I was Gwen Frost, that Gypsy girl who saw things. The girl you hired to find whatever was lost. I was good at figuring things out. Uncovering the truth about Jasmine's murder shouldn't be too difficult.

Besides, this was one secret that I was determined to discover—no matter what.

Chapter 7

I couldn't concentrate where I was sitting on the main library floor with all the other students who'd come to gawk, so I moved over to a table tucked into one of the corners in the stacks—the same corner that had the case with the strange sword in it.

I threw my messenger bag onto the table, then went over and stared down at the sword. The weapon looked the same as it had last night. Silver metal, long blade with faint writing on it, a man's face carved into the hilt.

I waited a minute, but the eye on the hilt didn't suddenly pop open and stare at me again. Good. Maybe I wasn't going crazy after all.

I sat down at the table, dragged a notebook out of my bag, and got to work, writing down everything that I knew about Jasmine Ashton. The more I knew about her, the easier it would be to figure out why she'd been in the library last night—and who might have killed her.

I didn't know much.

Jasmine was pretty, popular, and a total mean girl. A

Valkyrie who loved designer clothes and whose family had deep, deep pockets. And . . . and . . . and that was it. That was all that I knew about her. That was the complete sum total of her existence to me. I didn't even know what her other power was, besides her inherent Valkyrie strength.

For a moment, I was depressed. This was stupid. It wasn't like I was Veronica Mars or Batman or somebody, able to figure out complex mysteries with just a few clues. Maybe it had been some random bad guy who'd killed Jasmine after all, some Reaper of Chaos who'd just been after the Bowl of Tears so he could do Bad, Bad Things with it.

But then, I thought about my mom. Something about this felt wrong to me, and she'd always told me to trust my feelings, to trust my Gypsy gift. Besides, Grace Frost wouldn't give up so easily if she was investigating Jasmine's murder, and neither would I.

Okay, so I needed more information on Jasmine, and I knew of at least one place to get it—the Internet.

I pulled my laptop out of my bag and fired it up. Mythos Academy had the very best of everything, including free, campuswide Wi-Fi, so I was able to access the school Web site with just a few clicks of my wireless mouse. Every Mythos student was supposed to have his or her own personal school Web page to share interests, photos, and more with fellow students. Kind of like a Facebook account that was only accessible to the other kids at school. But some of the kids, including me, just didn't bother with it. I didn't have any friends at Mythos to start with, so who here would want to read my ramblings?

But, of course, Jasmine had a blog and more than two hundred friends, according to her campus profile. I scrolled down the page, scanning her blog, but there was nothing there. Just catty comments about who was wearing what, along with several dreamy posts about what a great guy Samson Sorensen was. Your typical high school popular rich girl angst. Or what passed for it. There were also several photos of Samson in his itty-bitty swim briefs at various meets. Dude *totally* had six-pack abs. Yeah, I looked at those pictures a little longer and a little more closely than the other ones.

But Jasmine hadn't posted anything on her page that told me anything really deep and meaningful about her, much less why she was at the library last night, which meant that I was going to have to go to another source.

Like her laptop. That's where the good stuff would be anyway. It always was. Even at my old school, kids had always been *frantic* when they'd lost their laptops, thinking about all the incriminating stuff that someone might find on them. Like e-mails about how drunk the kids had gotten with their friends the weekend their parents thought they went to band camp. Papers they'd downloaded and plagiarized for AP English. Porn.

I tapped my fingers on the table, thinking back to last night, calling up my memories of the scene of the crime, and sorting through them the way that I was able to do.

In some ways, my psychometry magic was better than watching a movie, because I had perfect color, picture, and sound every single time.

I hadn't seen a computer or any kind of bag lying on the floor next to Jasmine, just that blood-free dagger with the ruby set into the hilt. So Jasmine probably hadn't had her laptop with her. I knew that she had one, though, because I'd seen her with it yesterday on the quad. The most likely place to look for it would be in her dorm room.

I glanced back at the Web page in front of me. According to her campus profile, Jasmine lived in Valhalla Hall. I snorted. Of course she did. That's where all the Valkyrie princesses lived, since it was the plushest, poshest dorm at Mythos.

According to the whispered rumors that I'd heard today, Jasmine's room had been locked up until her parents could come and pick up her things. I wasn't a great detective like my mom had been, but the rumors told me two things. One, that Jasmine's dorm room should be empty. And two, that if I was going to break in and try to snatch her laptop I needed to do it now—like *right now.* Before her parents flew back from wherever they'd been vacationing in Greece or magically teleported in or whatever.

And most especially before I lost my nerve.

I sat there a minute, wondering if this was crazy. I was actually thinking about breaking into a dead girl's dorm room to steal her computer just so I could see what kind of info was on it. Just so I could find out why

she'd been in the library last night. Just so I could discover all of her secrets.

I sighed. Here I was again, thinking about another
girl's secrets and how I could find out all about them. I
was so totally dark and twisted sometimes. Despite
everything that had happened, I still liked my Gypsy gift
and how it let me know things about people, how it let
me see into them and get a sense of their true feelings,
the ones that they worked so hard to hide. Like Daphne's
massive crush on Carson. My psychometry was the
only kind of power that I had at Mythos, small though
it was.

But the cold, hard truth was that my thirst for secrets,
my own stupid curiosity, had gotten my mom killed.
Maybe if I hadn't wanted to know Paige's secret so
badly, my mom wouldn't have been working so late that
night and she would have never been hit by that drunk
driver on her way home.

Maybe my mom would have still been alive. Maybe
we'd be eating dinner together right now. Barbecue
takeout maybe, from the Pork Pit, tucked away in the
cozy kitchen of our old house, just the way that we used
to at least once a week. Mom would tell me about her
day, her violet eyes a little sad, but I was always able to
make her laugh and banish the shadows that cloaked
her face. After that, she'd ask me about school or what
comic book I was reading or even start teasing me about
some new boy I liked. Maybe we'd be doing all of those
things right now, right this very *second,* if things had
been different.

On the other hand, maybe Paige would still be being abused by her stepdad, too.

Maybe, maybe, maybe . . .

The pain and guilt over my mom's death knifed through my heart, and I rubbed my aching chest. Sometimes, I just didn't know what was right and wrong anymore, or what I was even supposed to do with my Gypsy gift in the first place. Deep down, I didn't think that I was supposed to find lost cell phones and crumpled bras for the rest of my life. But I didn't know if I was supposed to go snooping around in other people's business either. It was the whole Spider-Man dilemma about great power coming with great responsibility. Not that I thought my psychometry was the bestest power in the world or anything. I wasn't that vain or deluded. Not after seeing what some of the kids at Mythos could do.

Maybe . . . maybe I should just forget about my whole crazy plan and let Professor Metis do whatever she and the other teachers were doing to find Jasmine's killer.

But then, another memory flashed through my mind, and I remembered Jasmine lying on the library floor, staring up at the ceiling with her sightless eyes, blood all around her. Looking so still and absolutely dead.

I thought about all the mean things that I'd heard the other students say about her today. Maybe they were true, but somebody should care that Jasmine was dead. And it looked like that somebody was me. Now, it was time to actually *do* something about all of this, whether or not I even knew for sure if it was the right or wrong thing to do in the first place.

But it was a place to start at least, and it was way better than sitting around in the musty stacks brooding about my Gypsy gift, my mom's death, and staring at a strange sword out of the corner of my eye, wondering if it was going to stare back at me. Yeah, digging into Jasmine's death, however misguided it might be, had a lot more appeal than all that.

I packed up my things and left the library.

I'd been inside the Library of Antiquities longer than I'd thought, because twilight was starting to fall when I stepped outside. I checked my watch. After six already. Classes were over for the day, and except for a few kids going to and from the library, the grassy lawn was deserted. At this hour, most of the students were busy with club meetings, sports practice, or getting some dinner in the dining hall before they went back to their dorm rooms to finish their homework. But I didn't mind the gray twilight or the empty quad. The darkening quiet made for better skulking.

I hurried past the five main academy buildings, winding my way down one of the cobblestone paths until I reached Valhalla Hall. The girls' dorm was a three-story gray stone structure, covered with thick ivy vines just like all the other buildings. According to her Web profile, Jasmine's room was on the second floor, which meant that I couldn't just crawl in through an open window or something. Naturally, things just couldn't be that easy for me.

I didn't bother going around to the back of the dorm and trying to get in that way. I knew from living in Styx Hall that's where all the smokers liked to hang out, puffing on cigarettes and occasionally some pot. At Styx, you had to wade through clouds of smoke to get inside and then you reeked of tobacco until you could take a shower. So not worth it.

But all the doors on all the dorms had a machine that you had to swipe your student ID through to get inside. For security reasons and to try to keep the guys, the girls, and their various hookups to a minimum, your ID card only let you into your assigned dorm, which meant that my ID only worked at Styx Hall and not here at Valhalla. Frustration filled me. I'd forgotten about that pertinent detail in my hurry to get over here. Kids could buzz other kids into the dorm through an intercom system outside, but of course I didn't have any friends who roomed in this dorm who would let me in. I didn't have any friends at all.

But I wasn't ready to give up just yet. My eyes scanned the paths that wound by the dorms. After about ten seconds, I spotted a familiar face—a petite Valkyrie girl who was in my English lit class. A girl who'd probably never noticed me before and had absolutely no idea who I was—and, more important, that I didn't exactly belong here. It was worth a shot.

I walked up the steps to the front door of the dorm

and started rummaging through my messenger bag, like I was looking for my ID card. A few seconds later, the Valkyrie climbed up the steps. I turned to face her and moved off to one side.

"Forgot my ID card again," I said in a bright voice, and smiled. "Can you scan yours for me, please?"

The other girl gave me a strange look, but she slid her card through the machine, opened the door, and stepped inside. So much for that stellar security Professor Metis had been talking about last night. I followed the Valkyrie inside.

The inside of Valhalla Hall looked pretty much like my dorm. The first floor was a series of common areas linked together, including the living room that I was standing in right now, although it was a lot nicer than the one at Styx Hall, with upscale, expensive-looking furniture. Several couches and recliners ringed three huge TVs. One of them was tuned to some cheesy reality program, although the girl sitting in front of it was more interested in texting on her phone than watching the show.

I didn't waste time gawking but instead hurried up the stairs to the second floor. My luck held, and I didn't run into any more Valkyries. Just about everyone was still out on campus doing their own thing, and the dorm was still and quiet.

I quickly made my way to 21V, which was Jasmine's room, according to her online profile. The door was closed, but other than that, there was no indication that this was the room of a girl who'd been murdered. There was no yellow crime scene tape strung up or anything. Not that I was complaining, but it was just kind of weird, like everything else at Mythos.

I stood there a moment, looking at the door, wondering if this was really the right thing to do. But I'd come too far to back out now. And yeah, I was a little curious about what Jasmine's room looked like. Everyone had been talking about how great it was. Sue me for wondering. Besides, I'd already done most of the breaking—I might as well do the entering and stealing, too. So I drew in a breath, reached for the doorknob, and rattled it.

Locked. Shit.

Yeah, I'd expected the door to be locked, but part of me had also been hoping that the Powers That Were might have slipped up and left it open.

I bent down and looked at the door. Like the doors in my dorm, it wasn't as fancy and sturdy as it could have been and there was a small gap between the door and the frame. So I stuck my hand into one of the side pockets on my bag and fished around until I came up with my driver's license.

I'd been *thrilled* when I'd gotten my license last year, and I'd even been saving up money from my odd jobs to buy a car. But I hadn't driven since I'd been at the academy, mainly because I could walk everywhere I needed to go on campus and the Cypress Mountain bus went down by Grandma Frost's house every day. And when your mom dies in a car accident it takes the fun out of driving anyway. But my license had other uses, including one that my mom had shown me.

I slid the laminated card in between the door and the frame, gently guiding it down to the lock. It took some wiggling, but I managed to slip my license between the lock and the frame, popping it open.

The door swung inward.

Before I could think too much about what I was doing and how wrong it was, I stepped inside and shut the door behind me. To my surprise, it was light inside, thanks to the soft glow from a stained-glass Tiffany lamp on the desk. I stood there and stared around the room, trying to get a feel for the kind of girl that Jasmine Ashton had been—and who might have wanted to kill her.

It looked pretty much the way that I'd expected it to. Jasmine had the whole space to herself, of course, and it was more like a plush apartment than a dorm room. A bed was tucked away in one corner, covered with a blue Ralph Lauren comforter, a mound of matching pillows, and stuffed animals. Cats mostly, lions, tigers, and panthers, from what I could see.

A large, expensive white vanity table took up the opposite corner. A padded bench sat in front of the glass-topped table, while lights ringed the mirror above it. Makeup, hairbrushes, perfume bottles, and more cluttered the glass, while pictures were stuck in the edges of the gilded gold frame around the mirror. I scanned the pictures, most of which seemed to be of Jasmine, rather than of her friends or family. Somebody had liked looking at herself. I might have, too, if I'd been as pretty as Jasmine had been.

A door in the wall opened up into a walk-in closet full of designer clothes, shoes, and handbags, all carefully organized, while the other door led into the bathroom. I looked in the bathtub and opened the cabinet over the sink, but there was nothing interesting. Just pricey shampoos and lotions. No condoms, no birth control pills.

Maybe the rumors were true about Jasmine still being a virgin and not wanting to cash in her V Card with Samson Sorensen just yet. I wondered how Samson felt about that. He'd certainly looked happy enough rubbing her shoulders on the quad the other day. Jasmine had probably had the Viking wrapped around her little finger, willing to do whatever she wanted—even wait to have sex.

Once my tour of the room was complete, I went over to the heavy wooden desk that squatted next to a large, expensive TV and a couple of bookcases. The desk was almost always where the good stuff was. Books, papers, pens, fashion magazines. All your usual clutter littered the surface, along with Jasmine's laptop, half-buried underneath a stack of notebooks. Jackpot.

I pulled my hoodie sleeve down so that it covered my hand, grabbed the laptop, and slipped it into my messenger bag. I didn't want to touch the computer just yet. Not here. I didn't know what I might see with my psychometry magic, and I didn't want to do something stupid—like start screaming if there was a bad vibe attached to the computer. I'd do that later, when I got back to my own dorm room. Besides, I'd been in here several minutes now, and every minute longer that I stayed added to the risk of somebody catching me.

When that was done, I rifled through the desk drawers, still careful not to touch anything with my bare hands. But there was nothing in the desk that shouldn't be there and nothing that I thought I could get a real flash or vibe off of.

So I moved on and examined the bookcases that took up part of one wall. To my surprise, there were a lot of books there—a *lot* of books. Jasmine hadn't struck me as the kind of girl who loved to read. The really bizarre thing was that all the books were kind of... boring. Textbooks or encyclopedias with titles like *Common Valkyrie Powers* and *Mastering Your Magic*.

Maybe it wasn't so weird for Jasmine to have these kinds of books. Maybe she'd had a power besides her inherent Valkyrie strength—magic that let her call down lightning bolts from the sky or turn people to ice with her eyeballs. Okay, so most mean girls had that last power anyway, but here at Mythos a few students actually had the ability to deep-freeze whatever or whoever they wanted. I thought back, but I didn't remember hearing about Jasmine having any kind of special power, and I'd never seen her do any magic, like make storm clouds gather overhead or fog suddenly roll across the quad. Still, none of the books looked like they would be fun to read. Maybe they were just for show and nothing else. I just couldn't see Jasmine spending her time studying spells, researching magic, or learning about whatever kind of Valkyrie power that she might have had.

I was about to turn away from the books when a title caught my eye—*The History of Great Artifacts*. A memory clicked in my mind. Wait a minute. Last night in the library, Coach Ajax had called the Bowl of Tears an Artifact with a capital *A* and one of the Thirteen, whatever that meant.

Curious, I used my hoodie sleeve to pull the book off the shelf. A piece of blue paper was stuck in the top, almost like a bookmark. I put the heavy book down on the desk and flipped it open to that section—and was rewarded with a photo of the Bowl of Tears, along with a couple of pages telling all about its history and supposed magical, mythological powers.

My eyes narrowed. Maybe Jasmine hadn't been quite the innocent victim in all this that she'd seemed to be. Maybe . . . maybe she'd actually *helped* someone steal the Bowl of Tears before she'd been killed. Professor Metis had told me that some Mythos students had worked with Reapers before. Why else would Jasmine have this book with this particular page marked about the Bowl if she wasn't involved in its theft somehow?

I slid the book into my bag, right next to the laptop.

Then, I walked over to the very last part of the room that I wanted to look at—the trash can under the desk.

My mom had always told me that people left a lot of interesting things in the trash. Things that you just wouldn't believe folks didn't bother to hide if you were a detective searching someone's house and looking for evidence of all the bad things they'd done. My mom had always claimed that people put stuff in the cans and then forgot about it, like throwing it in the trash was the same as it getting taken off to the dump and buried forever.

So I pulled the can out from under the desk and sifted through the contents, still using my hoodie sleeve to keep from actually touching anything. Most of it was your normal, boring trash. A half-used tube of lip gloss. Some crumpled tissues. An empty bag of potato chips. But there was one thing that was interesting—a photo in the very bottom.

The photo had been torn in two, and I picked up both pieces, turned them over, and fit them together.

To my surprise, the photo wasn't of Jasmine. Instead, Morgan McDougall and Samson Sorensen smiled up at me. They had their arms around each other and were grinning for the camera. The photo looked like it had been taken sometime in the spring on the quad, because the tree behind them was green with new leaves.

I frowned. Why would Jasmine tear this particular photo in two? Was there something going on between Morgan and Samson? According to the rumors that I'd heard, Morgan had her eye on Samson now that Jasmine was dead. But this photo had to have been ripped up before last night, when Jasmine had been murdered.

Nothing made sense. Right now, I had more questions than answers—and a whole lot of trouble I could get into if someone found me snooping in here.

I put the torn photo in my bag with the rest of the stuff that I'd collected. Then, I crept over to the door, listening for voices or footsteps outside. I didn't hear anything, so I opened the door and slipped out into the hallway.

I went out the same way that I'd come in, hurrying down the stairs and walking through the main common room. A few more girls had come into the dorm by now, but none of them glanced at me as I went by. Luckily, I didn't have to swipe an ID card to get out of the dorm, so I was able to push through the front door and scurry down the stairs and back out onto the cobblestone walkway.

I glanced around to make sure no one was watching me, then headed around the side of the stone building so I could cut across one of the smaller quads and walk back to my own dorm.

I was almost clear of Valhalla Hall when a window on the second floor opened and a backpack sailed outside and plummeted to the ground in front of me. Somehow, I stifled the surprised scream in my throat. Especially since the backpack was followed a second later by a guy who landed in a low, perfect crouch. He got to his feet with ease, like the twenty-foot fall was nothing to him, and I saw who he was.

Logan freaking Quinn.

It was more dark than light now, and the Spartan looked even more dangerous in the blackening shadows. The pale, milky moon brought out the blue highlights in his thick, wavy black hair. Logan dusted a few leaves off his designer jeans, then glanced up to find me staring at him. His eyes narrowed in his chiseled face.

"Well, well, if it isn't the Gypsy girl out here in the dark all by herself." Logan's voice sounded deep and ominous. "What are you doing?"

I clutched my bag to my chest, as if that would some-how protect me from the Spartan and the fact that he could kill me with his pinkie finger. "Not sneaking out of some poor girl's dorm room like you so obviously are."

He moved closer to me, but I held my ground and didn't step back. Logan's lips quirked up into that amused smile again. He must have realized that I was scared of him, despite my acidic words.

But I was only a *little* scared of him, I told myself. And only because Jasmine had been murdered and I was the one who'd found her body. And, well, maybe be-cause I'd just broken into and searched her dorm room and had her laptop in my bag. Okay, so maybe I had several good reasons to be jumpy, in addition to the fact that I was standing here alone in the dark with Logan Quinn. The very sexy, very dangerous Logan Quinn.

"You're right," he said. "I had a date. And you? What are you doing out here?"

I clutched my bag with the stolen computer a little tighter. "Nothing. I was just on my way back to my dorm. Nothing, really."

We stared at each other. Logan's eyes were as pale as the moonlight on his face, more silver than blue now, while his skin resembled the marble statues that could be found on all the academy buildings. Cold. Remote. Hard. Perfect.

"Well, I think I'm going to go do *nothing* somewhere else," Logan drawled. "Maybe back in my dorm room. Care to join me?"

I couldn't stop my mouth from falling open. Had the infamous Logan Quinn just asked me to go back to his room with him? I rewound the last few seconds in my mind. Yes, yes, he had—a whole two minutes after he'd just jumped out of some other girl's window.

Disgust filled me. Egotistical pig. Did he think that I was that easy? That I'd sleep with him just because he asked? That I was that lonely and that desperate? That he was so sexy that no girl could resist him? My eyes drifted over his muscled body again. Well, maybe he had the right to be pretty confident there.

But even if I had been a raging slut like Morgan Mc-Dougall who gave it up just for fun, there was still the little problem of my Gypsy gift. Just touching a hair-brush had made me scream so loud and so long that I'd wound up in the hospital. Sex with somebody like Logan Quinn would probably fry my brain for good. I hadn't even kissed a guy in months now, ever since I'd broken up with Drew Squires, my first, and only, short-lived boyfriend. The last time we'd kissed, I'd felt him pretending that I was Paige Forrest. I'd dumped him right then and there.

"So what do you say, Gypsy girl?" Logan asked in a soft voice. "Want to go back to my room and do *nothing* together?"

"Sorry," I snapped. "I think I'm going to go call my grandma."

He raised an eyebrow. "The grandma who can rot off a guy's dick?"

I gave him a bright smile, although I wondered if he could even see it or me in the darkness. "The one and the same. I'll be sure and tell her all about *you*. Gotta run. Bye."

I skirted around him and hurried on, this time not even caring what kind of freak he thought I was. But before I stepped around the side of the building I glanced over my shoulder.

Logan Quinn was still standing underneath the girl's window. Still staring at me. Still watching me.

It might have only been my imagination, but I swear I thought I saw him smile again before I rounded the side of the dorm and he disappeared from sight.

Chapter 8

My chance meeting with Logan Quinn spooked me so much that I practically ran all the way back to Styx Hall. It was almost eight o'clock now, and darkness had fully fallen on the academy. The golden glow from the street lamps that lined the walkways and huddled next to the buildings did little to banish the black shadows. Or maybe that was just because I'd stolen a laptop and other personal stuff from a dead girl's room and now I was feeling all guilty about it.

I swiped my ID card through the machine and went inside the dorm. A few girls, Amazons mostly, hung out in the common area downstairs, texting on their cells, watching TV, or both. Once again, nobody paid any attention to me as I went up the stairs. I doubted they realized that I lived here at all.

My dorm room was the only one on the third floor, stuck in a separate little round turret that had been added onto the building for whatever reason. The walls were straight, although the roof rose up like a pyramid above my head. A couple of large picture windows were set into the turret, including one with a padded window seat that had an awesome view of the campus and the Appalachian Mountains that towered above it.

My room had the same stuff in it as Jasmine's did—a bed, a desk, some bookcases, a tiny TV—although mine were nowhere near as nice or expensive as hers. Still, I liked it. Grandma Frost had helped me decorate it with all my stuff from home, like my posters of Wonder Woman, Karma Girl, and The Killers. My superthick, purple and gray plaid comforter covered my bed, along with the big, fluffy pillows that I liked, while several Swarovski crystal ornaments shaped like snowflakes dangled in the windows.

The snowflakes were an inside joke between us. With a last name like Frost, it was kind of inevitable. I couldn't even remember when it had started, but every year for Christmas, Grandma gave me something with a snow-flake on it and I did the same for her. Last year, I'd bought her a snowflake-patterned scarf, and she'd given me the snowflake ornaments in return.

They were my favorite things in the room, along with the picture of my mom that sat on my desk, right next to the latest comic books that I was reading.

I opened the small fridge tucked in at the foot of my bed and grabbed a carton of milk and some pieces of the pumpkin roll that Grandma Frost had sent me back to the academy with. Then, I fished Jasmine's laptop out of my bag, along with the book and the photo that I'd taken from her room, and put everything on my scarred wooden desk. While I scarfed down the milk and the pumpkin treat with its sweet cream cheese filling, I plugged the laptop into the wall and waited for it to boot up.

It took *forever,* or maybe it just seemed that way because I was in such a hurry to start surfing through Jasmine's files. Finally, the welcome screen popped up—and asked me for a password.

I finished off my milk and cracked my knuckles. Then, I flexed my fingers and put my hands down onto the keyboard, waiting for the vibes and flashes to hit me, to fill my mind the way they always did.

Nothing happened.

I frowned. No, that wasn't quite true. Stuff happened. A couple of images of Jasmine sitting at her desk downloading music and shopping online flashed before my eyes. And I felt . . . satisfaction—the kind of smug satisfaction that came from getting exactly what you wanted no matter how expensive it was. Jasmine must have really been lusting after those cute black stiletto boots that she'd bought last week.

The problem was that I didn't get the big whammy that I usually did when I touched someone's stuff. Maybe I should have expected it. Computers were one of the everyday items that I could touch without getting much of a vibe off of, especially the ones in the library that were used by tons of kids. Maybe Jasmine just hadn't used her laptop enough to leave much of an impression of herself behind. Maybe there wasn't anything interesting on here. Maybe she didn't have any deep, dark secrets.

Maybe I'd just broken into a dead girl's dorm room for nothing.

I closed my eyes, reaching for my Gypsy gift once more, straining to see something, to feel something, anything that might give me a clue as to who had murdered Jasmine. Or at least what her password was so I could unlock her stupid computer.

I got a couple more images of Jasmine ordering stuff online—something that looked like a fancy knife or letter opener, along with a scarlet robe crusted with jewels. I got that same smug feeling of satisfaction, but that was it. Nothing else.

There wasn't anything in the images that would tell me her password, which was what I really needed right now. I might be savvy enough to slip open a loose door lock, but I wasn't computer literate enough to know how to break into someone's system. I'd need help with that, which was a major, major problem. It wasn't like I had a friend here at Mythos I could just call up and ask for a favor.

It wasn't like I had any friends here at all.

But I'd come this far. I wasn't going to let some stupid password stop me. So I fired up my own laptop and used it to log on to the academy Web site, clicking through the various pages and links until I found what I wanted—a list of all the kids in the Tech Club.

Mythos might be a place of magic, but it also happened to be inhabited by teenagers, some of whose parents owned computer companies and some of whom happened to be budding hackers themselves. For all the old-fashioned magic mumbo jumbo, the Powers That Were at the academy had realized that technology wasn't going away and had gotten with the times. Hence the establishment of the Tech Club.

So all I had to do was find someone willing to help me crack Jasmine's computer and keep quiet about it after the fact—

My eyes spied a name near the top of the alphabetical list. I blinked, making sure that I was seeing it right. *She* was in the Tech Club? Yes, she was, which meant that this whole thing might actually be easier than I'd thought. I looked at the name and sat there a minute, thinking about it.

Then, I smiled. Oh yeah. This part was actually going to be *fun*.

I stood in the back of the dining hall the next day at lunch, looking for her. Like everything else at the academy, the dining hall was *totally* pretentious. Instead of the long orange plastic tables at my old school, the Mythos cafeteria featured round tables covered with creamy white linens, fine china, and crystal vases full of fresh narcissus flowers. The tables were arranged around a large circular open-air garden that featured twisting grapevines, along with orange, olive, and almond trees. Marble statues of gods and goddesses like Dionysus and Demeter peeped through the greenery, watching the students eat. Suits of polished armor lined the walls, along with more oil paintings showing various mythological feasts. Somebody really cared about the ambiance in here, although I didn't know why. It was like eating lunch in a museum.

And the food? It was just as fancy and froufrou as everything else. We're talking veal and liver and escargot and other stuff that I didn't even recognize. Who wanted to scarf down slimy snails for lunch? Yucko. The salads were just about the only thing on the menu that I would even eat, and only because it was really hard to screw up raw vegetables. Still, the chefs at Mythos tried, always carving the carrots into elaborate curlicued shapes and fashioning the tomatoes into rosettes.

But the fanciest things were the desserts. Almost every one of them came in its own special serving bowl, was ridiculously small, and was served flambé. Seriously. A chef would come over and set your thumbnail-size chocolate-cherry soufflé on fire, if that's how he thought it should be served. Whatever. I'd rather have a tin of Grandma Frost's fresh-baked oatmeal raisin cookies any day. At least then I didn't have to worry about getting my eyebrows singed off because I needed a sugar fix.

I'd finished eating my usual grilled chicken salad five minutes ago, and now I was looking for the person who was going to help me break into Jasmine's laptop, even if she didn't know it yet.

It took me another two minutes of scanning the crowd before I spotted her sitting on the far side of the dining hall, a book on the table in front of her, even though her black eyes were fixed on the band geek next to her. I wound my way through the tables, heading toward them.

"...and so you see, there's lots of symbolism in *The Iliad,*" Carson Callahan lectured in a patient voice. "All you have to do is pick out your favorite god or hero and I'm sure I can help you come up with something to write your English lit paper on."

Daphne Cruz gave the object of her affection a dazzling smile that turned her from merely pretty into downright gorgeous. "You're so smart, Carson. It's all just gibberish to me."

Daphne eased a little closer to the band geek and put her hand on his arm. Carson's brown eyes widened behind his black glasses, and he blinked several times. The two of them were lost in their own little world.

I cleared my throat. "So sorry to interrupt."

At the sound of my voice, they started and jumped back from each other, as though they'd been doing something they shouldn't have. Daphne's head snapped up to me, even though Carson kept staring at her.

"Then why are you?" Daphne asked in a low, ugly voice.

She tapped a nail on her book, and pink sparks flickered in the air. The Valkyrie was annoyed with me for interrupting her pseudodate with her crush.

I smiled at her. "Because I need to talk to you, Daphne. About that special project that we've been assigned for myth-history class."

She frowned. "What project? You're not even in my myth-history class—"

"You know. The one we talked about in the girls' bathroom the other day. It was right after I told you about that charm bracelet that I found for Carson." I looked at the band geek. "How did that work out for you, Carson? You and Leta?"

Despite his dusky skin, the band geek still flushed an interesting shade of purple-red. "Um, well, I haven't actually, ah, done anything about that yet, Gwen."

"Well, you'd better hurry," I said. "The homecoming dance is Friday night. You wouldn't want to go without a date, now would you?"

Daphne's eyes narrowed, and her glossy pink lips pressed into a line that was so hard and thin that I couldn't even see them in her face anymore.

"Carson," Daphne said in a deceptively sweet voice. "I really do have to talk to Gwen. Maybe we can catch up later? Before last period and talk about my paper some more?"

"Sure," Carson said.

Daphne and I kept staring at each other. Carson's head swiveled back and forth between the two of us, not sure what was going on. Finally, though, after about thirty seconds of absolute silence, he got the idea that he should leave.

"Okay, then, I'll just . . . go," he said.

Carson stood up and started stuffing books and papers into his bag, before he looped the strap over his shoulder. He gave me another look before staring down at Daphne. The Valkyrie was too busy glaring at me to notice, but a sad, quiet longing crept into the band geek's gaze as he looked at her. Sweet, but I didn't have time for the Romeo and Juliet drama right now.

"Bye, Carson," I said in a firm voice, prodding him on his way.

Carson snapped out of his silent Valkyrie worship. "Um, bye, Gwen."

Carson gave Daphne one more longing look, then threaded his way through the tables and headed out of the dining hall.

I waited until Carson was out of sight before I sat down in his spot. Next to me, Daphne packed up her own books and papers as fast as she could, probably intending to leave me sitting here by myself since I'd driven off her crush.

"That was a cozy little scene," I said in a mild voice. "I didn't know you were such a flirt, Daphne."

The Valkyrie gave me a look that would have cut glass. "I wasn't flirting with Carson."

"Oh, sure you were. You were practically batting your lashes at him. And that *hand-on-the-arm* move? A *classic* flirting technique. Executed very well, by the way. Did Morgan McDougall give you some tips? I hear that she's quite popular with the guys."

Daphne glowered at me, but she didn't deny any of it. She knew that there was no use, not after the confession she'd given me in the girls' bathroom the other day. She sighed, leaned back in her chair, and crossed her arms over her chest.

"What do you want, Gwen Frost?" she snapped. "I've got an English lit paper to write, in case you didn't hear."

"I want you to help me with something."

She let out an angry snort. "And what would that be?"

I looked around to make sure that no one was paying attention to us, then leaned forward. "I want you to help me break the password on Jasmine Ashton's laptop."

Daphne frowned, as though she didn't understand what I'd just said. "Jasmine's laptop? How would you even—"

Her black eyes widened. "You have it! You have her laptop! You dirty little thief!"

"Sshh!" I hissed, glancing around to make sure no one had heard her. "Not so loud. I'm trying to keep this on the down-low. But yeah, I have her laptop. And some other stuff, too."

"What are you doing with Jasmine's laptop?" Daphne snapped. "You going to hock it and buy some more of those stupid hoodies you're always wearing?"

"No," I said in the calmest voice I could manage. "I want to see what's on it so I can figure out who killed Jasmine."

Daphne frowned again, but she didn't say anything. Instead, the Valkyrie sat there and stared at me, as though she couldn't believe what she was hearing. "Everybody knows that a Reaper killed Jasmine so he could steal the Bowl of Tears. Whoever he is, the guy is long gone by now."

I shrugged. "Maybe. But I see things, remember? And I've got a weird feeling about all of this."

Daphne's frown deepened. "But why do you even care what happened to Jasmine? She wasn't a friend of yours. You didn't even *know* her."

"No," I replied in a soft voice. "But I was there that night in the library when she was killed. And it could have just as easily been me as her who was lying underneath that glass case with my throat cut and blood everywhere."

I drew in a breath and told Daphne what had really happened that night. How I'd been in the library, heard a noise, and found Jasmine's body. A shiver slithered up my spine as I finished my story. It was a thought that I hadn't even let myself think too much about until now, but it was true. Whoever had stolen the Bowl of Tears was the same person who'd killed Jasmine and knocked me out. So why hadn't he stopped long enough to cut my throat as well? Why hadn't he killed me, too? That way, there wouldn't have been any witnesses at all.

"Look," I said in a quiet voice. "Everyone thinks that it was some anonymous Reaper who killed Jasmine and took the Bowl of Tears. But Professor Metis told me that Reapers can be anyone, even Mythos students. What if it wasn't some mystery bad guy? What if it was somebody we go to class with? That freaks me out."

Daphne didn't say anything, but I could see the agreement flashing in her eyes.

"I use my Gypsy gift to find things for people, so I thought I'd poke around a little and see if I could figure out what really happened. So yeah, I broke into Jasmine's dorm room last night and I took her laptop, hoping to find some sort of clue on it. Something to at least tell me why she was in the library. Maybe that makes me a thief, but at least I'm trying; at least I'm doing *something*. Everybody else doesn't even seem to care that she's dead. You were one of her friends. Can you say the same?"

Guilt flickered across Daphne's face before she could hide it.

The blond Valkyrie stared at me, her fingers drumming on the white linen tablecloth and shooting pink sparks of magic everywhere. "So why come to me? Why ask me to help? Besides the fact that I'm one of Jasmine's friends?"

"Because I know you're in the Tech Club, which means you can probably break the password with no problem. And because I've got something on you, which means you'll keep quiet about all this."

Her face tightened. "Carson."

I nodded. "Carson."

I didn't tell her what would happen if she didn't agree to help me. Daphne knew all too well. The rumor would spread through the academy like wildfire that she had a crush on Carson Callahan, of all people. It would go viral in about five seconds, and she'd be the laughingstock of the entire school. At least for this week.

She sighed. "What do you want me to do, Gwen?"

"Come up to my dorm room after last period today. Help me crack the password on the laptop and you never have to talk to me again."

"And you won't tell anyone?" she asked. "About Carson?"

I shook my head. "Not a soul."

Daphne stared at me, trying to read my face and figure out if I was telling her the truth or not. After a minute, the Valkyrie made up her mind, because she stopped drumming her fingers on the table. She sighed and nodded.

"All right. I'll do it. Not because I'm scared of you or whatever little rumor you might start, but because Jasmine was my friend. Okay?"

"Okay."

I wrote down my dorm and room number and told her to meet me there later.

"I can hardly wait," Daphne muttered before slipping the piece of paper into her giant Dooney & Bourke purse.

"Yeah," I drawled. "It's almost like we're BFFs already."

The Valkyrie gave me another dirty look before she slung her purse over her shoulder and stalked out of the dining hall.

Chapter 9

The rest of the day *dragged* by, especially Professor Metis's myth-history class. I stared out the window again, wondering if Daphne would really show up at my dorm room and help me with Jasmine's computer or if the Valkyrie would stand me up and rat me out to someone—

"...given the terrible tragedy and shock that we've all experienced, I thought that we would talk about the Bowl of Tears today and its importance in the Chaos War." Metis's soft voice cut into my musings.

My head snapped around to her. Metis was going to talk about the Bowl? The one that had been stolen? This might actually be useful, instead of the usual stuff that she went on and on and *on* about. All the talk about gods and goddesses and warrior whiz kids that I didn't quite believe. At least, that I hadn't quite believed before this week. The jury was still out on that one.

I wasn't the only kid who was suddenly showing

more interest. Everyone sat up straighter and stared at the professor.

Metis told us to look at page 379 in our myth-history books. I flipped to the page, and there it was—an illustration of the Bowl of Tears, the same bowl that Nickamedes had shown me in the library. It looked the same as I remembered. Round, brown, dull, plain. It didn't look like much of anything, certainly not like some powerful artifact that was worth killing over.

"Loki was always a trickster god, playing pranks on his fellow gods and mortals, but eventually, his mischief turned to evil, and his tricks became cruel. Among his many crimes, Loki was responsible for the death of Balder, the Norse god of light. Loki tricked another god into throwing a mistletoe spear at Balder, which pierced Balder's heart and killed him," Metis explained. "As part of his punishment for that and his other crimes, Loki was chained below a giant asp, or snake, which constantly dripped venom onto his face. A very harsh form of torture. Loki was supposed to stay there for all time, locked away so he could never hurt anyone again. But, of course, he eventually tricked Sigyn, his wife, into releasing him, and escaped."

"So where does the Bowl come in?" a girl across the room asked.

Metis smiled. "Patience, Skylar. We're getting to that. Now, the Bowl you see in your books is the one that Sigyn used to collect the snake venom. Despite his crimes, Sigyn loved Loki very, very much, and she held up the Bowl over his head, catching as much of the venom as she could to keep it from dripping on to her husband and burning him. But by standing there Sigyn also exposed herself to the venom, which severely burned her hands and arms."

It sounded to me like Sigyn was kind of . . . dumb. Loki was the one who got another god killed, not her. She should have let him be punished for it, not tried to lessen his pain, let him escape, and hurt herself in the process. Or maybe I was just being bloodthirsty since the cops had never caught the drunk driver who'd plowed into my mom's car. I wouldn't have minded seeing him, whoever he was, chained up under a giant snake with poison, acid, or whatever dripping all over his face.

"When the Bowl filled up, Sigyn would have to empty it, which let the venom drip freely onto Loki's face, causing him unimaginable pain. When Sigyn came back with the empty Bowl, before she would lift it up again, Loki's tears would drip into it, mixing with the venom. That's why it's called the Bowl of Tears," Professor Metis finished.

She told us to turn the page. There an illustration showed a giant snake curled around a tree, its head hanging down, its jaws open wide enough to reveal its curved fangs, a drop of fluid hanging off the end of each of them.

Loki cowered beneath the snake. The pen-and-ink drawing showed the god in utter agony, his mouth open in a silent scream, the muscles in his neck and arms bulging with the strain of trying to break free of the magical chains that bound him. His features were blurred in the drawing, but half his face looked like it was melted off. Because of the venom, I supposed.

"So, we know why Loki was chained up the first time—his actions resulted in the death of another god. But why was Loki chained up a second time centuries later and why does he remain imprisoned even now?" Professor Metis asked.

"Because he started the Chaos War," Carson piped up in front of me.

"Yes and no, Carson," Professor Metis replied. "Loki was chained up because he *was* Chaos. Each of the gods has his own place in the natural order of things. Loki was a mischief god. But Loki wanted more than to just pull pranks—he wanted to *rule* over the other gods. Over everyone and everything, gods, mortals, and all the creatures in between. Loki was smart and very, very clever. He knew that he couldn't overthrow the other gods by himself. He didn't have the power for that. So he started talking to others—gods, mortals, and all the creatures in between—whispering of how things would be different, of how things would be so much *better,* if he was in charge. He went from being a mischief god to sowing discord, to turning people against each other, to making them lust for power and do anything to get it—even kill each other."

I got the sense that it was a little more complicated

than all that, that perhaps Metis was dumbing it down for our teenage minds, but I got the gist of things. Loki: bad. Other gods: good.

"Eventually, Loki convinced others to follow him, and he created his own army of gods, creatures, and mortal warriors. He called them the Reapers of Chaos. And when he had enough followers, when he'd amassed enough power, Loki came out of hiding, rose up with his army, and challenged the other gods, who banded together with their own warriors and creatures to form the Pantheon," Professor Metis continued. "So the Reapers fought the members of the Pantheon, and the world was plunged into the Chaos War. Brother turned against brother, sister against sister; families were torn apart, slaughtered, or worse. It went on for the better part of a century, and Loki was on the cusp of victory when one god dared to challenge him to single combat. And who was that god?"

Nike, the Greek goddess of victory. Somehow, I knew the answer even before Metis said the words.

"Nike, the Greek goddess of victory," she finished. "Loki laughed, but he agreed to Nike's request, that the winner of the battle would also win the war. Which meant that the Chaos War would either stop or consume the entire world."

By this point, we were all on the edges of our seats, even me, Gwen Frost, the Gypsy girl who didn't really believe any of this. We all wanted to hear how it ended, how Loki was defeated when all hope was lost. Even if it wasn't true, it was still a great story, as good as any of the comic books that I had stashed in my dorm room.

"Of course, Loki thought he would win," Metis said. "He had grown impossibly strong by that point, and no one god, warrior, or creature could stand up against him. But he forgot one small thing—that Nike was the goddess of victory."

"So what?" a Viking guy asked behind me. "What did it matter if she was the goddess of victory if Loki had all this power?"

That was pretty much the same thing that I was thinking. But instead of being upset by his question, Professor Metis gave him a triumphant smile.

"Because Nike is much more than just the goddess of victory—she is the very embodiment of it, the very *spirit* of it. Just the way that every god is the essence of something. Nike is victory herself, and thus, she can never be defeated."

Metis paused, letting us all try to wrap our minds around that odd statement. Nike, a kick-ass warrior goddess. Got it. Like Xena, but cooler.

"But Nike wasn't without help. She took her great sword of victory into battle, along with a special shield given to her by one of the Spartan kings. And there were other artifacts that the members of the Pantheon used to overcome the Reapers. With Nike at all times was a single warrior, a personal guard who killed all those in the goddess's path so that she could reach Loki unscathed. Loki, of course, being the trickster that he was, tried to have Nike assassinated before she could reach him for their battle, but Nike's guard kept that from happening."

Metis paused a moment to catch her breath. A rosy flush painted her bronze cheeks, and her green eyes glinted behind her silver glasses. This was the most excited and animated I'd ever seen the professor. She must really enjoy talking about this particular battle. She was certainly making it come alive for me.

"So Loki and Nike fought a great battle. And it wasn't just them alone, fighting. All of their followers were there as well. Reapers and members of the Pantheon. Some historians claim that the battle lasted for days; others say it was weeks. But when she finally got close enough to strike, Nike did what no other god could do—she defeated Loki."

We flipped over to the next page in our textbooks, and there was a pen-and-ink drawing of Nike.

The goddess towered over a man on the ground beneath her. Her sandaled foot rested on his chest, her sword against his throat. A round shield hung down by her side. She looked proud, strong, and somehow serious all at the same time. Even though it was just a drawing, there was a cold, hard, terrible sort of beauty to her.

Her regal figure was in stark contrast to the man at her feet—Loki. He looked the same as he had in the other illustration. His mouth open in an angry scream, his eyes narrowed to snakelike slits, his melted features twisted into something dark, dangerous, and ugly.

For a moment, the image flickered in front of me, the

figures moving back and forth as though they were real, as though I was actually there watching the battle with my own eyes. I could smell the blood, feel the thick smoke clogging my lungs, hear Loki's vicious curses ringing in my ears—

I blinked. The feelings vanished, and I was once again looking at a simple illustration. That was a little creepy. I leaned back away from the book. Okay, a lot creepy.

"After the battle, Nike and her followers chained Loki once more, sealing him away from this world, the mortal realm, with the help of the artifacts that they and the Reapers had created. To this day, Loki remains imprisoned. But he still has his followers, his Reapers, people, gods, and creatures who want to free him and plunge the world into a second Chaos War. Which is why all of you are here."

Metis's bright green gaze went from student to student, face to face, until she'd looked at everyone in the room, including me. "You are all the descendants of the Pantheon's finest warriors, here to learn how to control and harness your magic and fighting skills so you can protect the world from Reapers and keep them from freeing Loki and plunging us all into a second Chaos War—"

The bell rang, cutting off the rest of Metis's lecture, but she'd captivated the entire class with her talk. Several students blinked, shaking off the spell of her words, before reaching for their bags. I did the same.

I got to my feet and had started to head to the door with the others when Metis waved at me.

"Gwen," she said. "Stay a minute, please."

I did as she asked, sinking back down into my seat. A few of the other kids, including Carson, looked at me, thinking that I was in some kind of trouble. I wondered if Metis knew that I'd broken into Jasmine's dorm room and swiped her laptop. That was the only thing I'd done that could get me into major trouble. But how could Metis know about that? There was just no way she could, unless Daphne Cruz had ratted me out to her.

Professor Metis straightened a few papers on her wooden podium, then walked over and perched on a desk in front of me. "We didn't get a chance to talk yesterday, but I wanted to ask how you were doing, Gwen. I know that what happened in the library . . . that finding Jasmine's body was a great shock to you."

So she didn't know that I'd broken into the Valkyrie's room after all. I tried not to let my relief show. "I'm okay, I guess. Just trying to . . . deal with it, in my own way."

I didn't tell her that my own way involved breaking, entering, and blackmail. So far. The day wasn't over yet.

Professor Metis stared at me, her green eyes soft and kind. "Well, if you want to talk about it, or anything else, anything at all, please know that I'm always here for you, Gwen."

For a moment, I wondered why she was so concerned about me. Yeah, I had sort of witnessed a murder, and I supposed that Metis was just a nice person that way. But I'd never seen the professor until the day that she'd shown up at my grandma's house and announced that I was going to Mythos. Now, it seemed like she was taking a special interest in everything I said and did—in and outside of class.

"Um, okay. So can I go now?" I asked, shifting in my seat. "I have an, um, appointment."

Metis smiled. "Of course. I just wanted to make sure that you were okay. I know coming to Mythos this year has been a bit of an adjustment for you, Gwen."

I let out a soft snort. She had no idea. None at all.

Metis went back up to the podium. I got to my feet, picked up my bag, and started to leave. But then I thought about something that Metis had said during her lecture. Something that had been bothering me ever since I'd come to the academy two months ago.

"Professor?"

"Yes, Gwen?" she said, turning to look at me.

"So if everything you said was true about all the kids at Mythos being the descendants of all these great warriors, then why am I here? I'm not a Valkyrie or an Amazon or a Spartan or a Viking. I'm not anything like that at all. I'm just a Gypsy. There are no great warriors in my family, at least not that I know of."

Some emotion flashed in Metis's eyes, but I couldn't quite see what it was through her thick glasses. The professor stared at me for several seconds before she spoke again.

"Not everyone at Mythos will turn out to be a great warrior," Metis finally said. "Some will be healers, scholars, or teachers. There are many ways to fight Reapers, and not all of them involve using a sword. You have your own gifts, Gwen. You're special in your own way. You're here at Mythos so we can teach you how to take full advantage of your powers, of your psychometry. It's quite a rare gift, you know, touch magic."

Touch magic? I wondered what Metis meant by that, since I'd never heard my psychometry called that before. And no, I didn't know how rare it was because no one had ever told me. It was just something that I could do, something that made me a Gypsy, whatever that really was. Everyone seemed to know but me.

Metis turned back to the papers on her podium, and I realized that she wasn't going to give me any more of an answer than that. At least, not today.

So I slung my messenger bag over my shoulder and left the classroom, once again with far more questions than answers about who I was, what I could do, and why I was stuck here at Mythos Academy—a place where I so obviously didn't belong.

Chapter 10

After class, I walked over to Styx Hall to wait for Daphne Cruz to show up and help me crack Jasmine Ashton's password like she'd promised. To my surprise, the blond Valkyrie was already sitting on the front steps of the dorm when I got there.

"You actually came," I said, walking up to where she was sitting.

She shrugged. "You didn't exactly give me a choice, did you, Gwen? So let's get this over with."

I swiped my ID card through the scanner, opened the door, and gestured for Daphne to follow me inside. "Come on in. My room's on the third floor."

I led Daphne up the stairs to my room in the turret. I went inside, threw my bag on the bed, and sat down on my desk chair, right underneath my framed Wonder Woman poster.

Daphne stood in the doorway, her black eyes scanning over everything just the way that I'd done in Jasmine's room last night. For a moment, I looked at my things, seeing them with a new eye. My bed with its purple and gray comforter and plump pillows. The crystal snowflake ornaments in the windows throwing out tiny rainbows of color. The bookcases crammed full of fantasy titles. The stacks and stacks of comic books and graphic novels on my desk. The superhero posters plastered on the walls. The half-eaten pack of gummi bears on my nightstand that I'd noshed on last night before going to bed.

I cringed. Shit. I'd forgotten what a total geek nest my room was. Daphne was the only other person who'd been in here besides me and Grandma Frost, when she'd helped me move in two months ago. The Valkyrie was going to think that I was even more of a loser than she did already. Great.

After a minute of staring, Daphne stepped into the room and closed the door behind her.

"Where's Jasmine's computer?" she asked.

I showed her where I'd set it up on my desk. "Right here."

I got up so Daphne could sit in my chair and have easier access to the laptop. I perched on the bed while she opened up the computer and turned it on. When the system had booted up, the Valkyrie looked at the password screen for a few seconds before starting to type.

"All right, baby," Daphne crooned. "Talk to Mama and tell me all your secrets. . . ."

Okay, that was a little weird. I didn't want to break

her concentration, so I didn't point out the fact that the Valkyrie was talking to a machine. Instead, I leaned back on the bed, grabbed the bag of gummi bears, and prepared myself for a long wait.

Three minutes later, Daphne hit a final key and pumped her fist. "Hah! Gotcha!"

I sat up. "You cracked it already?"

"Of course I cracked it already," she said in a smug voice. "It was just a simple password protection screen. It wasn't like Jasmine had any kind of *real* security on her computer."

"Well then," I said, moving to stand behind Daphne. "Let's see what's on it."

For the next ten minutes Daphne surfed through all the files on the laptop. Most of them were totally boring. History reports, essays, and all the other homework that Mythos students had to do. Lots of music and high-end shopping sites in Jasmine's Web-browsing history. She even had a database that was solely dedicated to cataloging and organizing all of her designer clothes, shoes, and handbags. Apparently, the Valkyrie liked to keep track of how many times she wore each one of her outfits— never more than once a month. Must be nice. All I had was a different-colored hoodie for every day of the week.

Then, Daphne pulled up Jasmine's personal, private e-mails—the ones that weren't posted on her Mythos Academy Web page for everyone to see. Now, those? They were *way* more interesting than anything else on the computer.

Jasmine might have been the prettiest, richest, most popular girl in our second-year class, but like Carson Callahan had said, she certainly hadn't been the nicest. There were catty, mean-girl comments about practically everyone at Mythos in her e-mails, especially Morgan McDougall, her supposed best friend—and Daphne, too.

"She told Morgan that I looked like a heifer in those pink skinny jeans? She's the one who told me to buy them in the first place! Bitch," Daphne muttered. "Let's see what else Jasmine wrote about me."

"Actually, I'm more interested in what she had to say about Morgan and Samson Sorensen," I said.

Daphne looked over her shoulder at me. "Why?"

I showed her the picture that I'd found of Morgan and Samson, the one that had been torn in two and shoved in the bottom of Jasmine's trash can. "I haven't touched it yet, but it's got to mean something."

"What do you mean you haven't touched it yet?" Daphne asked in a suspicious voice.

I sighed. "I mean I haven't *touched-it touched it* yet. That's how my Gypsy gift works. I have to touch something before I get a vibe off of it. Before I can see anything about the object or the person it belonged to."

"So why don't you do that now?" Daphne said in a cross voice. Reading Jasmine's comments had really pissed her off. "Because I don't plan on coming back here to help you again."

"Fine," I muttered.

I plopped down on my bed, picked up the two pieces of the photo, and held them up side by side, like I was trying to put the picture back together. For several long seconds I didn't feel anything, and I wondered if my psychometry was even going to work. If it had somehow gone on the fritz. I hadn't gotten any big flashes off Jasmine's laptop, and I hadn't gotten any vibes at all off her body or blood in the library. Maybe there was something wrong with me, something wrong with my Gypsy gift.

I was just about to put the photo down when I felt the faintest stirrings of something—a niggling worm of worry, wriggling deeper and deeper into my heart. As I held on to the photo, the worry intensified, ballooning up into a large ball of suspicion that felt like a lead weight pressing down on my stomach. The ball turned icy as cold knowledge sank into me. I recognized the feelings and what they meant. Wriggling worry, then heavy suspicion, and finally cold confirmation. Whatever Jasmine had thought was going on between Morgan and Samson, between her best friend and her boyfriend, she'd seen or heard something that made her think it was true, that it was really happening.

But the feelings didn't stop there.

The cold knowledge began to burn like acid in my stomach, growing hotter and hotter, as though I'd somehow swallowed a ball of fire. The burning spread through the rest of my body, making me sweat, my hands shake, and my heart hurt, like a giant fist was squeezing it tighter and tighter until it wanted to pop from the strain. I knew what this emotion was, too—rage.

An image of Jasmine filled my mind, one of her sitting and staring at the photo, tucked into the frame with the others in the mirror on her vanity table. Day after day Jasmine had looked at it, before she finally reached up, yanked the photo out of the frame, and ripped it in two, her face white with anger.

By this point, I could hear myself babbling, my voice getting sharper and louder with every word: "Bitch. I'm going to kill that bitch for doing this to me, for betraying me like this. Pay, pay, pay, she's going to pay—"

Daphne slapped me across the face, pink sparks of magic flicking off the ends of her fingers. The blow knocked me back onto the bed, but the Valkyrie wasn't done. She reached forward and ripped the two pieces of the photo out of my fisted hands.

It was like a switch had been shut off deep inside me. Slowly, the hate, rage, and jealousy that I'd felt faded, the pain in my heart eased, and I was in control of myself once more. I let out a long breath. That had been *intense*, even for me.

When I felt like it, I sat back up. Daphne stood over me, a worried look on her pretty face. She held the two pieces of the photo with the edges of her fingernails, as though they were something evil. Maybe they were, given the emotions that were attached to them and the awful things that Jasmine had been feeling whenever she looked at the picture of her best friend and her boyfriend.

"Geez," Daphne muttered. "Does that happen every time you touch something? Because that's some freaky stuff, Gwen."

I rubbed my aching head. "Tell me about it."

"So what did you see?"

I told Daphne about all the emotions that I'd felt, about seeing Jasmine staring at the photo over and over again and growing a little angrier every single time until she'd finally ripped it up in a fit of rage.

"So Jasmine thought there was something going on with Morgan and Samson?" Daphne asked in a doubtful tone. "You must be wrong. Because if Jasmine even *thought* that Morgan was putting the moves on Samson, she would have cut Morgan's throat—not ended up like that herself in the library."

I shrugged. I hadn't known Jasmine well enough to speculate on what she would or wouldn't do. All that I'd wanted was to learn what had really happened to her, why she'd come back to the library, and why no one seemed to care that she'd been murdered. Maybe it was my Gypsy gift, but I had a feeling that this was what I was supposed to do. That I was supposed to figure this out. That I *needed* to. That maybe I might even discover some secret about myself along the way.

I shook my head to chase away the strange feeling. "What else is on her computer? Anything about the Bowl of Tears?"

Daphne sat back down at my desk and turned her attention to the screen once more. "Nothing that I see that jumps out at me— Wait a second. Here's something.

Looks like Jasmine wrote her first myth-history report of the semester on the Bowl of Tears. Take a look."

I peered over Daphne's shoulder at the screen. Sure enough, Jasmine had written an essay about the Bowl and the fact that Nickamedes was taking it out of storage and putting it on display at the Library of Antiquities. I scanned through the report, but it didn't tell me anything that Professor Metis hadn't earlier. Maybe I'd been wrong. Maybe Jasmine had just had the *Great Artifacts* book in her room so she could do her report.

But that still didn't tell me why she was at the library that night. Had she just wanted another look at the Bowl? If so, why? Why then? So late at night when nobody else was around?

"Hey," I asked Daphne, "do you know what Jasmine was doing in the library that night? Why she was there? I remember seeing the four of you in there earlier—you, Jasmine, Morgan, and Samson. Why did she come back?"

Daphne shrugged. "We went back to our dorm and hung out awhile, watching TV and texting. Jasmine said she thought that maybe she'd left her sweater at the library and she was going to go back to look for it before the library closed. That was the last time that I saw her."

A shadow fell over Daphne's face, and she drummed her fingers on the laptop, causing pink sparks to flash and flicker around the room like tiny fireflies. I plopped back down on the bed, still trying to recover from having touched the photo and feeling all of Jasmine's pent-up anger, jealousy, and rage.

I tried to think what my mom, the detective, would do in a situation like this, where she would go from this dead end that I'd come up against. But nothing came to mind.

"Well, thanks for your help," I said. "I, uh, appreciate it."

Daphne took that as her cue to leave. She stood, picked up her designer purse from where she had set it down on the floor, and slung the oversize bag on her shoulder. Then, the Valkyrie looked at me.

"What are you going to do now?" she asked. "Because all you have is a myth-history report, a torn-up photo, and some feelings. It doesn't exactly tell you what's going on. Face it, Gwen. Some Reaper broke into the library to steal the Bowl of Tears, and Jasmine had the bad luck to get in his way. That's why she got killed. There's no big mystery, conspiracy, or whatever you think. These things just happen at Mythos."

I wanted to ask her why bad things like that happened here, why all the students were expected to grow up and take part in some stupid ancient war between the gods. Why didn't the gods and goddesses just fight it out among themselves and leave the rest of us alone? But Daphne would probably just give me the same answer that Carson had. The two of them had grown up with all this talk of magic. It was natural to them, even if it wasn't to me.

So I just shrugged. "I don't know."

She nodded. "Well, good luck with it, I suppose."

I nodded back at her, and she headed for my bedroom door.

"Daphne."

She turned to look at me.

"You really should give Carson a chance. Because he happens to be crazy about you." I didn't know why I was telling her this. Maybe because Daphne had actually been kind of cool about this whole thing, even if I had blackmailed her into helping me.

She frowned. "How do you know that?"

"Because when I touched that rose charm, the one that fell behind the desk when you picked up the bracelet?"

She nodded.

"Well, I didn't just feel your emotions. I felt Carson's, too. He really bought that bracelet for you, Daphne. He just told you that story about Leta Gaston to see what you'd say, to see if you actually liked the bracelet or not. He wanted to give it to you and ask you to the homecoming dance that night, but he chickened out."

Daphne's mouth fell open in surprise, and hope and wonder flashed in her black eyes. "Carson—Carson likes me? Really? He really likes me? You're not just making it all up?"

I shook my head. "He really likes you; I promise. I see things, remember? Trust me, I know."

A goofy, dreamy sort of grin spread across Daphne's

face. Then, she realized that I was still watching her, and she pressed her lips together into a tight line once more.

"You know what, Gwen? You might be okay, for a total geek with absolutely no fashion sense."

With those words and a small, sly smile the Valkyrie turned and left my bedroom. The strangest thing was that I found myself grinning back at her as she closed the door.

Chapter 11

I didn't get much sleep that night, mainly because I was still feeling the aftereffects of touching the ripped-up photo, still feeling the echoes of Jasmine's rage and the massive migraine it had given me.

Maybe I should have known better by now. After all, my Gypsy gift had let me see and feel a lot of things over the years—the good, the bad, and the just plain awful. But I still couldn't believe that Jasmine Ashton, the pretty, perfect rich girl who seemed to have everything, could feel that much rage at her best friend. Even if she did think that Morgan had something going on with Samson. Guys. They *so* weren't worth the drama.

My lack of sleep put me in a grouchy mood the next day, especially when it was time for my fifth-period gym class.

I *hated* gym class.

Going to a school full of the descendants of mythological warriors was bad enough. But the Powers That

Were actually expected me to be coordinated, too. Gym class at Mythos was completely different from what it had been back at my old school. There were no basketballs, softballs, or volleyballs in sight.

There were too many weapons crowded into the gym for that.

Like everything else at Mythos, the gym was enormous, with a ceiling that soared several hundred feet into the air. Colorful banners announcing various academy championships over the years dangled down from the rafters, while glossy wooden bleachers ringed the gym on two sides. Thick mats lined the floors, hiding the squeaky basketball court from sight, and racks of weapons butted up against one of the walls. Swords, daggers, bows, staffs, and other things that I didn't even know the names for but that looked like they would cut you to the bone if you so much as touched them.

The point of gym class at Mythos wasn't to score the most or run the most laps like it had been back at my old school. Oh no. Here? You were actually supposed to learn how to use all the weapons on the wall. How to kill, maim, and torture your opponent, whoever it might be.

At the moment, though, I was the one being tortured.

"Hee-yah!" the girl in front of me screamed before darting forward, raising her sword high, and bringing it down toward my head with every intention of killing me dead, dead, dead.

I winced, backed up, and raised my own sword. Her

weapon hit my blade, the sharp *clanggg* of it reverberating all the way up my hand and into my shoulder. The sword slid from my suddenly numb fingers and thumped onto the mat, the way it had five times already in the last five minutes.

"You're supposed to block my blow and try to hit me back. Not drop your sword every single time I hit you." Talia Pizarro rolled her eyes at me. "Geez, Gwen. You really suck at this."

"Tell me something I don't already know," I muttered.

At the start of gym class, we drew names to see who would fight whom. Talia had the misfortune of being my sparring partner today. She was an Amazon with ebony skin and short black hair who was almost six feet tall. Talia also happened to be the captain of the girls' fencing team and could make a pincushion out of me with her sword if she really wanted to. Like all the other Amazons, she was gifted with supernatural quickness. Talia looked like a blur when she moved. One second, she was in front of me. The next, she'd hit me with her sword six times already.

"Let's go again," Talia barked. "You might not get anything out of this, but I want to be able to pass my advanced weapons test next week."

Oh yeah. There were tests, too. I was actually being graded on how well I could chop off someone's head or put an arrow through his eye. I'd prided myself on my perfect 4.0 GPA at my old school, but gym was one

class at Mythos that I was definitely going to fail this semester and every other one. Students were required to
take gym and all the weapons training that went with it
every single semester until they graduated. Yippee-
skippee.

Since Talia was looking at me with murder in her
eyes, I sighed and picked up my sword again. I also used
the lull in the action to look over to my left, where Morgan McDougall was sparring with her own partner, another Valkyrie girl.

Gym was the only class that I had with Morgan, and
I'd been watching her all period long. Maybe it was
nothing or maybe I was just crazy and grasping at
straws, but I felt like there was some connection between Jasmine's murder and that ripped-up photo of
Morgan and Samson. Something obvious that I just
wasn't seeing.

I wasn't the only one interested in Morgan. Half the
guys in the gym kept sneaking looks at her, since Morgan filled out her tight, white T-shirt quite a bit better
than most of the other girls did theirs. And Morgan totally knew that the guys were watching her. Ten minutes
ago, she'd accidentally-on-purpose spilled water all
down the front of her shirt, plastering the fabric to the
black sports bra that she had on underneath.

Morgan and her partner finished their latest round of
combat. Then, Morgan looked down at her diamond-
encrusted watch, said something to the other girl, and
slipped out one of the side doors of the gym.

My eyes narrowed. Class wasn't even halfway over yet. So where was the Valkyrie going?

"Hold this," I said, passing my sword to Talia and hurrying after Morgan.

"Hey! Where do you think you're going?" Talia hissed, but I paid no attention to her.

It wasn't like I even needed to be in gym class. I wasn't descended from a long line of mythological warriors, and I certainly didn't have anything to do with the Pantheon, Reapers, or the Chaos War. But I did want to find out what had happened to Jasmine, which was something that spying on Morgan might actually help me with.

I kept to the edges of the gym, so I wouldn't draw attention to myself and the fact that I was trying to sneak outside in the middle of class. Since everyone else was absorbed in beating the crap out of each other, nobody noticed me.

Not even Logan Quinn, who was on the other side of the gym. Logan and Oliver Hector, another Spartan, were getting some pointers from Coach Ajax. The big, burly coach barked out some instructions, and the two guys bowed to each other before falling into crouching positions. Ajax held up his hand, then dropped it, and the two Spartans went at each other.

Smack—smack—smack!

The two staffs blurred together as Logan and Oliver fought, each turning, twisting, and doing his best to smash the other's skull in with the blunt weapon. The fight lasted maybe thirty seconds before Logan did some kind of fancy move, used his staff to sweep Oliver's feet out from under him, and darted forward, putting the edge of his staff against the other guy's throat. Winner: Logan Quinn.

Ajax barked out something else and clapped his hands, apparently happy with his star pupil. Logan smiled and stepped back casually, elegantly twirling the staff in his hand like it was a cheerleader's baton instead of a deadly weapon. Of course, *he* would love gym class. Beating up people was something that he seemed to excel at. Especially if you believed all the rumors about Logan and how wild, violent, and crazy he and the rest of his Spartan friends were.

And he looked good doing it. Logan wore a T-shirt with the sleeves cut off, exposing the muscles in his arms. The deep blue color of the shirt also brightened his icy eyes, making them seem like they were almost glowing in his face, even all the way over here on the opposite side of the gym. Logan raised up the end of his T-shirt to wipe the sweat off his face, exposing his flat, muscled stomach.

For a moment, I stopped, completely mesmerized. Just . . . *wow.* All that and washboard abs, too. Ones that put Samson Sorensen's to *shame.* I wondered if all the other Spartans at Mythos were as dangerous and sexy as Logan was or if he'd just been blessed with all the bad boy charm—

An arrow *thunking* into the target behind me snapped

me out of my reverie. I shook my head and moved on. I wasn't here to ogle Logan. I had a Valkyrie to spy on.

I hurried on and slipped out the same side door that Morgan had. The door led out to a small courtyard that connected the gym to the indoor swimming pool that was also part of the academy's massive stone sports complex.

In addition to a variety of hyacinths and lotus trees, the courtyard featured a round fountain with marble nymphs that sprayed water up into the air in a continuous stream. Like all the other academy statues, the nymphs seemed a little too lifelike to me, as though they were a breath away from leaping out of the water and stabbing whoever was closest with their sharp pointed tridents. Through the long tendrils of their seaweedlike hair, their sly, narrowed eyes all seemed to turn in my direction, watching me. Creepy. Especially since they were all naked. Yucko.

I scanned the courtyard, but I didn't see Morgan anywhere. Had she gone over into the pool area for some reason?

A soft giggle caught my attention, and I walked forward. A low voice murmured something, and the giggle came again, a little louder and a little flirtier this time. I slipped into the row of trees that lined one wall of the courtyard and followed the sound over to the far side, where a tall, twisting lotus spread its wide branches over the entire area. I drew in a breath and peeked around the tree.

Morgan McDougall and Samson Sorensen stood about twenty feet away from me, up against the back wall of the courtyard, half-hidden by a low bush.

And they were totally making out.

My mouth dropped open. I knew that Jasmine had suspected that something was going on between her best friend and her boyfriend, but it was something else to see it for myself. Especially when they were so obviously, um, *enjoying* themselves. If Morgan's tongue went any deeper into Samson's mouth, it would come out the back of his head. And Samson's hands were all over Morgan, squeezing and stroking everything he could touch—and she let him touch *everything*. Add to that the fact that Samson was just wearing a pair of swimming briefs and flip-flops and you had the makings of a porno. *Mythos Coeds Gone Wild.*

Finally, after a minute, the two of them broke apart, both breathing hard.

"Come on, baby," Morgan cooed. "Let's go to our usual spot in the locker room. I'm dying to put my hands all over that hard body of yours."

I snorted. It looked to me like she'd been doing that already, given the fact that she was plastered to him tighter than his wet Speedo was.

Samson gave her a grin but shook his head. "Sorry. Coach Lir is in there right now tearing into Kenzie Tanaka because his time dropped two seconds in the relay. You'll just have to wait until later tonight at the bonfire. Besides, it's not a good thing for us to be seen together right now, remember? I mean, Jasmine's only been dead a few days. How would it look?"

Morgan raked her nails down his bare chest, making green sparks of magic flicker up into what little air there was between them. "I don't care how it looks. I'm tired of sneaking around. You should have just broken up with her when she was alive."

My eyes widened, and I couldn't believe what I was hearing. Had the two of them actually done it? Had they murdered Jasmine so they could be together? That seemed kind of extreme to me, even here at Mythos Academy where very little made sense.

"Yeah, well, whoever killed her did us both a favor," Samson said. "You know that she was never going to let me go. She told you that herself. She thought we were going to get married and live happily ever after, when she wouldn't even sleep with me."

Morgan raked her nails down Samson's chest again. More green sparks fluttered in the air and her nails left welts behind on his skin, but Samson didn't seem to care.

"Jasmine also told me that she thought you were cheating on her with someone else." Morgan snickered. "She just never suspected that it was me."

Wrong, I thought. Jasmine had known that Morgan was screwing her boyfriend. Jasmine must just not have been able to do anything about it before she'd been murdered in the library.

"So I'll see you tonight at the bonfire?" Morgan

cooed, and wrapped her arms around Samson's neck once more.

"Absolutely. And after, too. We'll sneak away and have our own private party."

Samson gave her another sly grin. He dipped his head, and the two of them started kissing again—

A hand clamped over my shoulder, fingers digging into my skin through the fabric of my T-shirt. Somehow, I bit back a surprised yelp and turned around to find Talia Pizarro glaring at me.

"What arc you doing out here?" Talia demanded. "We're supposed to be sparring, remember?"

"I was taking a break for a second," I lied.

I walked toward her, forcing her to move back several steps. I didn't want Morgan and Samson to know that I'd been spying on them.

I made a show of gathering my brown hair up and waving my hand in front of my face, like I was trying to cool off. "In case you hadn't noticed, it's like a hundred degrees in the gym."

My explanation seemed to satisfy her, although Talia still gave me a dirty look for making her stalk all the way out here after me.

I fiddled with my hair some more, using that as an excuse to look back over my shoulder, but Morgan and Samson had disappeared from their love nest. Maybe they'd gone on to the locker room for their quickie after all. Still, I wasn't too disappointed. I knew where they'd be tonight. And I was going to crash the party.

Because there was definitely something going on between the two of them—and I was willing to bet that it
had a lot to do with Jasmine's death.

"Come on, Gwen," Talia snapped again. "I want to
get a couple more rounds of sparring in before class
ends."

Satisfied for now, I let the Amazon drag me back into
the gym.

Chapter 12

A bonfire was scheduled for that evening. Apparently, it was an academy tradition and the event was always held the night before the homecoming dance. The dance, of course, would be staged in the dining hall. Even at Mythos, the Powers That Were couldn't think of anywhere better to have the dance than the cafeteria. Some things stayed the same, no matter which school you went to.

Normally, I wouldn't have gone to the bonfire, as I hadn't been to any of the other after-school social events. It wasn't like I had any friends who were just begging me to go. Or like I was popular enough for people to care whether or not I put in an appearance at the Big Event. And it certainly wasn't like I was dating anyone and wanted to snuggle with him under a blanket by the fire.

But Morgan and Samson had made plans to meet at the bonfire, and I wanted to see what they were up to.

Hopefully, it would be something more interesting than dry-humping each other.

Maybe it was stupid, but I just couldn't shake off this feeling that the two of them had something to do with Jasmine's murder. Maybe they hadn't killed Jasmine, but there was something that just seemed wrong about this whole thing. Besides, it wasn't like I had any other Big Plans for the night, besides sitting in my room, eating junk food, and reading comic books.

The bonfire was being held in the outdoor amphitheater on one of the lower quads just down the hill from the Library of Antiquities. I took a shower, threw on some clean jeans, a T-shirt, and a purple hoodie, and walked over there. It was after seven now and already dark on this October night. The air was chilly, but not unpleasantly so, and the stars twinkled like the sequins on a prom queen's dress in the black velvety fabric of the sky.

A series of long, flat, shallow stone steps that doubled as seats made up the top of the amphitheater. The steps formed a semicircle as they gradually spiraled down to the raised dais that served as the stage. Unlike the stones of the other campus buildings, all the stones here were bone white and flecked with shimmers of opalescent color—sky blue, pearl pink, soft lilac. Four columns towered over the stage area, each one topped by a chimera crouching on a round globe, clutching the sphere with its curved claws and glaring out at where the crowd would sit.

By the time I arrived, the stage had been removed and

a small fire had already been built in a ring of white stones in the very bottom of the amphitheater. I'd expected the other kids to be laughing, talking, and halfway to drunk by now, but for once, everyone was quiet, somber even. Instead of forming their usual cliques and gossiping, the students stood single file in a line that snaked up the amphitheater steps. Since I wasn't sure what was going on, I hung back, staying away from the line and well out of the flickering firelight.

One by one, the students walked by a tall man wearing a royal blue cloak shot through with silver thread and a crown of silver leaves resting on top of his head. He was backlit by the fire, and it took me a few seconds to realize that it was Nickamedes, of all people. What was he doing? And why was he wearing that ridiculous cloak and crown? Was he dressed up for a night of playing Dungeons & Dragons or something?

Apparently, the other students didn't think the librarian's appearance was strange at all. No mocking whispers filled the air, no sly giggles, nothing. Everyone was as quiet as if they were at a funeral. As the kids passed Nickamedes, they reached into the large silver bowl that he was holding and pulled out a handful of whatever was inside. I watched the first girl in line as she walked over to the ring of stones. She stood there in front of the flames a moment, then tossed a fistful of silver powder into the heart of the fire.

WHOOSH!

Whatever the powder was, it made the fire blaze brighter and burn hotter, the orange flames taking on a faint silver tinge. One by one, the kids in line repeated the process, along with Metis, Coach Ajax, and some of the other professors. By the time the last student had finished, the flames arced as high as the top tier of the amphitheater and the heat from them shimmered like ghosts twisting in the air. More than the heat, there was a—a *charge* in the air. The same sort of old, watchful, knowing force that I always felt when Grandma Frost had one of her visions. I shivered and wrapped my arms against myself. I might not think all the magic mumbo jumbo that the profs spouted was true, but here, tonight, I could almost believe that gods and monsters were real—and that they were all watching us.

"We dedicate this fire to those who have fought before," Nickamedes said. "The light of their sacrifice will always banish the dark and bring order to the Chaos. We live because of them, and they live on in us."

"And they live on in us," everyone murmured, their words rippling out into the darkness.

For a moment the fire burned brighter and higher still, the flames more silver than gold. Then, I blinked, and the illusion was gone. There was only a bonfire crackling merrily in the ring of stone, its snaps of wood and sweet smoke filling the air—nothing more.

Just like that, the ritual was over and everyone relaxed. Hardly a minute had passed before the students drifted off into their usual cliques. It seemed like I'd barely blinked again before the scene shifted into what it should have been all along.

Kids stood around the fire, laughing, talking, and

giggling, while others sat in lawn chairs or huddled together under blankets on the stone steps. I hadn't noticed
them before, but several tables full of the academy's
usual fancy food and drinks had been set up a few feet
away from the bonfire. Some kids had already pulled
out long metal rods that they were using to roast puffy
gourmet marshmallows for s'mores.

The sight helped me shake off the strange feeling that
had gripped me earlier and remember why I was here in
the first place. Mmm. S'mores. One of my favorite
treats. I'd have to make myself some to take back to my
room—after I figured out what Morgan and Samson
were up to.

Metis, Coach Ajax, and a few other profs started pa-
trolling the edges of the amphitheater, making sure nobody did something stupid. Like, you know, grab a
blazing stick out of the bonfire and set someone's hair
on fire with it.

The profs were also here to keep an eye on the alcohol. Despite the supposedly strict no-booze-on-campus
rule, several kids took sips from small flasks when they
thought no one was looking. Some were even more
brazen about it, having poured beer, wine coolers, or
whatever into plastic cups. A few guys, Romans mostly,
even popped open cans and let beer foam and spew all
over them before chugging down the liquor and crushing the empty metal against their foreheads. But as long
as no fights broke out, Metis and the other professors
seemed content to let the students have their fun—at
least for tonight.

I skirted around the fringes of the bonfire, keeping to the shadows and looking for Morgan or Samson. I didn't spot them right away, but I did see someone else I knew—Carson Callahan. He was playing some kind of drum, a bodhran I think it was called, in an impromptu band that had parked themselves next to one of the refreshment tables. There was a guy with a guitar, a girl with a violin, and another guy with a pair of cymbals. The four of them were just jamming, playing fast, rocking Celtic music. They actually sounded pretty good together. I waved to Carson, but of course he didn't see me, and I walked on by.

But I wasn't the only person who had her eye on Carson. Across the flickering bonfire, I saw Daphne Cruz staring in his direction, completely focused on the band geek.

And Morgan McDougall was standing right next to her. Jackpot.

I kept walking around the bonfire, trying to look like I was going somewhere instead of spying on one of the most popular girls in school. Morgan was among the kids who were drinking, a plastic cup of beer in her right hand. Daphne was drinking, too, although her beverage of choice looked like a wine cooler.

I was so busy staring at Morgan and Daphne that I didn't watch where I was going and I once again slammed into someone familiar.

Logan Quinn.

The Spartan had been carrying a soda in his hand, and, thanks to me, it splashed all over the front of his long-sleeved T-shirt and jeans, completely soaking him. Uh-oh. Logan rocked back on his heels and opened his mouth, probably ready to curse me for ramming into him. But then he saw it was me, and the anger on his face melted into a sly, knowing smile.

"Well, well, Gypsy girl," he drawled. "We really have to stop meeting like this."

"I'll say," I muttered. "Sorry I ran into you. Again."

I was glad it was dark, so he couldn't see the red-hot embarrassment that stained my cheeks. Usually, I wasn't this clumsy and actually, you know, paid attention to where I was walking. Then, there was the fact that I'd never so much as spoken to Logan before this week and now I kept running into him over and over again—literally. The Spartan probably thought that I was stalking him or something. That thought made my cheeks burn that much hotter.

I started to step around him, but Logan blocked my path. I went the other way, and he blocked me again.

"What?" I snapped, getting more embarrassed by the second. Especially since Logan's wet T-shirt clung to his stomach, giving me a glimpse of his washboard abs—abs that I just couldn't seem to look away from. "Do you want something?"

"Just the pleasure of your company, Gypsy girl."

Logan smiled at me then, a small, sexy grin that curved his lips and made his eyes flare with a brilliant blue light. My brain must have shut down or something, because I was momentarily breathless, even as my heart pounded in my chest. *Thump-thump-thump.* If it got any louder, Logan would be sure to hear it, and then I'd be even *more* embarrassed.

After a few seconds of just staring at him, my brain kick-started once more, and I reminded myself who I was talking to. Logan freaking Quinn, the man-whore of Mythos Academy. He was probably only talking to me because I'd turned him down the other day and he wanted another shot at me. He probably thought I was so lonely, friendless, and desperate that I'd be an easy mark. Another girl whose mattress he could sign and then never speak to again.

Out of the corner of my eye, I saw Morgan say something to Daphne, then slip off into the crowd. Morgan had to be on her way to hook up with Samson, and Logan wasn't going to stop me from seeing what they were up to.

"Sorry," I said. "My company is going somewhere else."

Logan opened his mouth to say something, but this time I shoved past him and plunged into the darkness.

Morgan's tight light blue sweater and white skinny jeans stood out against the shadowy grass, making her easy to follow. Well, that and the fact that the Valkyrie was already drunk. She wobbled from side to side, occasionally stopping to take another drink from her plastic cup, as she left the amphitheater and slowly climbed the hill toward the library.

The Library of Antiquities didn't seem to me like the most romantic spot for a lovers' rendezvous, but I followed along behind Morgan, drifting from one group of kids to another, from one tree to another, so that she wouldn't see me. I shouldn't have bothered. The Valkyrie never looked behind her, not even once. So much for being discreet.

I wondered if this was how Jasmine had found out that her best friend was sleeping with her boyfriend. Just by following Morgan when she slipped off one night. I didn't think that Morgan McDougall was nearly as smart as she thought she was.

Morgan crested the hill, and I stopped and pretended to tie my sneaker to give her time to get across the upper quad. Then, I walked up the hill after her.

I reached the top and spotted Morgan weaving her way up the wide library steps. The library was closed because of the bonfire, and the Valkyrie headed to the left, staying on the open-air patio that wrapped all the way around the building. Wrought-iron tables and chairs perched on the patio, so students could sit outside and study when the weather was warm and sunny.

I didn't hurry up the steps after her but instead stayed on the quad, moving from tree to tree and going in the same direction that the Valkyrie did so I could keep her in sight.

Morgan had just rounded a corner when a hand reached out and dragged her into the shadows. I froze behind a tree, wondering if the person who had murdered Jasmine was lurking around the library after all, if he hadn't just taken the Bowl of Tears and left campus like everyone else thought.

But then Morgan let out a giggle and I heard a loud sucking noise. I rolled my eyes. Sounded like Samson had beaten her here already.

"About time you got here."

Sure enough, Samson's voice floated down from the semidark patio to me. I squinted. Thanks to the lights that ringed the library, I could just make out the Viking standing in the shadows.

"Mmm-hmm," Morgan agreed.

There were some more smacking sounds, and then something that sounded like a zipper being drawn down. Morgan giggled once more, and I heard some clothing rasp. A minute later, Samson let out a sharp gasp.

"Ah, yeah, baby. Harder. *Harder.*"

Morgan made some sort of sound in the back of her throat and obliged him.

I winced and resisted the urge to clap my hands over my ears and hurry back to the bonfire. I'd hoped to hear the two of them talking more about Jasmine's death, not listen to Morgan give her secret boyfriend a BJ. Yucko. Big, big yucko—

A shower of what looked like stone chips rained down from one of the library's upper floors, sounding like metal marbles as they hit the patio, but Morgan and Samson were too busy to notice. I moved out from underneath the tree and craned up my neck, grateful for the distraction.

One of the stone statues was closer to the edge than I remembered it being before. As I watched, the statue teetered back and forth before tipping over and starting its inevitable descent downward—where it would land right on top of Morgan and Samson.

"Watch out!" I screamed.

Startled, the two of them broke apart. Samson looked up and saw the statue plunging toward them. He threw himself at Morgan and managed to knock them both forward and out of the way. Behind them, in the spot where they'd been standing two seconds before, the statue hit the stone and shattered into a thousand pieces.

I ran up the closest set of library steps and hurried over. The two of them were sprawled on the patio floor. "Are you guys okay?"

"Get off me," Morgan muttered. "You're wrinkling my new cashmere sweater."

With a grunt Samson rolled off her and into a puddle of light. And I realized that all the clothes below his waist had been pulled down while Morgan had been going about her business. I quickly looked away.

"Um, are you guys okay?" I asked again, totally *not looking* while Samson got to his feet and stuffed himself back into his pants.

"We were fine, until you showed up, you freak," Morgan muttered.

She got to her feet, dusted herself off, and glared at me. She sniffed, then looked over at the wrought-iron table where she'd put down her drink. The table and her cup had both tipped over during the commotion, and the Valkyrie seemed more upset about her spilled beer than the fact that she'd almost had her brains splattered out of her head.

"What are you doing here anyway?" Samson asked, looking at me with narrowed eyes. "Were you spying on us?"

My mind went blank. "I—"

"She's a Gypsy freak. She's nobody. Who cares what she was doing?" Morgan said. "Let's go. Now. I told you this was a stupid idea anyway. We should have just gone back to the dorms. But no, you're the one who likes to sneak around and do it in public."

Samson snorted. "Oh, like you don't. You practically attacked me in the courtyard this afternoon."

Morgan put her hands on her hips, opened her mouth, and started to let Samson have it. But then the Valkyrie realized that I was still standing there and watching them.

I opened my mouth again to protest that I wasn't a Gypsy freak, that I wasn't a nobody, but Morgan gave me a dirty look, grabbed Samson's hand, and stormed past me, pulling him along behind her.

That hadn't gone well at all. I hadn't heard anything useful, and now the two of them thought that I was some sicko who liked to watch people have oral sex. I sighed.

But I pushed my failure and the embarrassment of the last few minutes aside and stared up at the library. As a detective, my mom, Grace, had never believed in coincidences, and she'd taught me not to put much faith in them either. So I couldn't help but wonder how and why that statue had come loose at exactly the moment that Morgan and Samson were standing under it.

Had someone else found out that they were sneaking around on the sly? Did someone want to hurt one or both of them? If so, who would do that? And why?

Jasmine was the only one who had reason to hate Morgan and Samson. That I knew of, anyway. But Jasmine was dead. I didn't know how every single thing worked at Mythos Academy, but I was pretty sure that dead people couldn't make statues topple off buildings.

I stared at the stone remains. The statue had been even bigger than I was, but there wasn't much of it left. It had been so old and the fall had been so high that it had pretty much been pulverized on impact. But there were some bigger pieces of rubble lying here and there. Maybe I could use my Gypsy gift to get some kind of reading off of it. Maybe it had just been an accident and the stone would tell me of its age and the wear and tear of the years on it. Or maybe, just maybe, someone had made it fall and I'd see exactly who that person was— and get that much closer to figuring out who had murdered Jasmine.

I'd just reached out my hand to touch the stone, to see if I could get some kind of vibe off of it, when a low, ominous growl rippled through the air behind me.

A growl that sounded like the most evil thing that I had ever heard.

I froze and slowly turned around.

A—a *monster* stood on the patio behind me. It looked like a panther, only bigger. Much, much bigger. The panther's shoulders came all the way up to my waist, and it was longer than I was tall. Its fur was completely black, although for some reason it seemed to have a faint reddish tinge to it. The panther's eyes were red, too—a deep, dark, burning red that made me think of fire, blood, and death. The creature was like one of the drawings in my myth-history book, a mythological monster come to life and ready to eat me.

The panther, cat, or whatever it was opened its mouth and let out another low growl. The outside library lights illuminated each and every one of its razor-sharp teeth.

Then, the panther snapped its jaws shut, licked its lips with its long red tongue, and headed toward me.

Chapter 13

Oh *no*.

I didn't know exactly what the panther was, what kind of mythological nightmare it had sprung from, but anything out here in the dark that had teeth that big wasn't going to be friendly.

As if reading my thoughts, the panther let out something that sounded like a low chuckle, like it was *laughing* at me. The evil hiss made my breath catch in my throat and my blood run cold. The panther smiled, showing me its teeth again, and then crept closer to me on paws that were bigger than my hands were—with curved needle-sharp claws to match. They clicked against the stone patio with every step the creature took, like the second hand on a clock, ticking down to my death.

I stood where I was. Partly because I was terrified and was pretty sure that my knees would buckle if I even tried to move. But also because I'd seen enough nature programs on TV to know that I couldn't outrun the panther. And, of course, I didn't have any weapons to try to fight it off with. Even if I'd had a sword, I doubted I could have used it.

For the first time, I wished that I'd paid more attention in gym class when Coach Ajax and the other instructors had been talking about this sort of thing and showing us how to kill Reaper bad guys. But then again, I hadn't actually thought that any of that stuff was actually *real*. But I was fast becoming a true believer. Because this creature? It was very, very real, and I could tell that its teeth and claws were very, very sharp.

The panther prowled around me in a loose, wide circle. Its mouth turned down, almost in a pout, and it seemed disappointed that I wasn't going to run away. Or scream, at the very least. Its tail, which was at least three feet long, twitched back and forth in what seemed to be annoyance. Or maybe anticipation. I didn't know. I'd always been more of a dog person.

I cleared my throat, and the panther stopped and flicked up one of its rounded ears. Listening.

"Um, nice kitty?"

The panther's eyes narrowed, fire blazing in the red depths, and it let out that hissing sound again. No, no, no. Not a nice kitty at all.

The panther stalked off to the far side of the patio. As soon as its back was turned, I reached down and picked up the biggest remaining piece of the smashed statue that I saw. I waited a second, wondering if I'd get a flash off the stone, but I didn't. Or maybe the feelings and images just couldn't penetrate my own cold panic right now.

I didn't know exactly what the statue had been shaped like, maybe a gargoyle. Whatever it had been made to look like, the creature had horns, one of which I was holding. I wondered if the point would be sharp enough to penetrate the panther's skin. Probably not. For the first time, I wished for a Valkyrie's strength or an Amazon's speed or a Spartan's skill with weapons—something, anything that would help me. That would save me from getting ripped to pieces. Sweat slicked my hands, and I struggled to hold on to my pitiful weapon.

The panther reached the edge of the patio and stalked back toward me. Its black nose quivered in its face, and its lips curled back into another smile. Yep, it was definitely smelling my fear. I reeked of terror.

The monster grew tired of playing its little stalking game, because it sank down onto its back haunches, getting ready to leap up and kill me—

The panther sprang, and I felt something ram into me. I closed my eyes, waiting for claws and teeth to tear into my skin. But instead, all I felt was my shoulder slamming into the stone floor and hands moving over my body, like they were searching for something.

"Give me that," a voice muttered in my ear.

Someone yanked the stone horn out of my hands, and I opened my eyes. What was happening? Why wasn't I dead yet? I looked up to find the last person I'd expected standing on the balcony between me and the panther.

Logan Quinn.

And he wasn't running away or screaming like he

should have been—like we both should have been. Instead, Logan stood in between me and the panther, clutching the horn in his hand like it was a real weapon or something.

The panther narrowed its bloodred eyes and circled one way, trying to get around Logan to get to me. But Logan stepped in front of the animal, tightening his grip on the stone horn. The panther let out another evil hiss, and a—a *smile* spread across Logan's face.

And then it hit me what he was doing. He was—he was actually going to *fight* that thing. Like . . . to the *death*.

Oh no!

I didn't even get to open my mouth to scream before the panther leapt at Logan.

Over and over, the two of them rolled across the patio, snarling, spitting, and hissing at each other. I scrambled to my feet and leapt back against the wall, not sure what else to do other than get out of the way. Not sure what else I could do. Maybe I should have been running the other direction, back toward the bonfire, trying to get some help. But for some reason, I didn't want to leave Logan out here by himself in the dark with the evil panther.

Not when he'd just saved me from it.

The panther was yowling at this point, and each sound it made felt like a dagger punching into my brain. I clapped my hands over my ears, wondering how Logan could stand being so close to that awful noise. Then I whirled around, looking for something that I could use to help Logan fight off the creature. My eyes landed on a metal chair sitting next to one of the tables on the balcony, and I grabbed it and hoisted it up over my shoulder.

By this point, the panther had Logan pinned beneath him and was snapping its jaws right in his face. I ran over, brought the metal chair up, and hit the creature as hard as I could with it.

I didn't do any real damage to it, but I definitely got the panther's attention. The monster lashed out, swiping its paw at me, but I held out the chair like it was a shield, keeping it between us. The panther's claws scraped down the chair with a horrifying screech, completely shredding the metal and sending up sprays of red sparks.

While I distracted the creature, Logan got his feet in between him and the panther and did some kind of fancy move to throw the animal off him. The panther sailed through the air and slammed into the side of the balcony wall. Then Logan flipped up onto his feet like he was a freaking Ninja.

Despite the fact that I'd almost been turned into catnip, it was seriously the coolest thing that I'd ever seen.

The panther got back up onto its feet, but it was too late. Logan dove on top of the creature and stabbed it with the stone horn.

The panther screamed in pain. It was the most horrible sound that I'd ever heard, a high keening, wailing cry that seemed to shred my eardrums from the inside out. It was almost like . . . the panther was calling out to something or someone, begging that person to help it, to stop its pain.

The noise didn't seem to bother Logan. With a grim face, he pulled the horn out of the creature's side and stabbed it again. The panther screamed once more and threw itself back on top of Logan. Then, they both started moving too fast for me to follow, just a wild tangle of arms, limbs, and claws lashing out, each one trying to kill the other.

I stood there with my shredded metal chair. I would have used it to hit the panther again, if I hadn't been afraid of accidentally braining Logan in the process. But I didn't get a chance to do anything.

The panther let out one more scream, and then it and Logan were both still.

Dumbfounded, I stared down at the huge pile of black fur in front of me, Logan trapped somewhere underneath.

The Spartan was dead. He had to be. Nobody could survive something like that. That was the thought that slammed into my brain. *No, no, no!* He was dead. He'd been trying to help me, trying to save me, and now he was dead. Sure, maybe he was a man-whore who slept around and seemed to enjoy annoying me for no good reason, but Logan hadn't been all bad. He had just saved my life.

Something let out a grunt, and I stepped back, wondering if maybe the panther wasn't dead after all. Anger filled me, and I raised my chair again, ready to pound the animal to death if I had to just for killing Logan—

"You think maybe you could put that chair down and heave this thing off me?" a strained voice muttered.

The chair slipped from my numb fingers and clattered to the patio floor. I fell to my knees beside the panther. "Logan! You're still alive!"

An arm trapped underneath the animal's heavy weight waved in my direction, although I couldn't see his face. "Of course I'm still alive. I'm a Spartan. Now, are you going to help me or not, Gypsy girl?"

"Help. Definitely help."

I got up on my knees, pushed up my hoodie sleeves, and held out my hands. I didn't want to touch the monster, didn't want to flash on the rage and pain that it had been feeling before Logan had killed it, but I didn't have a choice. So I gritted my teeth, put my hands on the animal's fur, and pushed as hard as I could.

Nothing happened.

The panther was far too heavy for me to move on my own. It weighed several hundred pounds, at least.

But the really weird thing was that I didn't get any kind of vibe off it. No flashes of images, no feelings, nothing. I frowned. Was something wrong with my Gypsy gift, my psychometry? This was the third time this had happened this week. First, I hadn't gotten any vibes off Jasmine's body in the library. Second, I hadn't flashed on her blood either, even though it had been all over my hands and clothes. And now I didn't feel anything when I was touching this dead creature either—

"What are you waiting for?" Logan muttered. "This thing is crushing my ribs and face, in case you haven't noticed."

There was no way that I could move the panther off him. I just wasn't strong enough— My eyes narrowed. But I knew someone who was—and she owed me.

"Stay here," I said, scrambling to my feet. "I'm going to go get some help. I'll be right back."

"What? Wait—"

Logan started to say something, but I'd already sprinted off the patio. I raced back across the upper quad in the direction that I'd come, then down the hill to the lower quad and the bonfire. While I'd been gone, someone had plugged a radio into the sound system, and the loud rock music added to the noise in the amphitheater.

It took me the better part of a minute to find Daphne in the crowd. She stood near the bonfire, standing in the shadows cast out by the flames and talking to Carson. Both of them were smiling, laughing, and shooting flirty little glances at each other when each thought the other person wasn't looking. I rolled my eyes. They really should just get on with things.

I reached them just as Carson put his drink down on the table, drew in a breath, and looked at Daphne.

"Daphne, I was wondering, I mean, I know it's kind

of last-minute, but if you don't have a date for the home-coming dance—"

I popped up next to Daphne, and Carson stifled a scream of surprise. Daphne jumped as well, as shocked by my sudden appearance as the band geek was.

"Hi there, Carson. Daphne. Sorry to cut this short, but you're coming with me." I grabbed one of the sleeves on Daphne's pink corduroy jacket.

"But—but—" That was all that Carson could get out, so I decided to make things easy for him.

"Yes," I said in a cheery tone. "Daphne would *love* to go to the homecoming dance with you tomorrow night. She thinks you're totally awesome. She's had a crush on you for *ages*. But right now, she has to come with me. She'll call you later, and the two of you can work out all the details. Color schemes, corsages, and whatnot. Bye now."

I dragged Daphne away from the band geek and started up the hill in the direction of the library. For the first few feet Daphne seemed just as stunned as Carson. But then she got with the program and stared back over her shoulder. Behind us, Carson was grinning like a fool—or a guy who'd just scored a date with his dream girl. Daphne's face alternated between absolute happiness and humiliated rage. After a few seconds, the rage won out.

"I'm going to kill you for this, Gwen," Daphne snarled. "Slowly."

I looked at her, but I didn't stop dragging her up the

hill. "Why? You got exactly what you wanted. A date with Carson. You should be thanking me, not plotting how you can rip my face off with your sparkly fingers. The two of you might have stood there for another *hour* before he worked up the nerve to ask you out. I just cut through the geek speak."

Daphne's black eyes narrowed, but she didn't contradict me. "Fine. So maybe you did me a favor. But what do you want now? I'm not your freaking sidekick, you know. I don't even *like* you. Not the least little bit. And we're certainly not *friends* or anything."

"Of course we aren't," I said. "I could never, ever be friends with a rich, spoiled, wannabe Valkyrie princess like you. But since you're one of the few people at the academy who will actually speak to me, you've been elected. Now hurry up. Logan's trapped. He may be hurt, too. I don't know."

"Logan?" Daphne asked. "As in Logan Quinn? *The* Logan Quinn? What have you gotten yourself into, Gwen?"

We reached the top of the hill, and I took off in a run. After a moment, I heard a muttered curse and Daphne fell in step behind me, her feet smashing the dewy grass along with mine. I led her back to the library and up onto the patio.

"I need you to help me move that thing, whatever it is," I said, pointing to the panther. "Logan killed it, and now, he's trapped underneath it."

Logan waved his arm again. Evidently, he'd heard us run up onto the patio.

"Dude!" Daphne whispered, her eyes wide as she stared down at the creature. "That's a Nemean prowler!"

I looked at her. "What's a Nemean prowler?"

"How can you not know what a prowler is?" Daphne asked. "*Everybody* knows about prowlers."

I shrugged. "I'm new here, remember?"

She shook her head. "Well, anyway, that's a Nemean prowler. Hercules killed a whole bunch of them way back when. Today, they're kind of like the mythological equivalent of a familiar. You know, like a witch's black cat?"

I nodded. "Sure."

"Except, of course, prowlers are much more than that," Daphne said. "Bigger, stronger, tougher. Their claws can tear through almost anything, which is one of the reasons that Reapers love them. Most Reapers don't keep them so much as pets as they do to kill people. They're really just big kitty-cat assassins. Man, those things are *nasty*. I can't believe that he actually killed it."

"Hello," Logan muttered, waving his arm again to get our attention. "Still trapped under here."

"Oh. Sorry."

Daphne bent down and dug her hands into the creature's fur, just like I had done a few minutes ago. With her Valkyrie strength it was easy for her to shove the prowler off Logan and roll it over to the side of the patio. Daphne bent over the creature, muttering that she'd never seen a prowler in person before and how cool it was that it was dead. And she thought *I* was a freak.

I dropped to my knees beside Logan, who was lying on his back, trying to get his breath back after being somewhat smushed by the prowler.

"Are you okay?" I asked.

"I think so." Logan stared at me, and a smile pulled up his lips. "But maybe you should give me mouth-to-mouth, just to make sure."

I rolled my eyes and stood up. "Do you ever think about anything besides sex?"

His smile widened. "Not when you're around, Gypsy girl."

My eyes narrowed, and I bit back a retort. Probably not a good idea to criticize the guy who'd just saved your life. But still. Logan Quinn seriously needed to be taught some manners.

"Um, guys," Daphne said. "You might want to look at this."

The Valkyrie backed up until she was standing next to us. Logan and I looked over at the prowler.

Which was disappearing before our eyes—literally.

The creature's fur, which had once been so dense, thick, and black, slowly wisped up into the air like it was made out of smoke. The mist curled up, and, for a moment, I could have sworn that I saw two eyes in the middle of it. The smoky eyes seemed to glare at me before a cool fall breeze swept over the patio and carried them away.

"Is that . . . normal?" I whispered.

"Not at all," Daphne murmured. "I've never seen a

prowler up close before, but they're as real as we are. They aren't supposed to disappear after you kill them. Only illusions do that."

Only illusions do that. Daphne's words echoed through my mind, and I felt a memory stirring in my subconscious. Something to do with illusions. Something that I'd seen or heard or read or thought about in the last few days. Something that was important. But the harder I tried to grab onto my thought, the more I tried to call up the memory, the deeper it sank into my brain—

Logan got to his feet and rubbed his chest. "Well, whatever it was, it was very heavy and very interested in killing me."

Whatever thread that I'd been following in my head snapped at his words, and the memory sank back down into the darkness. Still, I struggled to make sense of what I'd just seen.

"But if that prowler was an illusion, then it couldn't really hurt us, right?" I asked. "And why was it even here to start with? Are illusions like ghosts or something? Do they haunt certain places?"

Logan and Daphne exchanged a look, like I should have known exactly what was going on instead of asking such obvious questions.

"No, illusions aren't like ghosts," Daphne explained. "Illusions are created by people with magic, by warriors like us. And they can hurt you just as badly as the real thing can—sometimes even worse, depending on what type of illusion it is. The only difference between the illusion of a prowler that attacked you and a real prowler is that there's no body to get rid of, now that Logan's killed it."

I still didn't really understand why the prowler would have been able to kill me, if it was just an illusion to start with, but I didn't want to look completely stupid, so I kept my mouth shut.

There was nothing else for us to do but stand there and watch the prowler evaporate. Thirty seconds later, nothing remained of it at all, except for the crushed bits of stone that had sprayed everywhere when Logan had thrown it into the patio wall.

When the last remnants of the prowler were gone, Daphne turned and stabbed me in the shoulder with her finger.

"I think you've got some explaining to do, Gwen. So talk. *Now.*"

She wasn't going to take no for an answer, and I supposed that I owed Logan some kind of explanation since, you know, he'd almost gotten clawed to death because of me. So I told the two of them about everything that had happened tonight. About my spying on Morgan and Samson, what they'd been doing, the statue falling and almost hitting them, and then the prowler showing up and trying to take a bite out of me.

"So Morgan and Samson were out here getting busy when they almost got clobbered by that statue. Then, the prowler appears and almost eats you before Spartan boy kills it instead. Nice kill, by the way," Daphne said.

"Sticking it with that horn. Impressive. Even for a Spartan."

Logan grinned, accepting her backhanded compliment.

"So what does it all mean?" Daphne asked. "Do you think that statue fell on purpose? That someone was trying to hurt Morgan and Samson, then created that prowler illusion and sicced it on you after you warned them?"

I shrugged. "I don't know. The library's locked up tight for the night, and I didn't see or hear anyone on the patio besides Morgan and Samson. So who could have created the illusion? And why? Who would have a reason to want to hurt them or me to start with? Jasmine was the only one who cared about Morgan and Samson seeing each other, and she's dead."

"Maybe it was the same Reaper who killed Jasmine," Logan suggested. "Before he left the library that night, maybe he created some spells to make the statue fall and the prowler appear to help cover his escape. Maybe they just didn't work like or when they were supposed to, and you, Morgan, and Samson accidentally triggered them tonight."

Daphne nodded her head. "It's possible. Reapers are twisted that way. They love to leave booby traps behind."

"Do you think there are any more traps out here?" I asked, glancing around the patio.

Logan and Daphne both shook their heads.

"No," Logan said. "Otherwise, they would have gone off when the prowler illusion did. When you set off one booby trap, you set them all off. Reapers like to do as much damage as possible at one time."

Booby-trap spells? That seemed a little far-fetched to me. But so had Nemean prowlers until about ten minutes ago.

"I don't know. None of this makes any sense," I said.

I rubbed my head, which was suddenly aching. I felt like I was missing something—something obvious about this whole situation. But try as I might, I couldn't figure out what it was.

"C'mon," Logan said. "Whatever is going on, you aren't going to figure it out tonight, Gypsy girl. I don't know about you two, but I need to take a shower."

For the first time, I realized that Logan had blood all over his clothes from where he'd stabbed the prowler and it had fallen on top of him. The blood was black, just like the monster had been, and it had completely ruined his T-shirt and jeans. First I'd made him spill soda on himself, and now this. Graceful I was not.

"Sorry." I winced. "I'll buy you some new clothes. But you're right. Let's get out of here."

Daphne and Logan turned and walked down the library steps, but I hung back a moment, staring up at the spot where the statue had fallen from.

There was nothing up there, of course. Just more statues shrouded in more shadows. Maybe it was all the crazy things that had happened tonight, but I felt like there were eyes on me, like someone or something was watching me from somewhere higher up in the library—

"Gwen!" Daphne called out. "Come on, already!"

I shivered and pulled my gaze away from the library. But the cold, watchful feeling lingered as I stuffed my hands into my hoodie pockets and hurried to catch up with the others.

Chapter 14

Logan, Daphne, and I walked back down the hill to the lower quad.

The bonfire still burned, although by this point most of the students had plopped down into the chairs that surrounded the cheery blaze or crept up the stone steps for a bit more privacy. More than a few couples sat close together in the shadow-kissed upper levels, huddled underneath a comforter from someone's dorm room. The giggles, smacking sounds, and occasional squeals of laughter told me exactly what was happening underneath the covers.

More kids were drunk now, too, stumbling around so bad that Professor Metis and Coach Ajax were herding a group of them back to their dorms before they did something stupid, like pass out and fall into the bonfire.

"Hey," I said. "Do you think we should tell Metis what happened? You know, about the falling statue and the Nemean prowler being at the library?"

Maybe I should have gone straight to Metis in the

first place, but I'd forgotten all about the professor even being at the bonfire in my rush to get Daphne and drag her back to the library so the Valkyrie could heave the dead prowler off Logan before it completely smothered him.

"Sure, if we had some proof," Daphne said. "But the statue was smashed to bits and the prowler evaporated, remember? Besides, do you really want to explain to Metis why you were spying on Morgan and Samson and what they were doing? She's sure to ask why you were at the library in the first place, since it closed early tonight because of the bonfire."

I bit my lip. Daphne was right. I couldn't tell Professor Metis what had happened, not without getting into the whole weird story. Metis was cool, but I doubted that she'd think too kindly of me breaking into Jasmine's room, swiping her laptop, and then spying on the dead Valkyrie's best friend and boyfriend because I had a weird vibe about the whole situation.

"Too bad about the prowler, though," Logan mused. "I would have liked to have shown it to Coach Ajax. He would have been so impressed."

"True," Daphne agreed.

I looked at the two of them. "Geez. Do you guys really think killing a mythological monster is that cool?"

Daphne and Logan looked at each other.

"Totally," Daphne said.

"Absolutely," Logan agreed.

And they thought *I* was a freak. At least I had the good sense to be scared of things like prowlers. Things with big, sharp, pointy teeth that could rip me to shreds. I shivered again at the memory of the creature stalking me.

"Well," Daphne said. "I think I've had enough fun for one evening. I'm going back to my room. I still have that paper to write for English lit."

"Let me walk you to your room," Logan offered in a helpful voice. "You, me, and the Gypsy girl could have our own bonfire tonight."

Daphne and I stared at each other. I rolled my eyes while Daphne sniffed.

"Oh, please," she scoffed. "Like I need a *guy* to protect *me*. I'm a Valkyrie, remember? I could pick you up and break your back over my knee, Spartan. Like you were a piñata."

"Kinky," Logan said, smiling at her. "I like it."

She snorted. "Save the smarmy charm for Gwen. We all know that she's the one you're really trying to impress anyway."

We did? Because I hadn't gotten that message *at all*.

My eyes flicked to Logan. Something that looked like a guilty flush crept up the side of his neck, but the flickering flames of the bonfire made it hard to tell for sure.

Daphne snorted again and stomped off in the direction of her dorm, leaving the two of us standing there by the firelight.

"Don't forget to call Carson," I called out in a helpful voice. "The two of you have a date tomorrow night, remember?"

Daphne turned around and made a rude gesture with

her hand, telling me exactly what I could go do with myself. But she had a smile on her face while she did it. I found myself grinning back at her. Daphne Cruz was okay, even if she was a rich, spoiled, wannabe Valkyrie princess.

Logan looked at me. "You going to stomp off into the dark, too?"

"Oh no," I said, remembering the way that the prowler had licked its lips and hissed at me. Another shudder rippled through my body. "I'm more than happy to let you walk me back to my dorm."

We left the amphitheater behind and set off across the lower quad. A few people milled around the bonfire, but everyone else was wrapped up in their own little worlds beneath their blankets, macking on their hotties, and nobody paid any attention to Logan and me.

Good thing, since the Spartan was pretty much covered with black blood from head to toe. I winced when we passed by the fire and I saw exactly how much of it there was on him. Logan looked like he'd taken a bath in the prowler's blood.

I couldn't help but wonder what had made him follow me up to the library, and most especially what had made him step in between me and that horrible monster. Yeah, I knew that he was a Spartan and killing bad things was basically what he did, what he was here at Mythos learning how to do.

But there had to be more to it than that. Maybe if I'd been prettier, richer, or more popular it would have made sense. I wasn't exactly the kind of girl that guys tripped over themselves to help. Did Logan think that I'd be so grateful that I'd change my mind about him and just fall into his arms?

My eyes moved over his face and down his muscled body. Well, okay. That would have had some serious appeal, if he wasn't so icky looking right now. Okay, okay. It still had some serious appeal, even if he was all blood covered and nasty.

Logan saw me staring at him. "What are you looking at, Gypsy girl?"

This time, a flush crept up *my* cheeks. "Nothing," I muttered, and looked away from him.

We didn't speak as we left the light and warmth of the bonfire behind and stepped onto one of the cobblestone walkways that wound around the lower quad and led to Styx Hall.

"So," Logan finally said. "You're trying to figure out what happened to Jasmine, huh? Who killed her and took the Bowl of Tears?"

I shrugged. "Something like that."

"Why?" Logan asked. "Why do you even care? As you've probably guessed by now, Jasmine wasn't exactly the best-liked girl at Mythos. Sure, she was popular, but she terrorized people to get that way. People were afraid of her, and she was basically a coldhearted bitch. Why would you want to find out what happened to someone like that?"

Once again, I thought about Paige Forrest. She'd been a lot like Jasmine, well, except for the coldhearted bitch part. Paige had been pretty, popular, and sweet, but no one had known about the awful thing that was happening to her. Even now, I could still see her stepfather making Paige lie back on her bed while he touched her. My stomach turned over at the memory, and I shivered and wrapped my arms around myself.

I couldn't tell Logan all that, of course. That in some weird way Jasmine reminded me of Paige and that I wanted to help the Valkyrie like I had the other girl. It was too long of a story, and it probably wouldn't make sense to him anyway. Sometimes, my Gypsy gift and all the flashes, vibes, and feelings that went along with it didn't make much sense to me either. But my mom had always told me to trust my instincts, and that was what I was going to do.

"Because somebody should at least care what happened to her," I said in a quiet voice. "Somebody should be sorry that she was murdered, even if nobody really liked Jasmine deep down inside."

"Maybe," Logan said. "But Metis, Ajax, Nickamedes, and everyone else think that a Reaper killed Jasmine and stole the Bowl of Tears. The guy, whoever he is, is long gone."

I shrugged. "Maybe. But something about this whole situation just doesn't feel right to me. Maybe it's because my mom was a cop. She always told me to listen to my instincts."

"Was?" Logan asked in a quiet voice, picking up on the past tense.

"She died six months ago," I said. "She was killed in a car accident by a drunk driver. That's what the police said, anyway."

My throat closed up as I said the words, and I blinked back a wave of sudden hot tears. Once again, my pain, anger, and guilt over my mom's death twisted my heart, like a snake curling tighter and tighter around its victim until all the life had been squeezed out of it. That's how I felt right now. I couldn't even breathe without it hurting so *much*.

"I'm sorry," Logan said.

I nodded at him, but I didn't trust myself to speak.

We reached Styx Hall a couple of minutes later. The light burned over the front door, but the dorm was quiet. Everyone else must have still been over at the bonfire. I walked up the steps to the patio that wrapped around the dorm, and Logan followed me.

Logan drew closer to me until all that I could see, feel, and hear was him. Black hair, icy blue eyes, square chin, solid chest. He looked the same as always, a total bad boy who knew exactly how sexy he was. But somehow, Logan seemed nobler to me now, braver and stronger. Like there was so much more to him than just his killer smile, easy charm, and rumored ability to get rid of a girl's bra in under five seconds and her panties in another ten.

Maybe that was because Logan had saved my life tonight. That kind of thing would have made any girl think highly of him. Or maybe it was just part of who he was, part of his Spartan heritage, part of becoming the fierce warrior that he was so obviously meant to be.

I thought about the way that he'd so coolly faced that Nemean prowler, the way that he'd actually smiled when fighting the awful creature. Logan made me believe that there was some kind of purpose to all this. At least for tonight, anyway. That yeah, the Chaos War and Reapers and Loki were real, but that there were also good guys like Spartans and Amazons and Valkyries who were ready to stand up and fight the bad guys, too.

Whatever it was, the sudden feeling made me shiver, even as heat blossomed in the pit of my stomach like a flower slowly unfurling and stretching toward the sun. Just the way that I found myself wanting to reach out to Logan, to touch him, no matter how weird, wrong, or stupid it might have been.

"Can I ask you something?" Logan said, tilting his head to one side and looking at me.

"Sure."

"What's with you and all the comic books?"

That was just about the last thing that I'd expected him to say. I blinked. "What?"

"I saw them that day you ran into me on the quad and dropped your bag. Why do you like them so much?" Logan asked. "We pretty much go to school in a comic book. Tonight should have proven that to you. You don't really need to read them."

"I just like them," I said. "I always have."

It was true. I'd always loved the stories of people having amazing powers, of good guys doing good things and always thwarting the bad guys' evil plans at the last possible second. But lately I'd been reading more and more of them, burying myself in the colorful pages as though reading about someone else's heroic deeds would magically change everything around me. As though they would somehow make my life better or put everything back to the way that it had been before my mom died.

"I guess . . . I've been reading more of them since my mom's accident," I said, struggling to find the right words. "I guess . . . I like them because nobody ever really dies in a comic book, not even the bad guy. At least not for long. I guess . . . I keep hoping that one day, my mom's going to just show up, like the characters always do in comic books. That she's going to be fine and tell me that this has all been a bad dream. That she's been trapped in another dimension or that the person who got killed was really her evil clone or something. That she's going to take me away from Mythos and things will go back to the way they used to be. Pretty stupid, huh?"

I blinked a couple of times and scratched my nose like it was itching, even though I was really trying to hold back the tears in my eyes. I didn't want to cry in front of him.

Logan looked at me. "I don't think it's stupid at all, Gwen."

Some of the emotion clogging my throat eased up, and I smiled.

"What?"

"Do you know, I think that's the first time that you've ever said my name? I'm always just that *Gypsy girl* to you and everyone else."

Logan moved closer to me. "Really? Then, I'll have to say it again. Gwen," he whispered. "Gwen."

I stared into his ice blue eyes, mesmerized by the sudden softness that I saw there, even as Logan's head dipped lower. But then my brain kicked in and I realized that he was actually going to kiss me—and exactly what would happen the moment that his lips touched mine.

"No! Don't! Stop!" I stepped away from him, almost falling down the dorm steps in the process.

Logan frowned, and something like hurt flickered in his eyes.

"It's not that I don't want to— I mean, I do—I *really* do—it's just... my gift," I finished in a totally weak, lame voice.

He kept staring at me.

"My Gypsy gift," I said, trying to explain. "My psychometry magic. Whenever I... touch someone, I get flashes about him. Feelings and images. Kind of like a movie trailer of his life. Or at least what he's thinking about at that particular moment. It really just depends on the person."

The softness in Logan's eyes vanished, and his gaze was suddenly as cold as ice once more, his face harder than any marble statue in the Library of Antiquities.

"And you don't want to see mine," he said in a flat tone. "Because of who and what I am. Because I'm a Spartan."

He said "Spartan" like it was some sort of dirty word or terrible thing to be. I didn't know all the ins and outs of Mythos, but I knew that most of the other students were afraid of Logan and the others kids like him. Because they were Spartans, because they were such good fighters, because they were so fierce, so strong, and so full of life. And now he thought that I was scared of him, too, that I didn't even want to so much as *touch* him, much less let him kiss me.

"No! No! That's not it at all. I just didn't know if you would...want me to see...all those things about you," I finished in that same weak, lame voice. "Some people don't."

They don't want me knowing their secrets. That's what I wanted to say to him. Maybe that's what I should have said to him.

Or maybe I should have just come right out and admitted the fact that I was a total geeky loser who'd only ever kissed one boy in her entire life. And only a couple times at that, with very little tongue action involved. That I was worried my lack of experience would so obviously show and I wouldn't measure up to Logan's standards. That I wouldn't be able to kiss him back like he wanted me to—like *I* wanted to. That I didn't want him to laugh at me or make fun of me. And most especially, that I was starting to like him way, way more than I should, given the fact that he was who he was and I was who I was. Just Gwen Frost, that Gypsy girl who saw things, and not anyone special, exciting, or particularly interesting.

Logan kept staring at me, that same cold expression in his eyes. He made no move to try to kiss me again. The moment, whatever kind of moment it had been between us, was officially over. Spell, broken. Shattered was more like it. By me and my freak-out over my stupid Gypsy gift and what I might see and feel if I kissed him.

"Well," I said in an awkward voice, shifting from one foot to the other. "I guess I should go inside now. It's getting, um, cold out here."

"Yeah," Logan said. "Cold."

I stared at him again, wondering what I could do to make things better between us. We'd been on the verge of . . . something, something nice, I thought. But I'd ruined it, and I had no idea how to make it right.

"So, thanks, for, um, saving my life tonight."

"Yeah," he said again in that cold, hard voice. "Good night, Gypsy girl."

Logan turned, walked down the steps, and disappeared into the darkness. He didn't look back.

"Good night, Logan," I whispered, even though I knew that he couldn't hear me or see the tears in my eyes.

Feeling like a stupid, stupid loser, I trudged up the stairs to my dorm room, took a shower, and got ready for bed. Maybe it was the fact that I'd almost been eaten by a killer kitty cat or maybe it was my almost kiss with Logan, but I couldn't sleep.

But I just couldn't lie in bed, stare up at the pointed

ceiling, and do nothing either. At least, not without replaying the scene with Logan in my mind over and over again. Thanks to my psychometry, I could remember in crystal-clear, humiliating detail just how much I'd *freaked out* when he'd started to kiss me. I'd be lucky if he ever spoke to me again.

I had to do something to take my mind off all that, so I grabbed the last of Grandma Frost's sweet pumpkin roll out of my minifridge, turned on Jasmine's laptop, and once again surfed through the computer files that Daphne had unlocked for me. But I didn't find anything else that would tell me what was going on, what deep, dark secrets Jasmine might have had, or who had killed her.

I popped another bite of pumpkin roll into my mouth. Thinking. Maybe everyone else was right. Maybe a Reaper had been in the library to steal the Bowl of Tears all along. Maybe he'd murdered Jasmine simply because she'd been in the wrong place at the wrong time.

Thinking about the library and the Bowl made me remember the mythology book that I'd taken from Jasmine's dorm room. My violet eyes flicked over to the thick volume, which was sitting on the edge of my desk. It was the only thing I'd swiped from the Valkryie's room that I hadn't looked at yet.

Gingerly, I touched the book, my fingers skimming the surface, just in case I got another angry, hate-filled flash off it like the one that had been on the photograph of Morgan and Samson. I didn't want to start muttering to myself again—or worse, start screaming so loud that everyone came up to my room to watch the Gypsy girl have another mental meltdown. One had been enough.

No real emotions swept over me as I touched the book—just the feeling of old knowledge and the soft, well-worn impression of hundreds of hands turning and turning and turning the pages until they found the information they were looking for. I couldn't tell exactly how old the book was, but it had been around for quite a while.

I flipped over to the section that Jasmine had marked. To my surprise, it was the start of a whole chapter that dealt with Loki's Bowl of Tears. I moved over to my bed, propped some pillows up behind my back, and started reading.

> *The Bowl of Tears was what Loki's wife, Sigyn, used to keep snake venom from dripping onto the chained god's once-handsome face....*

Blah, blah, blah. The next several paragraphs were pretty much the same thing that Professor Metis had recapped for us in myth-history class, so I skimmed over those. Things got a little more interesting after that, though, because the book starting mentioning a bunch of stuff that Metis had left out, for whatever reason.

> *The Bowl of Tears is rumored to be one of the Thirteen Artifacts, the magical items that were present and used during the final battle*

of the Chaos War in which the goddess Nike defeated Loki. Six of the Artifacts belonged to members of the Pantheon, while six belonged to Loki and his Reapers, although scholars often disagree as to what the Artifacts were and on which side they were used. There was also a final Artifact, the thirteenth one, that was rumored to have tipped the scales in Nike's favor, but there is no known record of what it was, how it was used, or what became of it. . . .

After that, the next few paragraphs dealt with the various Artifacts, including what they might be and what powers they might have. A spear, a shield, a bow and a quiver of arrows, a drum . . . it was a pretty long list. Beside most of the items was the museum, library, or university where it was located—and more than a few were here at the Library of Antiquities. Geez. It was like a shopping list for bad guys. "Go here and steal this." Cue the evil laughter. "Wha-ha-ha."

I shook my head and skipped down to the section that talked about the Bowl of Tears.

After he managed to trick his wife, Sigyn, into helping him escape from his chains, Loki kept the Bowl of Tears and imbued it with his own godly magic, turning it into a powerful Artifact. It was rumored that Loki used the Bowl to bend people to his will. That once a person's blood was dripped into the Bowl the god—or whoever had the Bowl at that time—had complete control over him or her. It is also rumored that Loki's followers willingly spilled their own blood into the Bowl and that the god would then grant them special favors and powers for their show of loyalty. Reapers of Chaos were also known to use the Bowl when they sacrificed people to the god, which transferred the victim's powers and life force to Loki. Some believe that the Artifact could be used to help free the god from his current prison and allow him to draw closer to the mortal realm, where he could exert his Chaotic influence once more. . . .

So the Bowl of Tears supposedly had the power to let the person who was holding it bend someone else to his will. If, you know, he just didn't go ahead and sacrifice that person to Loki in the first place. I shivered. *Creepy.* Coach Ajax and Nickamedes had both said that the Reapers would love to get their hands on the Bowl. Now I understood why. Whoever had the Bowl would have a lot of power.

Still, though, I wondered why the person who'd taken the Bowl had killed Jasmine—and not me. Because I'd been there, too. Knocked unconscious and lying on the library floor right beside the dead Valkyrie. I'd been completely helpless. So why kill Jasmine and leave me behind—alive?

Oh, I knew that I wasn't any kind of *real* threat. Not physically or magically, and most especially not in a place like Mythos, where all the other students knew how to sling swords and shoot arrows through people's hearts. But it just didn't make sense. If I were going to steal a priceless Artifact from the Library of Antiquities, if I knew enough to somehow be able to beat Nickamedes's magical security system and take the Bowl out of the library, then I think that I'd be smart enough not to leave any witnesses behind. Didn't these people ever watch *NCIS* or *Law & Order* reruns?

I just didn't understand *why.* Why Jasmine had been killed, why my mom had been hit by that drunk driver, why Paige's stepdad had abused her, why I was here at Mythos Academy when I was nothing like the other students. When I had none of their powers, magic, or warrior skills.

But there were no answers to be found in the mythology book or even in my own troubled thoughts. So I closed the thick book, put it on my nightstand, and crawled under my soft comforter. But it was still a long, long time before I was able to put my questions aside and drift off to sleep.

Chapter 15

The next day was spectacularly boring. My classes dragged by, and I was as invisible as ever to the other students. All anyone could talk about was who'd hooked up and split up at the bonfire yesterday and how all that was going to affect the homecoming dance tonight. Even the professors seemed to have given up on getting the students to do any actual work today, because all my morning classes turned into study periods.

Really, though, they were all just raging gossip fests about the homecoming dance. Who was going with whom, what designer dresses everyone was wearing and how much they cost, which dorm was going to have the best after-party and the most kegs. Pretty much the same conversations that the kids would be having back at my old school. Except there I might have actually been going to the dance, instead of staying in my room all night long like I would be here.

In a way, though, I was glad that I wasn't going to the

dance. Because mixed in with all the talk about hookups and breakups were whispers of another ritual. Apparently, every year before the homecoming dance the staff and students at Mythos gave thanks to the gods for watching over them for another season, sort of like a harvest celebration. I shivered, thinking about the scene that I'd witnessed at the bonfire last night—the silvery flames and the old, ancient force that had stirred in the air around them. I'd already reached my limit of magic mumbo jumbo for the week—I had zero desire to see any more.

Everyone was so excited about the dance that there was almost no mention of Jasmine Ashton. Only a couple of days had passed since she'd been murdered, and it was like it had never even happened. Everyone else seemed to have forgotten about the Valkyrie already, even though she'd been the most popular girl in our class.

It made me sad and angry at the same time. Especially since I couldn't seem to let go of it. I still couldn't forget seeing Jasmine that night, her dead blue eyes staring up at me like she wanted me to help her.

I still couldn't forget the fact that it should have been me lying there in all those pools of blood.

Lunchtime rolled around. I got my usual grilled chicken salad, along with a bottle of Honeycrisp apple juice and a piece of chocolate-crusted key lime cheesecake that was depressingly small. Seriously. The pale, creamy sliver wasn't even as wide as two of my fingers put together. I loaded everything onto a clear glass tray and retreated to an empty table in the quietest, most re-mote corner of the dining hall that I could find.

I ignored the salad and all of its elaborately cut veg-gies, cracked open the sweet, tart apple juice, and drained half of it in one gulp. Not hard, since the drink portions were almost as meager as the dessert ones. I eyed the plastic container, wishing that I'd gone ahead and got-ten two juices like I'd really wanted to instead of just one—

A tray plopped down across from me, making me jerk back in surprise and almost drop my juice on the floor.

Daphne Cruz dumped her enormous purse onto the table. Her bag covered up Jasmine's mythology book, which I'd been planning on reading more of at lunch. But that wasn't the strangest thing Daphne did. She ac-tually sat down at my table.

Like—like we were *friends* or something.

I eyed the Valkyrie, wondering if she'd somehow been possessed or something. If somebody had dripped her blood into Loki's Bowl of Tears and made her a willing slave—

"So," the Valkyrie said, cracking open the lid on her Perrier. "This is where you eat lunch. All the way in the back here. What are you? A vampire who's afraid of sunlight or something?"

Vampires? Were vampires real, too? I wondered, but I didn't want to look stupid and ask, especially since I didn't know what Daphne was doing here in the first place.

"Yeah," I said in a guarded voice. "You caught me. I've got this whole superhero thing going on, so I sit way back here to keep the paparazzi and rabid fans at bay."

Daphne eyed me. After a moment, the Valkyrie's glossy pink lips crinkled up into a smile. "You've got a weird sense of humor. Superheroes are so *over.*"

"Yeah, but the actors who play them in the movies are still *so* rich. I think they'll get over the heartbreak of losing your approval."

Daphne snorted out a laugh, then picked up her fork and started stabbing her eggplant Parmesan to death. I waited a minute, then looked around the dining hall, wondering if this was some kind of joke. But I didn't see anyone looking in my direction and laughing behind their hands.

What I did see was Morgan McDougall and a couple of the other Valkyrie princesses all sitting at their usual table, deep into their lunchtime gossip and ogling every cute guy who walked by. But Daphne didn't look over at her friends, and they didn't seem to notice her sitting in the corner with me.

"Are you actually . . . going to eat lunch with me?" I asked.

"No," Daphne said, breaking a buttery breadstick in half and dipping it into the spicy marinara sauce on her plate. "I'm a figment of your imagination. You're only imagining that I'm sitting here eating with you. Because I'm just so freaking awesome that people daydream about being seen with me."

"Funny," I muttered.

The Valkyrie smiled at me and took a bite of her breadstick.

"But why?" I asked. "You hate me."

Daphne chewed and swallowed. "I wouldn't say *hate*, exactly. You're kind of like fungus, Gwen. After a while, you just start growing on people."

"So I'm mold. Wonderful. So why don't you just scrub me off and go sit with your Valkyrie friends like usual?"

"Because," Daphne said, dropping her black eyes to her Caesar salad. "The other night when you weren't looking, I forwarded all of Jasmine's e-mails to my account. And I found some things on there that I didn't like—things about me."

"Like what?"

Daphne sighed and pushed her salad away, like she'd lost her appetite. "Like the fact that Jasmine and Morgan were making fun of me behind my back. They knew about my crush on Carson, and they thought it was *hysterical*. And that was some of the nicer things they said about me. And it wasn't just them. Claudia, Kylie, Seraphina . . . all of them were swapping e-mails about me and each other. None of us seem to actually like each other very much."

"So?" I asked. "Isn't that what mean girls do? I mean, the Valkyries are the queen bees of Mythos. You girls make the kids on *Gossip Girl* look tame. Doesn't it all kind of go with the territory?"

"Maybe." Daphne shrugged. "But I'm sick of it. I've

known those girls since first grade, and they all just get shallower and stupider every single year. I think it's time that I made some new friends."

She drew in a breath and looked at me. "You did something really cool for me last night, hooking me up with Carson. I don't know why I was so scared of what everyone else would think about me and him, but I'm not anymore. And I'm not going to forget what you did for me, Gwen."

"So you've decided that I'm it then?" I asked. "That I'm your new BFF? Overnight? Just like that?"

For the first time, doubt flickered in Daphne's black eyes. "Hey, if you want to sit over here in the corner all by yourself and pout about how you don't have any friends, fine with me. *I* was just trying to be nice."

She grabbed her tray and started to get to her feet to storm off, but I held up my hands in a placating gesture.

"No, no, no," I said. "Wait; sit back down. I'd . . . love some company. Please. Stay."

Daphne stared at me another minute, then sank back into her chair. Geez. The Valkyrie was a little volatile. I'd have to remember that: Don't piss off Daphne, or she'll rip your heart out of your chest.

The Valkyrie clacked her nails on her fork, and pink sparks flashed and fluttered in the air the way that they always did when her fingertips scraped against something.

"Why do your fingers do that?" I asked. "Why all the pink sparks everywhere?"

Daphne shrugged. "It's a Valkyrie thing. It's just part of our magic."

"Magic? What kind of magic?"

"You know that all Valkyries are strong, right?"

I nodded. "Strong" was kind of an understatement when you could twist a guy's head off with your bare hands.

"Well, Valkyries have other magic, too, another power or ability that's special. Usually, Valkyries don't come into their power, whatever it is, until they're at least sixteen or seventeen. My magic hasn't quickened yet, so I don't know what kind of magic I'll have. But some Valkyries are healers, while others have enhanced senses. Some can do spells and make things happen, while others can control the weather or create fire with their bare hands. Some Valkyries can even create illusions."

Something stirred in the back of my mind. "Illusions? What kind of illusions?"

Daphne shrugged again. "All kinds. Think of it this way: You touch stuff and see things, right? Well, when I touch stuff, sparks of magic fly off the ends of my fingertips. It's just a thing that Valkyries do. The sparks are just little flashes of color, little pulses of light, and they fade away almost immediately, sort of like rainbows do. They can't actually hurt you or anything. Basically, my fingers are kind of like sparklers on the Fourth of July."

Okay, so it was a mythological quirk or something. Like Logan Quinn being a Spartan, picking up any weapon, and automatically knowing how to kill people with it. But there was one more thing I was curious about.

"Why pink?" I asked, thinking of the green sparks that I'd seen Morgan shoot off when she and Samson had had their little afternoon delight in the courtyard yesterday. "Why not blue or silver or some other color? Pink seems kind of odd. Kind of . . . girly."

"It has to do with our auras," Daphne replied. "The color of the sparks is tied to our emotions and personalities. And the more emotional or upset that we get, the more sparks you see."

I raised my eyebrows, wondering what kind of person had a princess pink aura. Daphne saw the question in my eyes.

"I like pink," she said in a defensive tone. "I think it's cool."

"Sure, sure it is," I agreed in a hasty voice.

Ugh. Every other thing I said seemed to offend the Valkyrie. It had been so long since I'd had a friend—or even since I'd had a lengthy conversation with anyone besides Grandma Frost—that I wasn't sure how to act anymore. Sure, I'd had friends at my old school, but I'd pushed them all away after my mom's death. I hadn't heard from any of them since I'd started going to Mythos, and none of them had tried to contact me. We'd all just gone on with our lives.

Maybe I felt so awkward because I was worried that you made friends differently at the academy, since everything else seemed to be so twisted and turned upside down. I mean, Daphne wouldn't want me to drink her blood or anything, would she? Because I was *so* not doing that. Potential friend or no potential friend.

Things got a little better after that, mainly because I asked Daphne about Carson and what the two of them had talked about on the phone last night. The Valkyrie's pretty face took on a soft glow, and more pink sparks flickered around her fingertips. She was a total goner where Carson was concerned, and she didn't seem to be afraid to admit it anymore. Then again, she was eating lunch with me, the Gypsy girl who was the academy's biggest outcast. A date with a band geek like Carson would be a definite social step up from being seen with me.

"Actually, I came over here to ask you something," Daphne said, a shy note creeping into her voice. "I was wondering if, um, you'd like to come over to my dorm room before the homecoming dance tonight. I bought a dress, just in case Carson or someone else asked me, but I haven't shown it to anyone."

Her words made me flash back to the last time that I'd done something like that. Something so . . . normal. Something so . . . fun.

It had been several weeks before the sophomore prom at my old school—and days before I'd discovered Paige's secret. I'd just broken up with Drew Squires, my boyfriend of all of three weeks, but I was still planning on going to the prom, mainly because my mom, Grace, and I had spent weeks shopping for the perfect dress and shoes. We'd finally found them both in this little out-of-the-way boutique in a run-down strip mall, including a violet dress that Mom claimed was the exact color of my eyes.

We'd brought it home that Saturday, and she'd died that next Friday, six days later. Of course I hadn't gone to the prom after that. But for some reason, I'd decided not to return the dress. In fact, it was hanging in the back of my closet in my dorm room—

"Are you okay?" Daphne asked, cutting into my memories. "You look like you're about to cry or something."

"I'm fine," I said, pushing away the memory.

The Valkyrie stared at me, and I fumbled for an explanation.

"I was thinking about my mom," I said in a quiet voice. "Back in the spring, a few days before she died, she took me shopping for a prom dress."

"Oh. *Oh.*" Daphne picked right up on the *dead mom* part, and she didn't say anything for a moment. "If you'd rather not, I understand—"

"No," I said quickly. "No, I'm fine. I'd love to help you get ready for your big date with Carson. What time do you want me to come over?"

Daphne and I made plans to meet up later in her room after I worked my shift at the library. The bell rang, signaling the end of the lunch period, and the two of us went our separate ways. And I realized that today was the very first time that I hadn't had to eat lunch or dinner by myself since I'd been at Mythos. It was nice to have someone to sit with, to have someone to talk to. I'd forgotten just how much I'd missed that. Well, maybe I hadn't forgotten. Maybe I just hadn't wanted to remember because it would have made my loneliness that much more painful.

Unfortunately, my good mood wasn't contagious, especially not when it came to my professors, and the rest of the day ground by. Finally, though, the last bell of the day rang at the end of my sixth-period myth-history class. I packed up my things as quickly as I could. I wanted to sneak off campus and go see Grandma Frost before I had to report to Nickamedes at the library. Despite the fact that absolutely no one would be doing something as boring as homework tonight, he was still making me work my usual Friday shift before the library closed early because of the dance.

"Are you going to the homecoming dance, Gwen?" Carson asked me as he stuffed his own books into his bag.

"Nah," I said. "But I am helping Daphne get ready. So you know she's going to look fabulous for you."

Carson smiled, and I found myself grinning back at the band geek. Maybe this making friends thing wasn't so hard after all.

I left the English-history building and walked across the quad. Today, instead of standing around talking and texting, just about everyone was hurrying on their way, off to make sure that they had everything they needed for tonight—dresses, tuxes, kegs, condoms, and all.

No one paid any attention to me, and I was able to stroll down to the main gate undetected. I stopped just inside the black iron bars and stared up at the two sphinxes on either side of the opening. Professor Metis had told me that Nickamedes was going to put extra magic, extra wards or whatever, on the closed gate to keep another Reaper from sneaking onto campus. Maybe it was my imagination, but it seemed like the sphinxes' features were even sharper and fiercer now than they had been the last time I'd been at the gate. Their eyes were narrowed to slits, and the edges of their claws glinted in the afternoon sun, like they were half a second away from erupting out of the stone and pouncing on whoever tried to slip past them.

For a moment I thought about turning back, but it had been a couple of days since I'd seen Grandma Frost. She'd be expecting me to come by, and I missed her. She was all I had left now, and I wanted to see her. It was worth the risk of tripping whatever magical alarm Nickamedes had put on the entrance. Besides, the sphinxes probably wouldn't kill me—right?

I tiptoed up to the gate, sucked in my breath, turned sideways, and slipped through the black iron bars.

Nothing happened.

No alarms sounded, and the sphinxes didn't leap down and rip me to shreds, if they could even do that in the first place. Apparently, Nickamedes had only strengthened the spells to keep Reapers out of the academy—not created a new one to keep students inside. Like everyone else, the librarian thought that the threat was outside the academy walls—not inside. Still, I was happy for his oversight, and I hurried across the street and hopped on the bus. Twenty minutes later, I was walking up the steps to Grandma Frost's house. I used my key to let myself in.

But for once, Grandma Frost wasn't busy giving a psychic reading in the other room. Instead, I found her in the kitchen, with its bright, cheery sky blue walls and white tile.

"Mmm. What smells so good?" I asked, throwing my messenger bag onto the table.

Grandma grabbed a dishcloth off the counter, reached into the oven, and pulled out a baking sheet full of homemade almond sugar cookies. I breathed in, the warm smells of melted butter, sticky dough, and crystallized sugar making my mouth water and my stomach rumble. Nobody baked as good as Grandma Frost did. The dessert chefs at Mythos could definitely learn a thing or two from her.

Grandma slid three cookies onto a plate and handed them to me, along with a glass of cold milk. Her usual colorful scarves fluttered around her body, the silver coins on the ends of them chiming together.

My eyes narrowed. "You knew that I was coming over today."

Grandma smiled her mysterious Gypsy smile, the one that she used on all her clients. "I am psychic, pumpkin. It comes in handy sometimes. Especially when I want to bake my granddaughter some cookies."

Grandma Frost grabbed a couple of the warm cookies for herself, along with another glass of milk, and the two of us sat down at the kitchen table to eat. We didn't talk much at first, both of us too busy stuffing our mouths with the sweet treats to bother with conversation. But eventually the cookies and milk disappeared and Grandma stared at me.

"Isn't there a big dance at the academy tonight?" she asked. "Something fancy and formal?"

I blinked. "How do you know that? Did you have a vision of me in a dress or something?"

"Of course not. I read about it in that electronic newsletter that your Professor Metis sends out every week." Grandma gave me a sidelong look. "Actually, I got two newsletters this week. The regular one about the dance and the cafeteria menu and all that. The other one was a little more serious—it was all about that poor girl's murder."

Uh-oh. I hadn't planned on telling Grandma Frost about Jasmine Ashton because I didn't want her to worry, but Grandma was too smart for me. She always was. I'd never been able to figure out if it was because she was psychic or just knew me that well. There was no use lying to her, so I drew in a breath and told her all about that night in the library and everything that I'd discovered about Jasmine since then.

"I know all the professors think that it was just some Reaper bad guy after the Bowl of Tears," I said, finishing up my story. "But I have this weird feeling there's something else going on. Something we're all missing.

Something obvious. Mom always told me to trust my feelings, my instincts, but I'm starting to wonder if she was wrong about that."

Grandma stared at me, a strange light flashing in her violet eyes. It wasn't the look that she always got when she was seeing a vision of the future. No, this was something else. Like I'd said something to upset her. I supposed that she was just freaked out about Jasmine's murder. I mean, who would want her only granddaughter to go to school where a student had gotten her throat cut?

"Are you okay, Grandma?"

She shook her head, and the light in her eyes vanished. "I'm fine. Just worried about you is all. I hate that you have to go to that school in the first place."

I hesitated. "Why *do* I have to go to Mythos? I've asked you before, but you've never really explained it to me."

Grandma sighed. "Because it's finally time for you to learn how to use your Gypsy gift, Gwen. Something that you'll do by going to Mythos."

"But I know how to use my psychometry magic already. I always have. I don't see how going to Mythos changes anything."

She shook her head. "It may not make sense now, but it will someday. Trust me, pumpkin, okay?"

I did trust her, more than anything, but I also wanted answers—answers about why my life had had to change so much. Why everyone at Mythos believed in things that I didn't. And most especially, why Professor Metis and Grandma Frost thought that I belonged there in the first place.

I thought about pressing my grandma for answers, but she looked so old in that moment, so sad and tired, like she'd used up all the life that was inside her and was nothing more than a hollow shell. And I just couldn't do it—not now. Or maybe it was because part of me was scared of what the answers might be. Knowing other people's secrets made me feel smart. Realizing there might be secrets that involved me made me nervous. Yeah, I could be a total hypocrite sometimes.

I didn't know why Grandma was keeping secrets from me, but she loved me and I loved her. It had always just been me, my mom, and Grandma Frost. My dad had died before I could even start to remember him, and we didn't have any other family that I knew of. With my mom gone, Grandma was all that I had. I didn't want to fight with Grandma—ever. Especially not over something as stupid as Mythos Academy.

"Anyway, I don't think you should be worried," I said, changing the subject and trying to reassure her at the same time. "Professor Metis and the others increased the magical security on campus. Besides, whoever killed Jasmine is probably long gone, despite what I think. Nobody else has gotten hurt, as far as I know, and nothing else has been stolen from the library."

I didn't mention what had happened outside the library last night. It wasn't like the falling statue had been directed at *me* or anything. Even if maybe I couldn't say the same thing about the Nemean prowler. But it was dead, vanished in a puff of smoke, and I wasn't, and that was all that really mattered.

Grandma Frost looked like she wanted to say something else, but then she shook her head and the moment passed. "I'm sure you're right, pumpkin."

"And they put more security on the dorms, too," I said, still hoping to ease her mind. "Which is where I'll be spending the night."

"You're not going to the dance then? It sounded like a big deal in the newsletter."

I shrugged. "It's just the homecoming dance. They're going to crown a king and queen in every class, and there'll be music and dancing and stuff. Just like at my old school."

I didn't say anything about the ritual that I'd heard the other kids talk about, the harvest blessing or whatever it really was.

"So why aren't you going?" Grandma asked. "You used to love getting dressed up for things like that before—"

She cut off her words, but we both knew what she'd been about to say. *Before your mom died.*

I shrugged again. "For one thing, I don't have a date. No one invited me. I don't want to go by myself and look like a total loser."

"Why not?" Grandma Frost asked. "You do lots of things by yourself. You always have."

"Yeah, but nothing like this," I said. "Nothing—"

This time, I bit off my words, but I didn't fool Grandma. She knew exactly what I'd been about to say.

"Nothing fun," she finished in a quiet voice.

Grandma Frost looked at me, her violet eyes soft and sad in her face. "It's okay for you to have fun again, Gwen. Your mom wouldn't want you to sit at home every night crying over her. She'd want you to go to the dance and have a good time, even if you didn't have a date. She'd want you to have as much fun as you could, as often as you could. Before—"

She cut off her words, and for a moment her whole body tensed. Her rings scraped together as her hands tightened into fists, and the coins on the edges of her scarves jangled together in harsh discord. Then, Grandma Frost realized that I was staring at her, and she forced herself to relax. Her hands unclenched, and the coins took on a sweeter, tinkling note.

"Before, well, before you're all grown up," she finished. "That's what your mom would have wanted. For you to go to the dance and have a wonderful time."

I knew that she would. Grace Frost would have wanted me to do exactly that. I bit my lip and looked away from Grandma's knowing gaze.

"It just doesn't feel . . . right," I said. "That I'm alive, and she's not. That she'll never do anything fun again. That I'll never see her smile or hear her laugh again."

Grandma reached over and took my hand. I felt the soft warmth of her love envelop me, the way that it always did. But this time, I felt her sadness, too, an ache so sharp and deep and fierce that it seemed like a sword slicing my heart in two. Sometimes, I forgot that Grandma had lost someone, too. My mom's death had hurt her just as much as it had me.

"I know it doesn't feel right, pumpkin. But your mom's death wasn't your fault. Life has gone on, whether you've wanted it to or not. I think that it's about time that you actually started enjoying it again, don't you? Even if it's just a little bit?"

I sighed, all the energy draining out of my body. "I guess. But it's just so hard, you know? I've been so . . . angry, and going to Mythos . . . I just don't fit in there. I don't know why I can't just switch back to my old school. I'm just not special like the other kids are."

"You're at that academy for a reason," Grandma Frost replied, an ominous note creeping back into her voice. "You'll find your own place there sooner or later. As for your mom, she's gone, but she wouldn't want you to mope around. She'd want you to get out and live and do everything that teenagers are supposed to do."

I raised an eyebrow. "Like come home drunk and high on pot after I have unprotected sex with my boyfriend behind the bleachers at the homecoming dance?"

Grandma's eyes narrowed, but she still grinned at me. "Well, everything except that. But you know what I mean. Now, I want you to go to that dance and have fun. Or at least promise me that you'll think about it."

I couldn't say no to her, but I also couldn't let go of my guilt, hurt, and anger long enough to say yes either. "Okay. I'll think about going. But no promises."

"That's all I wanted to hear, pumpkin."

Grandma kissed me on the forehead, then got up and started putting the rest of the cooling cookies into a tin so I could take them back to the academy with me.

I just sat there at the table, thinking about everything that Grandma had said and wondering if maybe it was time to get on with my life—and have a little fun.

Whether I really felt like it or not.

Chapter 16

Once Grandma Frost packed up the cookies, I slipped the tin into my messenger bag, got on the bus, and rode back up to Mythos Academy.

The quad was almost deserted by this point, as most of the students had retreated to their dorm rooms to get ready for the homecoming dance. Normally, I would have enjoyed the silence and watching the squirrels hop from branch to branch in the trees that towered over the lush lawn. But it was like the whole academy had suddenly turned into a ghost town. It was too empty, too quiet, especially for a school where one of the students had been murdered a few days ago. Once again, I felt like all the eyes on all the statues on all the buildings were looking down at me, watching my every move. I shivered, stuck my hands into my gray hoodie pockets, and hurried on.

The Library of Antiquities wasn't any better. Not a single student sat at the tables in the main space in front of the checkout counter. No professors either. Nobody was even manning the snack cart this afternoon, and most of the lights had already been turned off in the maze of glass offices in the center of the library.

I couldn't help but look to my left at the spot where the Bowl of Tears had been—and where Jasmine had been murdered. There was nothing left to see, of course, just like there hadn't been the last time that I'd been in here the day after her death. The blood, body, and Bowl of Tears were all long gone. Still, it felt like there was a watchful silence in the spot, like there was some kind of invisible force sitting there just waiting for something to happen.

Like, say, maybe a Gypsy girl to walk by so the big, bad monster could leap up out of the floor or wherever it was hiding and grab her. I shivered again. Okay, so maybe all that was just my overactive imagination at work, but right now just looking at the place where Jasmine had been killed seriously creeped me out.

My violet eyes flicked back to the dark offices. Maybe if Nickamedes wasn't here, I could just leave and forget about working my shift—

Something moved off to the right, heading quickly in my direction. I stifled a scream and turned . . .

To see Nickamedes come striding out of the stacks, several large, heavy books in his hands.

I leaned against the nearest table and sighed, my hand going up to my heart, as if I could somehow slow it back down to its normal speed just by touching my chest. Nickamedes's black brows drew together, pinching the rest of his face.

"Is something wrong, Gwendolyn?" Nickamedes said in his arch tone, putting the books down onto another table. "You're looking a little pale, even for you."

He was one to talk. Nickamedes had skin so white that he could have passed for a vampire, if they actually existed. Maybe they did. I didn't know what was real and what wasn't anymore.

Nickamedes's blue eyes checked the clock mounted behind the counter. I sighed. I knew what was coming.

"You're ten minutes late," the librarian sniffed. "*Again.*"

My previous unease vanished, replaced, as always, by annoyance. How could anyone be that prissy all the time?

"Oh, don't get your panties in a wad," I muttered. "It's not like there's anyone in here besides the two of us."

Nickamedes's gaze sharpened. "What was that, Gwendolyn?"

"Nothing. Nothing at all."

"Well then," Nickamedes replied. "I think it's time that you get to work. I've got several dozen books that need shelving before we close for the night."

He pointed over to the checkout counter, where three metal carts crammed with books sat. I just sighed again. So much for leaving early.

For the next hour I pushed the heavy, squeaky carts

back and forth through the library, putting all the books back into their proper places in the stacks. And, of course, every single cart had a loose wheel that pulled either this way or that, which meant that I had to wrestle with them every time I tried to move the carts down the aisles.

Eventually, my path took me past The Case, as I had come to think of it—the one with the strange sword inside it. I should have just shoved my squeaky cart right on past it, but I found myself stopping to stare down at the weapon again.

It looked the same as always—a long blade made out of silver metal. Maybe it was just me and all the weirdness that had been going on the past few days, but the man's face seemed even more pronounced in the hilt than ever before, as if he was an actual person who just happened to be resting his cheek against the metal. I half-expected the eye on the hilt to pop open and glare at me again. I held my breath, but that didn't happen.

Still, for some reason, the sword made me think about all the myths that my mom had read to me when I was a kid. She'd never told me any fairy tales, just myths, which I'd always thought was kind of weird. Maybe my mom had known something that I hadn't— like the fact that I'd wind up at Mythos someday—but she'd always insisted on reading myths to me. The stories where the hero always knew the answer to a tricky riddle or figured out how to vanquish the big, bad unbeatable monster. Like all it would take would be the

right person touching the sword in front of me and Stuff
Would Happen, just like it always did in the myths.

I was suddenly aware of this weird charge in the air,
like static electricity slowly building and building around
me. My palms itched, and I had a sudden urge to open
The Case and pick up the sword. I didn't know why. It
wasn't like I actually knew how to use the weapon or
anything. Not like Logan Quinn. Still, something made
me want to pick it up. It was almost like I *needed* to
pick it up. Mesmerized, my fingers stretched out toward
The Case—

"Gwendolyn!" Nickamedes's voice boomed through
the library, echoing up to the ceiling and back down
again. "You've got five minutes to finish shelving those
books. Hurry up!"

Startled, I snapped out of my trance, dropped my
hand, and backed away from The Case. What had I
been thinking? I didn't know whose sword that was or
what kind of psycho-killer vibes might be attached to it.
The last thing I needed to do tonight was touch something and have another screaming fit, thanks to my psychometry. *Geez, Gwen. Pull yourself together.*

"Gwendolyn!" Nickamedes shouted again.

I rolled my eyes, walked back over to the cart, and
steered it farther down the aisle. Still, for some reason, I
turned around and gave the sword one more longing
glance before I rounded the corner and it disappeared
from sight.

* * *

Thirty minutes later, I found myself standing outside Valhalla Hall, staring up at the gray stone building and the ivy that wrapped around it from top to bottom. Only this time, instead of sneaking in to steal Jasmine's laptop, I was actually here as an invited guest. Weird, how things could change in the space of a few days.

A Valkyrie I recognized as a third-year student was on her way out, so I was able to step inside without having to hit the intercom button by the front door and ask Daphne to buzz me in.

I walked into the same living room that I'd been in before, the one with all the recliners, couches, and TVs. It was after six now, and some of the other girls had already come down to the common room to wait for their dates, since the dance started at seven. They all perched carefully on the edges of their chairs, careful not to wrinkle their dresses, as they eyed each other and gossiped.

Everyone had seriously glammed up for the occasion, with long, slinky, glittery dresses that I could tell were wicked expensive and jewelry that sparkled too much not to be real. No rhinestones here at Mythos, that was for sure. Everyone's hair was also done just so, their makeup was picture-perfect, and their shoes, purses, and cell phones had all been color-coordinated to go with their gowns. It was all very matchy-matchy.

I stared out at the sea of diamonds, sequins, and glossy pouty lips. I hadn't thought the homecoming dance would be this formal. This was like all the proms at my old school rolled into one—times ten. It was just . . . dazzling. It took me a few seconds to quit blinking and staring at all the shiny objects.

A few of the girls looked at me, but once they saw that I wasn't dressed up for the dance and thus they couldn't critique who and what I was wearing, they turned back to their friends. I put my head down, hurried through the room, and headed up the steps.

And almost ran right into Morgan McDougall.

The Valkyrie was coming down the stairs just as I was going up. Morgan looked gorgeous and totally slutty at the same time. Her skintight gown matched the deep black of her hair, while smoky shadow rimmed her hazel eyes. Her lips were a crimson heart in her pretty face. The front of her dress had some sort of wire in it that pushed her boobs up to impressive heights, while the slit in the leg almost went all the way up to the promised land. I'm sure Samson Sorensen would approve of it—and so would every other guy at the dance.

Two other girls—Morgan's usual entourage—surrounded her, looking just as glitzy as she did, although not quite as slutty. The three of them had stopped a couple of steps up from the bottom, and their conversation drifted down to me.

"Of course I'm going to be the homecoming queen of the second-year class," Morgan said in a loud, proud voice. "Professor Metis told me as much during myth-history when she said that the other profs had decided to crown an alternate winner instead of Jasmine. They didn't want to bring everyone down by mentioning *her* tonight. And, of course, Samson's going to be homecoming king. It's only fitting, since he's my date. Tonight is going to be perfect and just the way it was always meant to be."

The two Valkyries nodded their heads, agreeing with everything she said. Even though Jasmine, their previous fearless leader, had only been dead a few days.

Morgan tossed her hair back over her shoulder, struck a model pose, and then slinked down the last few steps, ready to go claim her homecoming crown, her new boyfriend, and her rightful place as the new queen of Mythos Academy. The Valkyrie walked past me like she didn't even notice me standing on the first step. Maybe she didn't. I imagined it was hard for Morgan to see anything but her own perfection.

"Aren't you even sorry that she's dead?" I called out.

I'd never spoken to Morgan before, and I certainly had no real reason to talk to her now. But the image of Jasmine lying on the library floor, sprawled across the sticky puddles of her own blood, flashed through my mind, and the words came out before I could stop them.

Morgan turned around to stare at me, along with her two Valkyrie followers. "Are you talking to me?"

"Of course I'm talking to you, Morgan. You were Jasmine's best friend. Aren't you sorry that she's dead? Even just a little bit?"

Morgan frowned at me, her red lips turning down into a perfect pout. "Well, of course I'm *sorry.* I mean, she was my best friend and all, and I'd known her for, like, *ever.* But just because she's dead doesn't mean that we all have to act like we are, too. If you had known Jasmine, you'd realize that's what she would have wanted. She would have wanted us to pull together, to go to the dance and have fun without her."

It sounded like some little speech that Morgan had rehearsed in front of the mirror while she was putting on her lipstick. Some pat little answer that she could just pull out and use like an emotional stun gun if anyone else asked her the same question that I had. Of course, it was also more or less the same thing that my Grandma Frost had told me, but at least I knew she meant it. Morgan? Probably not.

I rolled my eyes. I was willing to bet that I knew Jasmine a lot better than Morgan ever had. Morgan hadn't even realized that Jasmine knew that she was sleeping with Samson behind Jasmine's back. But I did, thanks to the flashes that I'd gotten off the picture that I'd dug out of Jasmine's trash. With best friends like Morgan, who needed enemies?

But I didn't say anything. There was no use trying to tell Morgan any of that. Girls like her never listened to freaks like me.

Morgan gave me a haughty, superior look, as though she'd just won some kind of war of words with her quick answer. Then, she turned and strutted out of the dorm on her black stilettos, with her two new BFFs trailing along behind her.

I shook my head and went up the stairs to the second floor, where Daphne's room was. I knocked once on the door, and, a moment later, the Valkyrie threw it open.

Daphne had already put on her dress—a pink princess ball gown with tiny spaghetti straps, a sweetheart neckline, and a poofy skirt dusted with glittering pink sequins. She'd twisted her blond hair up into a sleek bun on top of her head, and her pink lip gloss matched her dress perfectly. The Valkyrie looked like she'd just stepped out of a Disney movie. I half expected singing birds and animated mice to come scurrying out of her room, pleased by their work for the night.

"Um, so what do you need me to do?" I asked. "Because you look pretty perfect to me already."

Daphne's face creased into a smile. "Do you really think so? Do you really like the dress?"

I came inside and shut the door behind me. "I really do. And I think that Carson will, too."

Daphne beamed at me, then turned and went over to stare at herself in the mirror over her vanity table once more.

I used the opportunity to study the Valkyrie's room. She had the same dorm room furniture that we all did, more or less. A bed, a vanity table, a desk, a TV, some bookcases. But Daphne had meant it before at lunch when she'd said that she liked pink, because it was *everywhere*. The comforter on her bed, the pillows, the curtains. All some shade of pink. Even the walls and ceiling were painted a pale, pearly pink.

But the strange thing was that there were also tons of computers in the room. I counted three monitors, a couple of laptops, and some plastic boxes that looked like servers—and that was just on her oversize desk stuck in the back corner. Wow. I'd thought her being in the Tech Club was just a fluke or something, but it looked like Daphne was really into the computer stuff. A Valkyrie princess computer geek—who would have thought? I would have had a hard time believing all the equipment was hers—if the computers, monitors, and servers hadn't all been covered with pink cases and Hello Kitty stickers.

Daphne smoothed down her dress and turned to look at me. I stood there in the middle of the room, feeling awkward and underdressed once again.

"So . . . what do you need me to do, exactly? Because you're already dressed and stuff."

Daphne shrugged. "Nothing, I guess. I just wanted . . . somebody to talk to before Carson comes and picks me up."

"He's a nice guy, Carson," I said, sitting down on the bed. "You two make a cute couple."

"Do you really think so?"

"I do."

We fell silent, each one of us trying to figure out what we could talk to the other person about. This friend thing was harder than I remembered it being. A lot harder.

"So . . . ," Daphne said, still standing so her dress

wouldn't get wrinkled. "I take it that you're not going to the dance. At least, please tell me you're not going in that awful hoodie."

My eyes narrowed. Catty I could do. Being nice was what was so difficult. "I like my hoodie just fine, thank you very much. But don't worry. I'm not wearing it to the dance because I'm not going. No one asked me, as if you hadn't guessed. Like you pointed out at lunch today, I don't have any friends at Mythos, much less a boyfriend."

It might have been my imagination, but I thought Daphne winced a little at my harsh words.

The Valkyrie hesitated. "You know, you could come along with Carson and me. . . ."

I raised an eyebrow. "And ruin your first big date? I don't think so. Even I'm not that much of a bitch."

"Yeah, it might be a little awkward."

"You think?"

We both looked at each other, rolled our eyes, and laughed. That broke the ice between us, and we started talking about all the juicy gossip that we'd heard today. About who was going with whom to the homecoming dance, who would get drunk before it was halfway over, and who was planning to go All the Way tonight with their boyfriends and girlfriends.

And I suddenly realized that I felt almost . . . *normal.* Almost like I still went to a normal school with normal kids—and even that I was normal myself. It felt . . . nice . . . fun, even.

Finally, we quit gossiping and giggling about the other kids, and Daphne gave me a sly look.

"So what's going on with you and Logan Quinn?" she asked.

I blinked. "What do you mean?"

She raised an eyebrow. "I mean the two of you looked awfully cozy last night at the bonfire. And he did go all Spartan and kill a Nemean prowler that was trying to eat you. Which is *totally* sexy, if you ask me."

"Logan Quinn doesn't strike me as a guy who gets cozy with a girl unless he wants something from her. Like the chance to sign her mattress," I said in a dry tone. "Yeah, he saved my life last night, saved me from that awful prowler. But you should have seen him. It was almost like he was *happy* that it was trying to kill him. That he actually *enjoyed* fighting it. I think he killed it more for himself than for me. Like to prove to himself that he could or something."

Daphne shrugged. "Well, he *is* a Spartan. Killing things is what they do. What did you expect? That he'd send you flowers and write you bad poetry? That dead Nemean prowler is pretty much as close to a stuffed animal as you're ever going to get from a Spartan like Logan Quinn."

I gave her a blank look. "What does being a Spartan have to do with stuffed animals?"

Daphne sighed. "You've been here, what, two months and you still don't get it, do you, Gwen? How things work around here? Why we're all really here?"

I shrugged.

Daphne stared at me, her black eyes serious in her pretty face. "We're all here, all of us—Valkyries, Spartans, Amazons, and all the rest of us—because we're *magic*. Because we're descended from myth. You know all those stories that talk about how brave the Spartans were at the Battle of Thermopylae? How such a small group of them held off all those thousands and thousands of other warriors? Well, it's not just a story. It's *real*. Just like the ancient Valkyries escorted the dead to Valhalla, just like the Trojans totally got punked by the Greeks and that wooden horse during the Trojan War. All the myths, all the legends, all the magic is real. And it's all a part of us, a piece of us. We keep it alive, and we use it to keep Chaos and darkness from swallowing the world."

A week ago, I would have laughed at her. But now I was actually starting to believe her, to believe in all the myths, magic, and monsters. Too many weird things had happened the past few days for me not to. Jasmine's murder. The Bowl of Tears disappearing. The statue almost hitting Morgan and Samson. The prowler stalking me, then evaporating in a cloud of smoke after Logan killed it. That strange sword in the library that I couldn't stop staring at.

"Okay," I said. "Maybe Logan is a Spartan and that explains why he went all berserker last night. Maybe you're a Valkyrie who can crush diamonds with your bare hands and shoot pink sparks off the ends of your fingers. But all that doesn't tell me anything about *me*.

I'm the only Gypsy here. That I know of, anyway. The only one who isn't like the rest of you. I'm not a great warrior. All I do is touch stuff and see things. I don't fit in with everyone else."

"I wouldn't say that," Daphne said. "You have magic just like the rest of us do."

"Maybe, but I don't know why my magic makes me a Gypsy and not something else. Do you?"

She shrugged. "I've heard about Gypsies over the years, but nothing concrete about your powers or anything. I even asked around school after you first approached me about stealing Carson's bracelet, but none of the other kids knew anything either. Neither did the professors that I asked. Or if they knew, they wouldn't tell me. I always thought Gypsies were warriors, like Valkyries, Amazons, and the rest of us. Just with a different kind of magic."

"Until you met me," I said in a bitter voice. "And realized just how much of a warrior I'm not."

Daphne tilted her head to one side. "How did you even wind up here in the first place? I've been wondering about that."

I told her the story about Paige Forrest and how her stepdad had been abusing her. And how seeing all that had led to my mom's death.

"The next thing I know, Professor Metis is knocking on my Grandma Frost's front door telling me that I'm going to Mythos Academy this fall," I said, my voice still angry and bitter. "But she never told me why. I asked her the other day, and she still didn't give me a straight answer. My grandma knows something about all this, too, but she's not talking either. She just keeps telling me to give the academy a chance, that things will get better for me."

"I don't know your grandma, but Metis is a crafty one," Daphne said. "She's not quite like the other professors. Some people say that she's really a Champion."

"A Champion? What's that?"

Daphne rolled her eyes. "You really need to pay more attention in myth-history class, Gwen. After the Chaos War ended, all the gods and goddesses agreed to a truce. That basically, they wouldn't use their powers against each other or interfere with things here in the mortal realm. But, of course, none of them could just sit back and do nothing, so they created Champions instead as a kind of loophole to the truce. Champions are people who are chosen by the gods to be, well, their Champions. Their heroes—or villains, depending on which god it is. A good Champion helps carry out the god's desires and keep bad stuff from happening. Champions kill Reapers, guard artifacts, or even mentor other people and help them understand their magic. It's dangerous work, being a Champion. Most of them don't live too long."

Well, that answered my question about why the gods and goddesses didn't fight things out among themselves. They'd agreed not to and were using the rest of us to do their bidding instead, which was so totally *Clash of the Titans*. Being a Champion sounded exactly like something that Metis would do. Not the killing or guarding part, but the mentoring others. Although if the professor had been trying to do that for me, it wasn't sinking in yet.

I shifted on the bed. Maybe everything that Daphne had said was true, but it still didn't explain why I was here and what I had to do with myths, gods, the Chaos War, or any of the rest of it. I was just a Gypsy girl who touched stuff and saw things. Hardly special at all. Not like Logan and his killer warrior skills, or Daphne and her incredible strength and sparking fingers.

Some kind of alarm beeped, and Daphne's black eyes flicked to the clock in the corner of the room. "It's seven o'clock already. Carson is probably waiting for me downstairs. How do I look?"

She twirled around, making her dress swing out in an arc around her, before she smoothed it back down into place.

"You look beautiful," I said in a truthful voice. "Now go have a great time."

Daphne smiled at me, grabbed her purse off the bed, and went over to the door. She stopped and looked back over her shoulder at me.

"Thanks for coming over, Gwen," she said. "I had fun."

I smiled at her. "Me too."

"Can I call you later?" the Valkyrie asked in a shy voice. "If it's not too late?"

"You'd better," I warned in a tough voice. "Because I want to hear all about what a good kisser Carson is."

Daphne laughed and held out her hand. I got up, and

she looped her arm through mine, resting her hand on my hoodie sleeve.

Arm in arm, we left her room, the beginnings of a real friendship shimmering in the air between us, just like the bright pink sparks fluttering up from the Valkyrie's fingertips.

Chapter 17

I escorted Daphne down the stairs. Carson was waiting in the main common room.

He wore a classic tux that made him look like a tall, lanky penguin, but I didn't say anything to Daphne. Because the band geek's face lit up at the sight of the Valkyrie, just like hers did when she saw him. More pink sparks flashed around Daphne's fingers, and if Carson's grin got any wider, his lips would pop off his face.

"Hi," Daphne said in a soft voice, stopping in front of him.

"Hi," Carson whispered back. "You look *beautiful.*"

Daphne blushed. Carson kept staring at her. Neither one moved or said another word. Finally, I cleared my throat to make the band geek get on with things.

"Oh! This is for you." Carson jerked forward and held out a plastic box with a single pink rose inside, as if he'd just remembered that he'd been holding it all along.

"Thank you." Daphne took out the flower, handed

me the empty box, and slipped the simple corsage over her wrist.

I got a little flash off the box, an image of Carson clutching it in his sweaty hands and wondering if he'd picked out the right color rose. It was a sweet, nervous feeling, that he'd be worried so much about something so small. I could feel that Carson wanted everything to be perfect tonight, right down to the corsage.

The two of them stood there staring at each other, before Carson cleared his throat.

"Well, I guess we should be going. We wouldn't want to be late." He frowned. "Or would we? What's cooler?"

Daphne laughed. "I'll tell you all about it on the way over to the dining hall."

Carson held out his arm, and Daphne slipped hers through his. The Valkyrie turned to wave at me; then the two of them left the dorm. I watched them go and smiled. They really did make a cute couple.

Now that they were gone, I had no reason to stick around Valhalla Hall. But instead of heading over to my own dorm, I turned and walked back up the stairs to the second floor. Everyone had left for the dance already, and the dorm was still and quiet, like no one lived here at all.

Nobody saw me use my driver's license to pop the lock and slip back into Jasmine's room.

It looked exactly the same as it had the first time that I'd been in here a few days ago. Bed. Vanity table. Desk. TV. Bookshelves. I pulled out Jasmine's desk chair and sat down, still holding the empty corsage box in my hands. My eyes scanned over the room, hoping for a clue or a vibe or something that would tell me what had really happened to her.

But everything was exactly the way that I'd left it during my last break-in. Pictures of Jasmine stilled lined the mirror over the vanity table. Makeup still cluttered the glass surface. And her bookcase was still full of reference books with titles like *Common Valkyrie Powers, Mastering Your Magic,* and *Manipulating Magical Illusions.*

I stared at the books a minute. Something about them stirred a faint memory in the back of my mind, some vague, half-formed thought. My eyes kept going back to the last book. Illusions, illusions . . . it was something to do with illusions and magic. Something that I'd seen or felt or heard someone say. But even as I reached for it, I could feel it slipping away. Whatever it was, the memory, thought, or idea wasn't ready to come to the surface of my mind yet. Sooner or later, it would, though. They always did.

I didn't know why I'd come in here. What I thought I'd find, if anything. It just seemed . . . sad. That someone could be forgotten so easily so soon, even if Jasmine hadn't been the nicest person at Mythos Academy. Nobody ever wanted to be forgotten.

But there were no real answers to be found in the quiet room, so I got up and left.

I made it back to my own dorm, went inside the turret, and closed the door. Everyone who lived here was at the dance, too, and my dorm was just as quiet as Valhalla Hall. I was probably the only person left inside. Alone again. Naturally.

I flopped down onto the bed and stared up at the ceiling. There were things that I could do. Read the last of the new comics that I had, take a shower, watch some lame reality show, eat the rest of Grandma Frost's almond sugar cookies.

I still had that report due for Metis's myth-history class, the one where we had to pick a god or goddess and write an essay on them. Maybe I'd choose Nike, I thought. The Greek goddess of victory seemed to be in the thick of things when it came to Loki, Reapers, and the Chaos War.

Instead of reaching for my myth-history book, I found myself sitting up and staring at my closed closet door. After a few seconds, I heaved myself up off the bed, went over, and opened it. My usual assortment of jeans, graphic T-shirts, hoodies, and sneakers filled the closet, along with a few other things. My heavy purple plaid winter coat. A couple of pairs of dressy black pants. Thick gray fishermen's sweaters for when the weather got really cold. The scratchy black dress that I'd worn to my mom's funeral.

I didn't have a black dress back then, and Grandma Frost had taken me shopping the day before the burial to get one. I'd picked out the very first dress that I'd seen in my size, not caring what it looked like or who saw me in it. I'd hated the fact that I'd had to wear it at all, that my mom was dead and never coming back.

My fingers hovered over the fabric, but I didn't touch it. I didn't want to remember that day and how miserable I'd felt in that dress, how devastated I was that my mom was gone forever because she'd been trying to help one of my friends instead of staying home where she belonged with me. How her accident was all my fault because I'd been so damn nosy and so determined to learn another girl's secret. I never wanted to put that dress on again. Just looking at it made my stomach twist with a sick, guilty feeling, like I was responsible for my mom's death instead of some anonymous drunk driver. . . .

I slid the metal hanger aside, careful not to touch the black fabric, and pulled out the garment buried in the very back of the closet—the prom dress that my mom and I had bought the weekend before she'd died.

It was a curious shade, somewhere between purple and gray—that same soft violet color that my mom always teasingly claimed my eyes were. The gown had a kind of Greek goddess vibe to it—cap sleeves with a high empire waist and a long, flowing skirt. Silver sequins ran across the dress in a slim band where the waist was and rimmed the circular neck, adding a bit of soft shine to it.

I drew in a breath, pulled out the dress, and brushed my fingers against the fabric.

There were no weak feelings, no faint flashes, associated with the dress. Instead, all at once, I was assaulted with images. Mom and me laughing in the food court at the mall over the chocolate milk shakes we'd ordered for lunch. The two of us flipping through rack after rack of dresses, trying to find just the right one. Always coming up empty, but still having a good time together. Mom deciding to try a little boutique she knew across town as a last resort. And finally, the look on my mom's face when she'd spied this dress and shown it to me.

I closed my eyes and concentrated, trying to bring the images into even sharper focus. My fingers stroked the silken fabric of the dress, and I breathed in, almost imagining that I could smell the sweet, soft lilac perfume that my mom had always worn. I'd liked it so much that she'd given me a bottle of it for my last birthday, but I hadn't worn it since she'd died. It just reminded me of how much I missed her.

Slowly, the waves of feeling and the images started to fade, the way they sometimes did with an object like this. If they weren't used, or in this case worn, emotions and feelings leaked out of items over time, like water dripping out of a cup with a hole in the bottom of it, until there was nothing left. Sometimes, the old images were imprinted with new thoughts, feelings, and emotions as new experiences were had or new people used the object in question. Sometimes, they just faded away altogether, leaving nothing behind but faint echoes of who and what had been before.

I started to put the dress back in the closet, but the images that I'd just seen, the feelings that I'd just experienced, wouldn't let me.

Maybe it was the way I'd felt when I'd first tried it on, like I'd be the prettiest girl at the sophomore prom. Maybe it was the smile on my mom's face when she'd seen the dress, when she realized how perfect it would look on me. Maybe it was knowing that a little piece of her that I'd thought I'd lost forever had been right here hanging in my closet the whole time.

But suddenly I wanted to go to the homecoming dance, and I wanted to wear this dress, if for no other reason than it would have made my mom happy. Grandma Frost was right. It was time to start living again.

Morgan had said the same thing about Jasmine, that that's what Jasmine would have wanted everyone to do after her death. Except in my mom's case I knew that it was true, that it was what Grace Frost would have wanted for me, her daughter.

I could feel it in the fabric of the perfect dress that she'd bought for me.

And I realized that's what I wanted, too.

So I slipped the dress off the hanger and put it on the bed. The sequins winked up at me like eyes, each one blinking with encouragement.

"Here goes nothing," I muttered, unzipping my hoodie and letting it fall to the floor.

Chapter 18

By the time I got ready, it was after eight, which meant the dance had been going on for an hour already. I'd missed the part where the homecoming king and queen would be announced for each class, the couples the other students had voted for two weeks ago. But like Morgan had said, who else was it going to be in our second-year class besides her and Samson now that Jasmine was gone?

I stared at myself in the mirror in the bathroom. Violet dress and eyes, wavy brown hair loose around my shoulders, freckles splashed across my winter white skin. I didn't look like a beautiful fairy princess like Daphne had, but at least I didn't come off as a total slut like Morgan either. I didn't know what I was, other than that Gypsy girl who saw things. But I was determined to have a good time tonight—or at least fake it well enough so that no one else would know the difference but me.

I left my dorm and walked across the campus quad. Everyone else was already at the dining hall, so the quad was even more deserted than before. A cold breeze gusted across the lawn, bringing the fall chill with it, along with the faintest bite of winter. I wrapped my arms around myself, wishing that I'd thought to grab a coat before I'd left my room, but I didn't want to go back for one now. If I did, I doubted that I'd make the effort to come back and go to the dance at all.

Finally, I reached the dining hall. The front doors were open, the light spilling outside and banishing some of the shadows. Several students stood around the entrance, a few of them taking drags off cigarettes or something stronger when they thought no one was looking. Some kids were drinking, too, and the sour stench of beer mingled with the clouds of sweet, choking smoke.

I walked past the other students and went inside. To my surprise, the dining hall had been completely transformed since lunchtime. The usual round lunch tables were gone, replaced by a single long banquet table that stretched down the left wall. Crimson and pumpkin-colored autumn leaves twined with greenery and baby's breath clustered around an enormous ice sculpture shaped like a giant cornucopia. Candles also flickered on the banquet table, highlighting the gourmet food that covered the surface. More leaves and greenery hung from the ceiling, along with strings of silver and gold lights that bathed the area in a soft, romantic glow. Even I had to admit that it was all very classy, very elegant, and very beautiful.

I'd missed the harvest ritual, which had been held before the dance had started, but I could see the remnants of it. Tall bronze rods topped with beeswax candles burned in the open-air garden, and golden bowls full of fresh-picked grapes, oranges, almonds, and olives sat at the feet of the various statues of the gods there, including Dionysus and Demeter. Everything in the garden seemed to have a warm bronze tinge to it tonight, including the goblets full of wine that had been placed next to the bowls of fruits and nuts, and the air smelled sharp and sweet, like citrus. I waited a moment, wondering if I'd feel the same kind of invisible force that I had at the bonfire last night. But whatever presence that might have been summoned by the ritual had vanished already. I let out a breath. No more magic mumbo jumbo tonight. Good.

I didn't know how many students went to Mythos, but it looked like every single one of them had shown up for the dance. Couples wearing glittering gowns and tuxedos held on to each other and swayed back and forth on the dance floor. Some sat at the tables that had been set up on the far side of the hall, kissing, giggling, and whispering into each other's ears. Others clustered around the food table, dipping strawberries and other fresh fruits into a dark chocolate fountain that spewed out a never-ending stream of warm, gooey goodness. I even saw a few kids eating the caviar that had been put out as part of the buffet. Yucko.

I'd been right about the homecoming kings and queens having been crowned already. Morgan McDougall stood on the edge of the dance floor holding court with her fawning Valkyrie friends. A glittering tiara topped Morgan's head, and a triumphant smile curved her crimson lips. This was her coming-out party, and she wanted everyone to know it. Morgan had her arm looped through Samson Sorensen's, her body plastered to his side. Samson looked handsome in his tux, although he was holding on to his garish gold crown instead of actually wearing it. He bent down and slobbered a kiss onto Morgan's neck while she talked to her friends.

I couldn't help but wonder what Jasmine would do if she was here right now. If she saw how easily Morgan had stepped into her place as queen of the second-year Mythos students. I imagined that Jasmine would go over, snatch the crystal crown off Morgan's head, and start beating her friend and Samson with it. The Valkyrie had certainly been capable of doing something like that, given all the rage that I'd felt when I'd picked up that photo in her room. The one of Morgan and Samson that Jasmine had ripped up.

My eyes roamed over the rest of the dining hall. Students weren't the only ones here tonight. More than a few professors could be seen in the crowd, including Metis, Coach Ajax, and Nickamedes. The three of them stood off to one side of the hall, drinking punch, talking, and occasionally stepping forward to keep the dry-humping on the dance floor to a minimum. Ajax and

Nickamedes both wore tuxes, while Metis looked soft and pretty in a green evening gown.

Finally, I spotted Daphne and Carson deep into a slow dance. Daphne had her head on Carson's shoulder, and the band geek had a goofy, dreamy look on his face. Morgan said something to the two Valkyries standing next to her and pointed at Daphne and Carson. The three of them laughed and snickered, making fun of the new couple. But Daphne and Carson were so into each other that they didn't see or hear the Valkyries. I doubted it would have bothered them anyway. Not tonight.

Since I didn't want to tromp through the crowd to get to Daphne and Carson, I skirted around the edge of the dining hall and headed for the refreshment table, just to have something to do. Just so no one would see that I was a total loser who was here by myself. Coming here had been a mistake. I'd thought it would be fun, but now I wasn't so sure. Because my only, sort-of friend was totally into her date, which meant that I didn't have anyone else to talk to—much less dance with.

So I got in line, piled a plate high with fresh fruit, and dipped everything into the dark chocolate fountain before grabbing a glass of sparkling fake champagne punch. I headed for the tables in the back of the dining hall, but all the seats were occupied by couples. I stood there, feeling stupid and awkward, food in one hand and drink in the other, with nowhere to sit down and eat and absolutely no one to talk to.

I sighed. I didn't know what I'd been thinking, coming here by myself. I was going to take my food back to my room and stuff my face before reading comic books the rest of the night. Which was what I should have done in the first place instead of coming here and trying to fit in, trying to pretend like I actually *belonged* here.

I turned and walked back around the edge of the dance floor, weaving in and out of the couples who crossed my path. I was about halfway toward the exit when someone stepped in front of me. The guy had his back to me, so he didn't even see me. I had to jump back to keep from slamming into him, and the sharp motion made the punch slosh out of my glass and splatter down the front of my dress, staining it. Great. Just great.

"Hey," I muttered. "Watch where you're going."

The guy must have heard me, because he turned around and glared at me, and I found myself staring up at Logan Quinn.

I hadn't talked to Logan since last night when he'd tried to kiss me and I'd totally freaked out about it. I hadn't been able to get close to him in gym class, but I'd looked for him the rest of the day out on the quad, hoping to apologize again. I hadn't seen him then, but now that I finally had, I couldn't stop staring at him.

Logan looked absolutely *gorgeous* in his black tuxedo, although he'd already undone his tie, as if it was choking him. The jacket stretched over his shoulders, highlighting just how totally muscled they were. His black hair glistened underneath the silver and golden glows from the twinkling lights, and his eyes glittered like ice in his face. I stood there, breathless.

Logan glared at me another second before doing a visible double take. His eyes slid down the front of my dress, lingering on the punch stains that dotted the long skirt. My cheeks started to burn. Why did I have to run into him now? Why couldn't I have at least seen him before I managed to splash punch all over myself?

"Excuse me," I muttered, and moved past him.

I hurried over to the buffet table and put down my plate and glass, having lost my appetite for, well, everything. I turned around, and there he was again, standing right behind me, still staring at me.

"Gypsy girl?" Logan asked in an uncertain voice, as if he wasn't quite sure whether or not it was me.

"Spartan," I replied, crossing my arms over my chest to try to hide some of the sticky stains on my dress. "Enjoying the dance?"

Logan looked at me another moment, then shrugged. "As well as any other, I suppose. They're all the same— long and boring."

I didn't say anything. I didn't know how to talk to him when he wasn't teasing me—or when he wasn't saving my life. And I certainly didn't know what to do now, when he looked so freaking sexy in that tux.

"Do you want to dance?" Logan asked in a low voice, his eyes gleaming in his face.

My heart leapt up into my throat. I'd never realized until just this second how much I wanted that very thing. How much I wanted to step into his arms, even if it was only for tonight. But I couldn't answer him. I just couldn't make myself say the words.

I didn't have to. Logan put his hand around my waist, careful not to touch the bare skin of my arms, and pulled me out onto the dance floor along with all the other swaying couples. I let him, as if in a trance, mesmerized by the sensation of his hand on my waist. I could feel the heat of his fingers even through the silky fabric of my dress.

"So," Logan said once we stood in the middle of the floor. "How are we going to do this? Because I can't touch your skin or anything, right?"

I just stared at him. If there was anyone I'd want touching me, it would be Logan. But I couldn't risk it. I just . . . couldn't. For once, I didn't want to know someone else's secrets. I didn't want to touch Logan and realize that he was really laughing at me deep down inside. That he was thinking about how pathetic I was and how sorry he felt for me. I wanted to pretend like he actually cared about me, even if it was just for this one dance.

"No," I finally said. "You can't touch my skin, not without me flashing on you. So, just, uh, put your hands on my waist or something, and I'll put mine on your shoulders. Okay?"

He gave me a crooked grin. "Whatever you say, Gypsy girl."

Logan's hands curled around my waist, and I settled mine on his shoulders, somehow resisting the urge to reach up and run my fingers through his thick ink-black hair. Slowly, we began to sway in time to the music, some old, sad song about lost love.

We didn't speak. I could feel Logan's ice blue eyes on my face, but I didn't look into his. I didn't want him to see everything that I was feeling right now. I wasn't touching him, not *really*, not touching his skin anyway, but I still felt so much. The lean strength of his body. The gentle way he held on to me. How easy it was to move to the music with him despite the fact that I was totally uncoordinated and sucked as much at dancing as I did at gym class. It was the first time in a long time that I was completely overwhelmed with sensations, even though I wasn't using my psychometry magic at all.

A sharp stab of longing pierced my heart, making my whole body quiver with its aching intensity. Because I knew that I was very close to developing a major, *major* crush on Logan Quinn. If I wasn't a complete goner already.

I don't know how long we danced before he cleared his throat.

"You look beautiful tonight, Gwen," Logan said.

He wasn't flirting with me or talking about sex like he usually did, but, for once, I almost believed him. It was like...I could almost *feel* him telling the truth, even though I wasn't touching his bare skin. Or maybe that was just because I was lying to myself, trying to convince myself that this dance, this moment, meant as much to him as it did to me.

"Thank you. So do you. Um, not beautiful, but handsome. Very, very handsome," I finished in a lame tone.

The truth was that he was beautiful—far more beautiful than I could ever be. Logan looked like one of the illustrations out of my myth-history book come to life— like some ancient warrior dressed up in modern clothes. A mix of old and new that seemed like everything to me. That seemed completely wonderful to me.

We kept dancing, and the rest of the room fell away. The other dancers, the kissing couples, the kids hanging around the refreshment table, Morgan and her catty entourage. It all just fell away until there was nothing but Logan and me.

Logan holding me, his eyes on mine, his head slowly dipping lower and lower, my eyes fluttering closed, my breath catching, catching in my throat in anticipation of something that I knew would be completely wonderful—

A sharp tap on my arm snapped me out of my reverie, and a hot spurt of annoyance surged through me at the contact. I jerked to one side, causing Logan's lips to slide past my cheek and into my hair. The sharp tap came again, and more annoyance filled me. Whoever was stabbing me with her finger, she wasn't very happy.

I dropped my arms and stepped away from Logan. A girl moved around me and slid in between the two of us. I recognized her as one of Talia Pizarro's Amazon friends, although she was just my size and not as tall as the other girl. Still, the Amazon was beautiful, with a blaze of red hair and eyes that were greener than the emerald necklace she wore around her pale throat. She wore a form-fitting seafoam-colored dress that hugged her curves in all the right places.

Pop! went my pseudo-Cinderella moment, and I suddenly felt like a giant grape next to her. One that was about to get squished.

"What do you think you're doing with *my date?*" the girl asked in a sharp, angry voice.

I looked at Logan. He stared at me, then her. After a moment, Logan looped one arm around her waist and hugged her close.

"We were just dancing, Savannah," he said in a light tone, smiling down at the other girl just like he had at me a moment ago.

Hurt filled me—hurt that Logan could dismiss me so easily. That he could almost kiss me, then look like he was about to do the same to another girl seconds later. Maybe he could, though. Maybe he didn't feel the things that I did when we were together. Maybe he never had.

I shook my head to clear away the rest of the stupid romantic fog. *Of course he didn't,* I chided myself. He was Logan freaking Quinn, the guy who went around Mythos Academy and signed the mattresses of all the girls he slept with. What had I been thinking? Because there was fun and then there was insanity. And anything to do with Logan fell squarely into the latter category.

"Yeah," I said in a cold voice. "We were just dancing. And now we're not."

Logan looked at me, guilt flickering in his eyes. He opened his mouth like he wanted to say something to me, but I didn't give him the chance. I turned on my heel and walked away, leaving him to his date for the evening.

Chapter 19

I walked away from Logan as fast as I could, slithering through the crowd of dancers, careful not to brush up against anyone so I wouldn't accidentally flash on them. Coming here tonight had been a bad, bad idea. What the hell had I been thinking? Everyone had a place at Mythos—everyone except me. No, wait. That wasn't right. I had a role here, too, now—that Gypsy girl who had just made a complete fool of herself. The class idiot, in other words.

I hurried out the front entrance of the dining hall. More kids clustered outside around the doors now, passing cups of beer and silver flasks of who-knew-what from one hand to another, along with cigarettes and even a few joints.

For a moment, I thought about stopping and asking for a drink from one of them. Maybe a couple. I'd never been drunk before, so I didn't know exactly how many it would take. But they probably wouldn't share with me anyway. Besides, I doubted that getting drunk would drown out these feelings that I'd suddenly developed for Logan Quinn. I didn't think anything would help me with that, except maybe a total lobotomy.

I couldn't go back in to the dance, but I didn't want to go back to my room either. I already knew that I was a stupid, stupid loser. I didn't want to sit around and think about it the rest of the night. Besides, I'd put on my damn prom dress. I was at least going to wear it for more than an hour, even if it killed me.

Not really thinking about where I was going, I turned left and stepped onto the circular cobblestone path that wound past all five of the buildings that ringed the quad. I just started walking the huge circle, trying to find a quiet spot where I could sit by myself and . . . and do something. Maybe scream. Maybe cry. I didn't know.

I wasn't the only one who'd left the dance early. Couples sat on every one of the iron benches close to the dining hall. They all stared dreamily into each other's eyes, giggling and kissing. One guy even had his hand down his date's dress, and the two of them were practically lying on top of each other.

It all made me sick.

Because even out here, I couldn't get away from everyone's perfect little dance—

Something winked in the shadows up ahead, distracting me from my dark thoughts. The bright flash came again, bobbing up and down, and I spotted another lone figure moving across the quad. Was she . . . wearing something on her head? I squinted, but I couldn't quite make out who it was. Then, she stepped into the glow from one of the streetlights that lined the walkway, and I was able to get a good look at her.

Morgan McDougall.

The homecoming queen plodded across the quad, heading toward the Library of Antiquities. Probably so she and Samson could hook up on the outside patio again. I rolled my eyes. Slut. The flashes that I'd seen had come from the homecoming queen tiara that Morgan wore on top of her head. The expensive crystals winked at me with every step the Valkyrie took.

I frowned. For some reason, something about Morgan seemed . . . off. I kept trailing after her, wondering what it was. Finally, I realized that it was the way she was walking, so slow and steady with careful, measured steps. It wasn't the way a normal person would walk, especially a girl who was eager to hook up with the hot guy she'd been sleeping with on the sly. Morgan stepped through the glow of another streetlight, and I realized that she had a weird look on her face, too. One that was totally . . . blank. She reminded me of a zombie or something, like she wasn't really herself. Like she was possessed or being controlled by someone else—

Little warning bells went off inside my head, and they only got louder the longer that I stared at the Valkyrie.

I glanced around, but by this point the dining hall and all the couples were several hundred feet away. Nobody else had noticed Morgan. They were all too absorbed in their own little dramas, in their own little bad romances, to notice her—or me.

So I started following her.

I didn't know why. Maybe because I was pissed at myself for being such an idiot in front of Logan. Maybe because I didn't have anything better to do. Or maybe it was because of this ... this *feeling* that I had. That something about this was very, very wrong. I almost felt like I *needed* to follow Morgan for some reason. That something really, really bad would happen if I didn't.

It was the exact same feeling that I'd had right before I'd picked up Paige Forrest's hairbrush.

Morgan walked across the quad, still heading toward the library. I frowned. Weird. The library was closed tonight because of the dance, and only a few lights burned inside the building. So why would Morgan be going there? Especially tonight of all nights? Yeah, maybe she and Samson were going to hook up again ... except the two of them didn't have to hide the fact that they were a couple anymore. Everyone had already seen them together at the dance. So why would they meet at the library again? Why wouldn't they go to one of their dorm rooms? What was the Valkyrie doing? And why did she have that blank, empty look on her face?

Morgan plodded up the front steps of the library, still moving in that slow, steady zombie way. I picked up my skirt and hurried after her. Did the Valkyrie actually think that she was going to get inside? The doors were shut, and I'd watched Nickamedes lock them after my shift this afternoon—

Morgan pulled open one of the double doors and stepped inside the library, disappearing from sight. I slowed and stopped at the bottom of the steps. I bit my lip and stared at the structure before me. All the stone statues, towers, and balconies seemed especially sinister tonight, as though the whole building was a living thing just waiting to swallow me. I blinked, and, for a moment, it seemed like the entire library just... *rippled.* Like there was something crawling around underneath the stone. Something old. Ancient. Powerful. Evil.

I shivered, wrapped my arms around myself, and looked back over my shoulder. In the distance across the quad, the lights of the dining hall seemed warm, bright, inviting. I should go back there. Go grab a plastic cup of beer from someone, smoke some pot, get completely wasted, and pretend like tonight had never happened.

But I couldn't do that, any more than I'd been able to stop myself from reaching for that damn hairbrush. In the end, I always wanted to know people's secrets, no matter how dark and twisted they were. Maybe it was my Gypsy gift or maybe just my own paranoid imagination, but I felt like there was one lurking in the library tonight—maybe the biggest secret of all. Somehow, I knew it to the very depths of my soul. Who killed Jasmine, who stole the Bowl of Tears, even the reason that I was here at Mythos Academy in the first place. It was all inside the library, just waiting for me to walk in and discover it for myself.

Come inside, and all will finally be revealed, a voice seemed to whisper in the back of my mind. Or maybe it was just my own wishful thinking.

Whatever it was, I picked up my skirt, walked up the stairs, and slipped inside.

*   *   *

I'd been wrong before, when I'd thought that there had only been a few lights on in the Library of Antiquities. The double doors that led into the main floor stood wide open, and the golden glow from inside spilled out into the hallway, showing the way. But there was something strange about the light tonight. It seemed to cast out more shadows than it actually banished and gave a black, sinister air to everything it touched, from the suits of armor that lined the hallway to the mythological creatures carved into the marble walls.

Once again, the stone eyes of the gryphons and Gorgons watched me, tracking my movements as I crept forward. The weird light splashed across the carvings, making the creatures look even fiercer and more lifelike than ever before—like they could spring out from the stone at any second and tear me into pieces. I shivered and dropped my gaze from the walls.

Morgan had already disappeared from sight, but the clack of her stilettos on the floor inside the main space echoed through the entire library. I stopped a moment to slip off my own heels, then followed her. The floor was as cold as ice on my bare feet, but at least now I wouldn't make as much noise as the Valkyrie had.

From the hollow echo of her footsteps, it sounded like Morgan had gone down the main library aisle, walking right toward whoever or whatever was waiting inside. I wasn't so naïve or stupid to think that there wasn't someone or something else here. Somebody had had to turn on the lights and open the doors for Morgan, and I doubted it was Nickamedes, since I'd just seen him over at the dining hall, chaperoning the home-coming dance.

Since I wasn't so sure that I wanted to run into who-ever else was waiting inside, I headed over to one of the side doors that led into the main floor, opened it up, and slipped in that way. I wasn't sure what was going on, but I wasn't going to bumble right into the middle of it. Not if I could help it, anyway.

I was going to do the right thing this time. The smart thing. Get a quick look at whatever was happening, at whoever had made Morgan come here, then slip out and go get help from Professor Metis, Coach Ajax, or even Nickamedes back at the dining hall.

I moved through the stacks, trying to get a look at Morgan through the rows of musty books that sepa-rated us. The sound of her footsteps was louder in here, echoing all the way up to the ceiling and back down again, and she was still walking at that slow, steady pace.

Through the bookshelves, I caught a glimpse of the Valkyrie. Morgan still had that blank, empty look on her face, like she wasn't even aware of what she was doing, like she wasn't even in control of herself any-more. Like she was . . . possessed.

Like somebody had dripped her blood into the Bowl of Tears.

The thought erupted from the bottom of my brain, bursting through to the surface. I flashed back to last night in my room when I'd been reading Jasmine's book, the one that had all the information about the Bowl of Tears in it. I focused on the memory, and the words on the page popped into my head.

> It was rumored that Loki used the Bowl to bend people to his will. That once a person's blood was dripped into the bowl the god—or whoever had the Bowl at that time—had complete control over him or her. . . .

The words triggered other memories of all the things that I'd seen and done over the past few days. Nickamedes talking about the Bowl and the fact that whoever had stolen it shouldn't have even been able to take it out of the library in the first place. The ripped-up photo of Morgan and Samson that I'd found in Jasmine's room. The rage that I'd felt when I'd touched the picture. All those books about magic and illusions that had been on Jasmine's bookshelves. The stone statue almost braining Morgan and Samson when they were getting busy outside the library. The prowler showing up, then evaporating after Logan had killed it.

But the one thing that I kept coming back to over and over again, the *biggie,* was the fact that I hadn't felt anything, that I hadn't gotten any kind of flash or vibe at all off Jasmine's body that night that I'd found her in the library. The night that I'd thought she'd been murdered. I'd thought that there had been something wrong with my Gypsy gift, my psychometry magic, but maybe . . . just maybe there hadn't been anything there for me to feel in the first place. Not really.

The more I thought about it, the more sense it made. My Gypsy gift always let me see *something,* whether I wanted to or not. But not with Jasmine, which was the first time I hadn't seen anything at all. *Ever.* All the images, all the memories and feelings, suddenly came together in my head, clicking into place like the pieces of a jigsaw puzzle. I thought I had a pretty good idea who had killed Jasmine, stolen the Bowl of Tears, and why.

Oh *no.* If Morgan was walking toward who I thought she was, then the Valkyrie was in big trouble, and so was I—

I was so busy figuring things out that I wasn't really looking where I was going and I bumped into one of the glass artifact cases. But not just any case—The Case, the one with the strange sword in it. The one with the hilt that looked like half of a man's face. I hit The Case so hard I jiggled the sword inside—causing the eye in the hilt to snap open.

I froze and blinked several times, thinking, no, *hoping* that it was just a figment of my imagination. That the eye would disappear the way that it had before and I could tell myself that I was just seeing things because I was in a bad, bad situation and feeling a little stressed. Okay, a *lot* stressed.

I blinked and blinked, and nothing happened. The eye was still there, and it was still staring at me.

The eye was a peculiar color, somewhere between

purple and gray, the kind of color that made me think of a softly falling twilight, that sliver of time after sunset just before the world went dark for the night.

I was in an awkward position, half-sprawled over The Case, my fingers leaving streaks all over the glass, but I couldn't move. I just couldn't look away from the eye in the sword. I felt this peculiar sensation in my chest, a sort of euphoria. For some reason, looking at the weapon made me *happy*. The same way that fighting seemed to make Logan happy. I shivered. Why would a sword make me happy? I didn't even know how to use one—

The eye suddenly narrowed, as if sizing me up, as if it knew every single one of my secrets just by looking at me. I felt like I was somehow falling into it, drowning in its twilight gaze, that I could never look away from that single, piercing stare and that, strangely enough, I didn't really want to.

I don't know how long I would have stood there, just staring at the unblinking eye, if I hadn't heard something hiss behind me.

A low particular evil hiss that I'd heard only once before. The kind that made my blood run cold and my heart turn to ice. The noise cut through my dazed reverie and snapped me back to reality. I thought about what had happened the last time that I'd heard that awful sound.

Oh *no*.

I slowly turned around and looked over my shoulder. A Nemean prowler stood behind me.

It looked just the same as the one had outside the library last night. A black, pantherlike creature with big claws and even bigger teeth that could kill me as easily as it could breathe. If it actually breathed at all and didn't just exist on pure evil alone. I still wasn't sure about that part.

The prowler hissed at me, its lips curling back to show off its fangs. Which, of course, glinted *magnificently* in the strange twisting golden glow that filled the library. I swallowed, but it didn't dislodge the hard lump of fear stuck in my throat. This time, though, I didn't bother to say, *Nice kitty.* There was nothing nice about it, especially not the way it was looking at me.

For a moment, I thought the prowler was going to pounce on me right there and tear out my throat with all its many, many teeth. But instead, a low whistle sounded and the creature moved off to one side so its master could come closer toward me.

A figure wearing a long scarlet cloak crusted with jewels strode down the aisle. The crimson cloth billowed out as the person drew nearer. The rippling fabric made me think of a river of blood. I shivered again. The sight of it shouldn't have surprised me, though. After all, I'd seen an image of her buying it online when I'd touched her laptop. I just hadn't thought anything of it at the time. Veronica Mars I was not. The person wearing the cloak was definitely smarter than me. Smarter than us all. Because she'd pulled this whole twisted scam off beautifully so far.

The cloak had a hood on it, so I couldn't get a good

look at her face. All I saw was a hint of a smile on her pink lips and the flash of white teeth. For some reason, hers scared me even more than the prowler's did.

"Hello, Gypsy," a low voice murmured from the depths of the hooded cloak. "I was wondering when you were going to show up."

If I'd had any doubt before, now there was none, because I knew that voice. Knew exactly who it belonged to. The last time I'd heard it she'd been laughing out on the academy quad, the day this whole thing had started.

The figure reached up and pushed back the hood of her cloak. Strawberry-blond hair, blue eyes, perfect skin, gorgeous face.

I once again found myself staring at Jasmine Ashton—only this time, she was as alive as I was.

Chapter 20

Nobody ever really dies in a comic book, not even the bad guy. At least not for long.

The words that I'd spoken to Logan last night whispered in my mind, mocking me as I stared at Jasmine. Because the girl standing in front of me was definitely not dead. My eyes fell to her throat, which was just as smooth as mine. Nope, *definitely* not dead. I had a feeling the same wouldn't be said about me, though, before the night was through.

"You're—you're *alive,*" I finally said.

The Valkyrie let out a soft giggle that bounced off the library walls. "So I am, Gypsy. So I am. Be a good girl, go stand next to Morgan, and I'll explain it all to you. The only problem with plans like this is that there's never anyone around to gloat to."

My eyes slid past Jasmine to the open door at the far end of the stacks, as I wondered if I could run past her and sprint out it before she, oh, I don't know, *killed* me until I was dead, dead, dead. But the prowler saw what I was looking at and let out another evil hiss.

I wet my lips. "Is that thing an illusion? Like the one last night was?"

Jasmine walked over and put her hand on the creature's back, stroking its black fur. The prowler's blood-red eyes brightened, and it let out a little purr of pleasure that made me wince.

"Oh no, Gypsy. This prowler is very real. But it wouldn't really matter, either way. Illusions can tear you to shreds just as much as real teeth and claws can."

Daphne had said something similar to me outside the library last night, but I hadn't quite believed her. How could something that wasn't even real hurt you? But I was beginning to realize there was a lot about myths and magic that I just didn't understand.

I didn't have any choice but to do what Jasmine told me. Otherwise, the prowler—real or illusion—would rip me to shreds, something that I desperately did not want to happen. So I walked down an aisle and rounded the corner, stepping into the main, open part of the library.

Morgan stood to my left in the same spot where the glass case had been that had once housed the Bowl of Tears. The Artifact that had supposedly been stolen the night Jasmine had supposedly died.

The Bowl that Morgan was now holding.

It looked the same as I remembered it. Small, round, brown, plain. A simple bowl with no paint, carvings, or extras of any kind on it. No gold, no jewels, nothing. Still, just looking at it tonight made me sick to my stomach. I didn't always have to touch an item to get a vibe off it. If an object had enough emotion tied to it, had enough memories embedded in it, then it could radiate those feelings, sort of like an aura. Like Daphne and her sparking pink fingers.

And tonight the Bowl radiated cold, black evil.

"Stop," Jasmine said.

The prowler hissed in time to her command.

I paused where I was, next to one of the study tables. A couple of books lay on the edge of the table, the ones that Nickamedes had come out of the stacks with earlier today. For whatever reason, the librarian hadn't put the books away. I leaned back against the table and casually put my hand on the top one. I got the same vibe that I always did off the library books—one of old knowledge. It wasn't much and it certainly wasn't a weapon, but it was something at least. I'd take every little thing I could get right now, starting with an explanation.

"So you faked this whole thing," I said, turning to face Jasmine. "The theft of the Bowl, your body, all the puddles of blood. All of it was just an illusion, right?"

"Well, well, well," Jasmine said. "The Gypsy has a brain after all. You're right, of course. I faked everything you saw that night, and a lot of stuff since then."

Jasmine moved past me to where Morgan stood, still staring blankly ahead. The prowler paced around the library tables, moving back and forth and weaving through them like they were some sort of giant kitty-cat obstacle course. But the creature never took its red eyes off me, not even for a second.

Jasmine stopped in front of Morgan, staring at her best friend, hate burning in her blue gaze. The Valkyrie reached up and plucked the homecoming queen tiara off Morgan's head. Morgan stared straight ahead, no emotion flashing on her face, no sort of acknowledgment of what was going on flickering in her hazel eyes at all.

I'd been right when I'd thought that Morgan had been possessed. Jasmine was using the Bowl of Tears to control her best friend. For the first time, I noticed there was something in the Bowl that Morgan was holding—something dark, red, and sticky looking. Blood.

"How did you do it?" I asked. "How did you get Morgan's blood in the Bowl? I know you had to do that, had to drip her blood into it and chant some kind of magic mumbo jumbo. Otherwise, you wouldn't be able to control her the way that you are."

Jasmine kept staring at the crystal crown in her hands. "Oh, that was actually the easiest part. There was a blood drive on campus a couple of weeks ago. Morgan and I both gave blood. It was easy to swipe the bag with hers in it when the nurse wasn't looking."

Geez, what was she? Some kind of freaking criminal mastermind or something? Because that's not something I would ever think to do, especially not to my supposed best friend.

Jasmine turned the tiara this way and that, watching the crystals catch the light and wink it back at her. She scraped her nails against it, and ugly red sparks flickered in the air around her. Then, the Valkyrie snapped the crown in two with her hands. Crystals zipped through the air, and I flinched at the sharp cracks they made as they hit the marble floor.

"I always wondered what it would be like to be homecoming queen with Samson by my side," Jasmine murmured. "I hoped you enjoyed it, Morgan. Because it's the last thing you're ever going to enjoy."

Jasmine took one end of the splintered crown and raked it down Morgan's face, drawing blood. Then, the Valkyrie twisted the pointed end, digging it into her best friend's skin that much more. Red sparks winked around the two of them like fireflies, flashing on and off, warning of danger, hate, death.

I bit back a scream and started forward to try to do something to help Morgan. But the prowler let out a warning growl, and I stopped where I was.

It didn't matter anyway, because Morgan didn't move a muscle. She didn't flinch, scream, or even cry out in pain. It was like she was a lifeless doll, frozen in place. I wondered if she even felt Jasmine shredding her face with the crown, or if her mind was gone forever.

Jasmine yanked the bloody end of the crown out of Morgan's face and drew her arm back, getting ready for another strike.

"Stop!" I called out. "Stop hurting her! She's your friend! Your best friend!"

Jasmine turned and stared at me, as if she'd forgotten that I was even standing in the library with the two of them. "Correction: She *was* my best friend before she started screwing my boyfriend behind my back six months ago."

Jasmine threw the end of the bloody crown down and stalked around Morgan, her face as dark as a storm cloud. I didn't know what the Valkyrie would do next, but I had to do my best to distract her. I didn't want her hurting Morgan again. Or worse, killing the other girl in front of me.

"Is that why you're doing all this?" I asked in a shaky voice. "Just because your boyfriend cheated on you?"

"He didn't just *cheat* on me," Jasmine snapped. "He did it with *her*. My supposed *best friend*. For *months*. And they both lied to my face about it the whole time. I was getting suspicious, you know? Samson was acting strange, kind of distracted. He cut a couple of our dates short, wouldn't answer his phone in front of me, that sort of thing. I thought that he might be cheating on me, that he might be seeing someone else on the side, so I told Morgan about it. Actually *confided* in her about it. And do you know what she said?"

I shook my head.

"That I shouldn't worry. That Samson was crazy about me and had told her so himself. That he was cut-ting our dates short because he loved me so much and it was hard for him to control himself around me when we were together. I can't believe I fell for her bullshit." Jasmine let out a bitter laugh.

She paced around Morgan again, muttering some-thing under her breath. I reached my hand behind me, my fingers curling around the edge of the book. The prowler circled around a table and paced back this way, stalking away then toward me, its bloodred eyes fixed on my face the whole time.

"Do you know what the worst part is?" Jasmine asked. "The reason Samson slept with her in the first place. Do you know why he slept with her?"

I shrugged. The ripped photo of the couple had shown me a lot of things, but that hadn't been one of them.

"Because I wouldn't," she muttered. "I wanted to wait, and Samson said he did, too. That we weren't ready yet. That it was better to take things slow and wait for the right moment. That it would be more *romantic* that way. And the whole time, the two of them were screwing like rabbits behind my back."

"I found that picture of Morgan and Samson. The one that you tore up and dumped in your trash can. How did you even find out about them?" I asked in a calm voice, even as my eyes scanned the library, trying to figure a way out of this mess. But nothing came to mind, no way that I could get myself or Morgan out of here. Not alive, anyway.

Jasmine shrugged. "Morgan lied to me about where she went on summer break. She said that she and her family were going to their house in the Bahamas for a month. But a week later my brother texted me that he'd seen Morgan up in the Hamptons. Why would Morgan lie? It made me suspicious, especially since Samson's parents have a summer home there. So I borrowed my daddy's jet and flew up there. I snuck out to Samson's house, and I saw them together on the beach. They were all over each other. It was disgusting."

"But that was in the summer," I said. "That was months ago."

Jasmine gave me a cold, satisfied smile. "I know. The two of them never suspected a thing. They never even had a clue that I knew about them."

"So what?" I asked. "You've spent the last few months planning how to fake your own death to get back at your best friend for sleeping with your boyfriend? Don't you think that's a little extreme?"

Jasmine's blue eyes narrowed in her face, and she opened her mouth, probably to bark out some command to the prowler to come over and kill me, but I cut her off.

"I mean, yeah, it completely sucks, and I can totally understand why you would want revenge. The two of them hurt you real bad. They deserved to be punished."

Jasmine nodded. "Exactly. I *loved* Samson; I really did. But he's a guy, after all, and he's always thinking with his dick. I expected this sort of thing from him. But Morgan and I grew up together. She's almost like a sister to me, which made her betrayal all the worse. That's why she's going to pay for screwing my boyfriend."

I guess that explained why Samson wasn't standing next to Morgan, all zombied out the way that she was. Kind of sexist of Jasmine if you asked me, only blaming the other girl and not her precious boyfriend, too. From what I'd seen, Samson had been a very willing participant. In his own way, he was just as big a slut as Morgan was.

"So why not do something a little more . . . reasonable to them?" I asked. "Why fake your own death? What was the point?"

"Because I wanted them to *miss* me," she snapped in an angry voice. "I wanted to hurt them. I wanted them to feel guilty about what they'd done. I wanted the guilt to eat them alive until they couldn't stand to even *look* at each other. Only . . . it didn't."

No, it didn't. I thought of how the whole school, how all the other students, had just gone on with their lives after Jasmine's supposed death like it had never even happened. Morgan and Samson had been happy that she'd died so they could finally be together out in the open. Everyone else had just been relieved that Jasmine wasn't around to terrorize them anymore. Everyone but me. The Gypsy girl who saw things and decided to stick her nose into someone else's business yet again, to try to learn all of Jasmine's secrets. And look how well that was working out for me.

"How did you do it?" I asked. "And why here in the library?"

Jasmine shrugged. "Illusion powers run in my family. My mom's really good at creating them, and she taught me tons of them over the summer when my magic finally quickened. It was easy to make one of my own body just lying there with my throat cut open. My mom used to create dozens of dead body and zombie illusions every year for Halloween when I was a kid and we'd have a haunted house."

So I was right. I hadn't gotten a vibe off Jasmine's body or blood that night because there hadn't been anything there to start with. Nothing real, anyway.

"But if it was all an illusion, how did your blood wind up all over my clothes?" I asked.

I still had the purple hoodie and jeans crumpled up in the bottom of my laundry basket. The last time that I'd looked, the bloodstains had still been on them.

"Because once a person believes in an illusion, it's real to them. Once you believe in something, you give it life and form and substance. You thought you saw my blood, so it ended up all over your clothes. Just like Metis, Ajax, and Nickamedes thought they saw my body, so they packed it up and put it in cold storage in the basement of the math-science building. That's where they keep all the bodies, you know."

No, I hadn't known that, and I kind of wished she hadn't told me. A morgue in math-science? Creepy.

I jerked my head at the pacing prowler. "And what about your kitty cat there? How did you get it onto campus? When? And why?"

Jasmine shrugged. "Another illusion. I made it look like a hungry stray cat that came onto campus looking for food tonight. The sphinxes on the main gates didn't even glance twice at it, much less attack it like they're supposed to do to intruders. Nickamedes isn't quite as clever with his spells as he thinks he is. As for why, well, I thought that it might be good to have the real thing handy since your Spartan boyfriend killed my illusion last night."

"You're talking about what happened with the statue," I said. "So you pushed it over the side of the library, trying to hit Morgan and Samson with it?"

"I did." Jasmine's eyes flicked to Morgan. "I was enjoying a little fresh air out on the fourth-floor balcony when I saw what they were doing. I admit my temper got the best of me and made me want to kill both of them right then and there, instead of sticking with my plan for tonight. But lucky for them, you were there to shout out a warning. Of course, that made me rather angry at *you,* which is why I conjured up that prowler illusion. I was going to let it claw you to death for getting in my way. But, of course, Logan Quinn showed up and got the best of it instead."

"And the Bowl of Tears?" I asked. "Why steal it?"

Jasmine let out another laugh that reminded me of the prowler's hiss. "Oh, I didn't *steal* it at all. The Bowl's been right here in the library the whole time, just like I have. There's a storage room on the fourth floor where nobody ever goes. I've been sneaking stuff up there ever since the semester started: food, clothes, a sleeping bag. That's where I've been staying the past few days, along with the Bowl. Nickamedes put so many enchantments on the Bowl that it can't leave the library, enchantments that I couldn't break. So I used my illusion magic to hide it, to make everyone think that the Bowl had been stolen and taken somewhere far, far away. And it worked, too. It all worked—but then you started snooping around."

I shifted on my feet.

Jasmine stared at me, tilting her head to one side. "You know, I've been watching you the past few days, and I just can't figure out why you cared so much about me. You weren't one of my friends. You didn't even know me."

"No," I said in a quiet voice. "But I didn't think that you deserved to die like that. I wanted to find out what happened to you. I felt sorry for you, that you had died."

Jasmine's face hardened. "You? Felt sorry for me? You're nobody, Gypsy. You don't have any friends, and you don't belong here. You're pathetic."

The sneer in her voice made me stand up a little straighter. "I have a name. It's Gwen Frost. I'm not *nobody*. And you think I'm pathetic? I'm not the girl who faked her own death just so she could get some sort of twisted revenge on her best friend. *That's* pathetic."

Jasmine's face darkened at my insult, but she let out another laugh. "You think this is just about me getting revenge on Morgan? Oh, Gypsy, you really have no idea what you're dealing with, do you?"

I shrugged. "So tell me. You're just going to kill me anyway."

"Oh yes," Jasmine said, dashing any hope I had that

she'd let me live. "But this is about so much more than Morgan and the fact that she can't keep her legs closed. This—this is about Chaos."

When she said the word "Chaos," a sort of . . . breeze gusted through the library, some sort of force that made the bookcases creak and my skin crawl. But the weirdest thing was the Bowl of Tears. Morgan was still holding it in her hands, but, for a moment I thought that I saw a face shimmer in the air above it. A twisted, evil, melted, screaming sort of face. The sight made my stomach knot up.

"You're—you're actually a Reaper of Chaos?" I asked in a whisper. "One of the bad guys? You actually serve the god Loki and want to bring him back into this world?"

Jasmine nodded her head. "Now you're catching on. You're not as dumb as you look, Gypsy. There are lots of Reapers at Mythos, kids and profs. And it's not just me. My whole family are Reapers. We always have been. Sshh. Don't tell anyone at the academy, though. All the professors think that my family is so good, that I'm so well-bred. Metis would really get her panties in a twist if she knew that my family's been serving Loki for centuries. When they announced in my myth-history class that Nickamedes was bringing the Bowl of Tears out of storage and putting it on display in the library, well, it was just too good an opportunity to pass up. A way to get back at Morgan and serve my god at the same time."

"But—"

"Enough!" she snapped. "Enough talking. I'm bored now. It's time to get on with things, starting with the sacrifice that Morgan is going to make tonight."

She turned to look at the other Valkyrie, who had remained silent and frozen through all of this, although blood still dripped down her cheek from where Jasmine had stabbed her with the homecoming crown.

"Morgan," Jasmine said, her voice sounding exactly like the prowler's hiss. "Go lie down on top of one of the tables and take the Bowl with you. And don't spill a drop of the blood inside it."

Morgan jerked forward, as though she were a puppet and Jasmine were the one pulling her crazy strings. I watched, horrified, as Morgan climbed up onto the closest library table, lay down on it, and put the Bowl in the middle of her chest. And just like Jasmine had commanded, she didn't spill a drop.

From the depths of her crimson cloak, Jasmine drew out a dagger with a ruby set into the hilt. I recognized it, too—it was the same one that I'd seen on the floor in the library the night I'd thought she'd died. Now I knew why the dagger hadn't had any blood on it—because the puddles had all just been illusions to start with.

My brain kicked into gear, and I finally realized what she was going to do with the dagger—she was going to sacrifice her best friend to an evil god. Jasmine was actually going to kill Morgan right in front of me, and there was nothing that I could do to stop it.

"Stop!" I screamed, starting forward. "Get away from her!"

Jasmine looked over her shoulder at me and gave a dismissive sniff.

"Kill her," Jasmine ordered the prowler, and turned back to Morgan.

The creature licked its lips and sprang at me.

Chapter 21

Before I could save Morgan, I had to save myself from the prowler.

I didn't have time to think about what I was doing, so I threw the book that I'd palmed at the prowler. I got lucky, because the thick volume hit the creature square in the nose, making it hesitate and throwing it a bit off balance. I dove underneath the closest library table, and the creature landed on top of it, instead of on me.

The prowler dug its claws into the wood, ripping it apart like it was made of toothpicks. I crawled out from underneath the collapsing table, scrambled to my feet, and ran toward the open double doors. But the prowler was quicker than I was. With a mighty leap, it flew through the air over my head and landed in front of me, putting itself between me and my escape.

I immediately backed up. The prowler growled and started stalking me again, enjoying the game of big, big cat, little, little mouse.

Out of the corner of my eye, I saw Jasmine turn away from Morgan to stare at me.

"You won't get away from it again," she said. "This one isn't an illusion, and this time, the Spartan's not around to save you."

"That's where you're wrong," another voice called out.

Logan Quinn stood in the doorway of the library. He still wore his tuxedo, but he'd stopped to pick up two other accessories along the way—a shield and a spear. The silver shield was strapped to his left arm, while he held the spear in his free hand. Somehow, he looked right with them, like they belonged to him and him alone. I thought about what Daphne had said about why the other kids were here. Logan knew his destiny as a Spartan, as a warrior. I just hoped that I wouldn't be the death of him tonight.

The prowler hissed again as soon as it saw Logan, recognizing him as the real threat. The Spartan tightened his grip on his shield, and a sort of cold calm filled his face. He wasn't going to run away from the prowler—he was going to fight it to the death just like he had before. Only this time, the creature wasn't an illusion. Somehow, I knew that made it even bigger, stronger, and deadlier than before.

After a moment, Logan's icy eyes flicked to me. "Gwen, go! Get help—"

That was all Logan got out before the prowler threw itself at him.

Instead of doing as he asked, I picked up the book

that I'd thrown at the prowler before and ran back to the middle of the library, where Jasmine still stood over Morgan, the dagger glinting in her hand. While I would have loved nothing more than to run away, find Professor Metis, and tell her every twisted thing that was going on, I knew that if I did, Jasmine would kill Morgan and finish whatever bizarre ritual she'd started. My mom had never run from a fight when she'd been a detective, and I wasn't going to now.

Jasmine saw me coming and stepped away from Morgan, pointing her dagger in my direction. Not good. But I was too committed to back down now. For all I knew, the second I turned my back Jasmine would throw the dagger and kill me that way. She could do it. She was a warrior, too, and had been training to be one for years.

"You should have just let it go, Gypsy," Jasmine murmured, stepping up to meet me. "You should have just not paid any attention to my death the way that the others did."

I skidded to a stop in front of her. "Tell me one thing: Why didn't you kill me that night in the library when you had the chance? The night you hit me on the head, I assume with that stupid dagger you're holding, and knocked me out. Why didn't you just slit my throat then?"

She shrugged. "Because you were nobody. I didn't even know your name. You didn't have any real power, nothing that I could take or use, so what was the point in killing you?"

My fingers tightened around the book, and for a moment I thought about Paige Forrest. She hadn't had any power either. According to my mom, Paige's stepdad had told her that if she didn't do what he said, if she didn't let him touch her, then he'd go down the hall to her little sister's room. That's why Paige hadn't told anyone what was going on. So she had done the only thing that she could—she'd given me her hairbrush to touch.

Because she knew what I could do. Paige knew that I had power, that I had magic, even if she didn't understand it. Even if I didn't understand it.

"I'm not a nobody." I ground out the words.

Jasmine rolled her eyes. "Whatever. You're still going to die."

She threw herself at me. The dagger slashed through the air with an evil hiss that matched the prowler's. Acting on pure instinct, I brought up the book, putting it between me and the dagger. The weapon sank into the pages, its sharp tip piercing all the way through to the other side—and only stopping an inch away from my eye. Yeah, I totally screamed at that.

Jasmine let out a loud curse and tried to pull the dagger back out of the book, but I tightened my grip and twisted it away from her, ripping the hilt of the weapon out of her hands. Then, I threw the book with the dagger still embedded in it as far as I could. It hit the slick marble floor and rolled across it, turning end over end, before finally stopping on the other side of the library underneath one of the tables.

"Bitch," Jasmine said. "That was my favorite dagger."

She had a favorite dagger? Seriously? And she thought that I was a freak.

Before I could move away from Jasmine, she slapped me across the face, then punched me in the stomach, using her Valkyrie strength to her full advantage. The pain of her blows was bad enough, but her skin touched mine, and I felt all of her pent-up rage and anger at Morgan, Samson, and everyone else at school who'd ignored her fake death. It burned through me like acid. I fell to my knees, gasping for air and trying not to vomit.

Jasmine stared down at me, shook her head, and walked back toward Morgan, who was still lying on the table and staring up at the ceiling at nothing in particular.

The Bowl of Tears rested on Morgan's chest, and the blood inside it began to bubble up. Even across the library, I could feel some sort of power emanating from it. If I'd thought the Bowl had been evil before, it radiated the ugliest sort of black hate now.

Jasmine reached down and pulled a long sword out from underneath the table. Where the hell had that come from? Jasmine turned and headed back in my direction, slicing the sword through the air like she just couldn't wait to cut into me with it.

I was dimly aware of Logan fighting the prowler in the back of the library near the doorway. The prowler's relentless hisses filled the room, as did the clang of its claws on Logan's shield as it tried to rip away the barrier so it could tear into the Spartan once and for all. I even thought that I heard Logan call out my name, telling me to turn around and run, that Jasmine would cut me to pieces with the sword. I rolled my eyes. Like I didn't already know that. I might suck at gym class, but I wasn't completely *stupid*.

So I got to my feet, turned around, and ran toward the nearest door—the side door I'd used to slip into the library. But just before I reached it, the door slammed shut. Behind me, Jasmine laughed.

"Stupid Gypsy. Everything in here is under my control, including the doors. You can't get out, so why don't you just be a good girl and come here so I can kill you?"

I didn't know what kind of Valkyrie magic she was using, whether it was just an illusion or if the door was really and truly shut. So I ran toward the next door set into the wall. It too slammed shut just before I reached it. I wrapped my hand around the doorknob and tried to open it, but it wouldn't budge. Whatever magic Jasmine had, she'd sealed us all in the library with her. Or at least made us all think that she had. Which was really the same thing as actually doing it. At least, I thought that it was. This illusion stuff made my head hurt.

Since the doors weren't working, I scurried over to one of the windows. It was locked as well, and it wouldn't budge. Outside on the quad, a flash of movement caught my eye, and I spotted Daphne and Carson walking hand in hand, making the same slow circle around the quad that I'd started to earlier tonight.

"Daphne! Carson!"

I yelled, screamed, and pounded on the glass, but they

didn't hear me. They were too caught up in each other for that. I'd have to make them hear me. Frantic now, I looked around. A study table was tucked in next to the window, along with a wooden chair. I picked up the chair and slammed it into the window.

The glass erupted with a roar.

Whatever magic Jasmine had, she hadn't thought to use it to completely secure the windows, only the doors. So the chair shattered several panes of glass, leaving behind a jagged hole just above my head. I would have hoisted myself up and crawled out it, if there hadn't been a couple of iron bars in the way. So I stood on my tiptoes and got as close to the glinting shards as I dared.

"Daphne!" I screamed as loud as I could. "In here!"

My voice echoed through the quad. Daphne and Carson froze, and their heads snapped in this direction.

I waved at them, but I couldn't tell if they saw me or not. Something whistled behind me, and I ducked. Jasmine's sword slammed into the iron bars, throwing red sparks everywhere. I turned to stare at her. Jasmine had a wild look to her now. Her blond hair streamed down her face, and her once-blue eyes glowed that same eerie red that the prowler's did. *Creepy.*

"Stand still so I can chop off your head," she muttered.

Jasmine swung the sword at me again, and I ducked back out of the way. Again and again, she came at me, swinging the blade, but every time I managed to avoid it. Maybe some of the gym class training had sunk in after all, because I couldn't believe that I was still alive.

On her next pass, Jasmine's sword slammed into one of the bookcases and got stuck in the thick wood. Cursing, she wrapped her hands around the hilt and tried to pull it out. Since she wasn't focused on me, I ran around behind the bookshelf and rammed my shoulder into it as hard as I could.

"C'mon," I muttered, and pushed again and again, finally managing to rock it back and forth. "C'mon! C'mon!"

I gave it a final, vicious shove. With a loud, unhappy creak, the bookshelf tipped over. A second later, it landed on top of the Valkyrie, burying her under hundreds of books.

For a moment, all I could hear was the sound of my own raspy, panicked breathing and the thumping rush of blood in my ears. Then, Jasmine let out another evil laugh.

"You forgot that I'm a Valkyrie, Gypsy," she said. "I'm strong, much stronger than you are. This will only slow me down. It won't stop me from killing you. Nothing can do that now."

The heavy case began to shift back and forth, as Jasmine wiggled her way out from under it and the mountain of books I'd buried her in. I backed up, wondering what I could do now to stop her. There was nowhere to run, not really, not since I couldn't get out of the library, and it was only a matter of time before Jasmine wormed free.

I didn't know what was going on with Logan and the prowler, but I could still hear the creature yowling, which meant it wasn't dead yet. Even if Logan could kill it without dying himself, I wondered if he could defeat Jasmine, too, because she'd had the same warrior training that he'd had and if the prowler injured him, he'd be at a serious disadvantage.

I bit my lip and looked around, trying to stay calm, trying to think what my mom would do in this situation. Okay, so maybe my mom had never gone up against a crazed Valkyrie who wanted to sacrifice her slutty best friend to an evil god, but she had faced plenty of bad guys while she'd been a detective. I remembered watching her come home sometimes, take her gun off her belt, and—

My eyes narrowed. Of course. I needed a weapon.

Not that I knew how to really *use* a weapon of any sort, but it was better than running away from Jasmine or, worse, letting her hack me into little pieces with her sword.

My bare feet seemed to move of their own accord, and I raced back into the stacks. I didn't even really think about where I was going until I skidded to a halt in front of the glass case.

The Case—the one with the strange sword in it.

I fumbled with the clasp, hoping that it wouldn't be locked or magically sealed. To my surprise, it opened immediately and I didn't get any unwanted vibes off it. I threw back the top of The Case, reached for the sword—and stopped. I didn't know exactly what would happen if I picked it up. What kind of flashes or vibes that I might get off it. But I knew that it would be something—something *big*. Something that would change my life forever.

Behind me, there was an enormous roar, and Jasmine's laughter filled the library once more. She'd gotten free of the bookcase. If I didn't pick up the sword, the rest of my life was going to be short. Very, very short.

"Gypsy," Jasmine hissed, her voice echoing over to me. "I'm going to enjoy killing you."

Quick footsteps sounded, running in my direction. Time was up, so I reached down into The Case and grabbed the sword.

Chapter 22

As soon as my fingers brushed the hilt, the eye snapped open and regarded me with its gray-purple gaze once more.

"Gypsy," an old, crusty voice seemed to murmur in my head. *"At last."*

Okay, so apparently it talked, too. *Supercreepy,* but I was too far gone now to care. My fingers closed all the way around the hilt, and I yanked the sword out of The Case. The way the hilt was designed, my hand covered the lower half of the man's face—from the mouth down. His nose hooked over my hand, a wrist guard, I think it was called, with the open eye clearly visible above that—the eye that was still staring at me. For a moment, nothing happened.

And then, the emotions hit me.

The sword was old—*ancient* even—in the way the Bowl of Tears was. So many things flashed through my mind. So many images. Battles, mostly. Hundreds, thousands of them, all happening in a single second. Big, small, quiet, loud. I smelled smoke and blood. Heard screams of rage and pain. Felt other swords, other blades, slicing into my own skin in a way that made me cry out in pain and completely furious at the same time.

I couldn't do anything but stand there and see the images and ride the waves of emotions pouring through me. I couldn't have let go of the sword even if I'd wanted to. After a second, the images slowed down enough for me to make some sense of them. I realized that I was watching battles from throughout history. Different times, different places, different enemies. Clothes, weapons, armor, people. They all changed, becoming more and more modern with every passing fight.

But one thing was the same in every image—in every battle, a woman wielded the sword. One after another, their faces flashed through my mind, almost too fast for me to follow. But I felt them, felt their emotions, felt all the things they had felt when they'd been wielding the sword. Pride. Power. Fear. Anger. And most of all, a sense of duty and honor.

There were gaps, too, times when the sword wasn't in the images, when it was just the women, one after another, being born, growing up, having daughters of their own, growing old, and finally dying. The images skipped on from one to the next, and I got the sense that this was a long, unbroken chain of women stretching back to the time when the gods themselves walked the earth.

Among the images, I saw a familiar face—Grandma

Frost. Her features flickered before me for an instant, before they were replaced by another face—my mom's face.

"Mom?" I whispered.

Grace Frost smiled at me, and her mouth opened, almost as if she was trying to say something to me.

"Mom!" I stretched out my hand to her, as if I could somehow reach into the vision and touch her.

And I felt myself falling, falling, falling. . . .

With a gasp, my eyes snapped open, and I found myself standing in the middle of the Library of Antiquities, in the spot where the glass case that had once held the Bowl of Tears had been. I still had the sword in my hand, and I whirled around, looking for the others.

They weren't here.

There was no Jasmine coming to kill me. No Morgan lying on the table looking at nothing. No Logan fighting off a Nemean prowler. It was just me in the library—alone.

"Hello?" I called out. "Is—is anyone here?"

My voice echoed through the library, a frightened lonely little sound that seemed to stretch on forever—

"Hello, Gwendolyn," a soft voice murmured.

I bit back a scream and turned around. A woman stood behind me, right in front of the closed double doors. At first glance, there was nothing remarkable about her. Average height, slender, but with some muscle on her. Her hair fell to her shoulders in soft brown ringlets that seemed to shimmer with a metallic bronze sheen. She wore a gown that reminded me of a toga—long flowing fabric in a sweet lilac color. A silver belt looped around her waist, and some kind of silver flowers ringed her head like a crown. Laurels, I thought, wondering how I even knew that to start with.

But the more I stared at her, the more I realized that she was simply the most beautiful woman I'd ever seen. Not because her features were beautiful, but because there was an aura about her, a presence, a sense of peace and serenity and eternity. For some reason, it comforted me, even now, when I probably should have been screaming my head off at all the weirdness that had happened in the last hour. In the last freaking *minute*.

The woman walked closer to me, her gown flowing around her body like water. For the first time, I noticed that she had a set of soft, feathery wings attached to her back, kind of what I'd always thought an angel's would look like. Was I dead? Was this some sort of heaven?

The winged woman stopped in front of me and regarded me with eyes that were neither gray nor purple but the soft shade of twilight in between.

"Who are you?" I whispered.

She tilted her head to the side and smiled. "I think you know."

And suddenly I did. The knowledge filled my mind. I'd seen her picture before in my myth-history books and had heard Professor Metis talk about her. I'd even seen her statue in this very library. I looked up at the spot on the second floor where the marble statue always stood, but it was gone. Maybe because she was standing in front of me.

"You're Nike, the Greek goddess of victory," I said in a small voice.

She nodded. "That's right. And you are Gwendolyn Frost, daughter of Grace Frost, granddaughter of Geraldine Frost, and so on and so forth."

"You know my mom? And my grandma?"

A mysterious smile curved Nike's lips. "I know all of your ancestors, Gwendolyn. The women in your family have served me since time itself began."

Okay, I felt like my head was going to explode. I mean, here I was, talking to a goddess. A real goddess. And not just any goddess, but Nike, the kick-ass chick who'd defeated Loki and pretty much saved the world from destruction. And she knew me and all about my family. Yeah, my brain was *definitely* exploding inside my skull.

"Um . . . should I bow or something?" I asked, feeling like I was standing outside of myself, like this was all happening to another person. "Because I didn't pay attention in myth-history class, so I really don't know the proper etiquette for the whole talking-to-a-goddess thing. Sorry."

Nike's smile widened. "No, Gwendolyn, you don't have to bow to me. But we do need to talk about some things."

"Like what?"

She nodded at the sword in my hand. "Like that."

I realized that I was still holding the sword. I held it up. The single gray-purple eye regarded me with a skeptical gaze.

"I don't know about this, goddess," the sword said. "She doesn't look like much to me."

I felt the cold, metal mouth move underneath my palm, tickling my skin. I shrieked and dropped the sword. The weapon clanged to the ground.

"Oh, bloody hell," the sword grumbled, its face on the marble floor. "She can't even hang on to me."

"This is Vic," the goddess said, bending down to pick up the weapon. She rubbed at a spot on the blade just above the hilt. "He's going to help you face what's ahead, the danger that's coming."

Danger? I didn't like the sound of that. A minute ago, I'd been in plenty of danger already, what with Jasmine trying to kill me and everything.

Vic almost seemed to preen under the goddess's gentle touch, like he was her favorite pet that she was giving all of her love and attention to.

"You know about the Chaos, don't you, Gwendolyn?" Nike asked in a soft voice. "About Loki and his Reapers?"

I nodded.

"Well, Loki is closer to returning to your world, to the moral realm, than anyone thinks. His prison is weakening, and his followers are gathering strength every day. Which is where you come in, Gwendolyn. You're going to help me fight the Reapers and keep Loki from plunging the world into a second Chaos War."

"Me?" I squeaked.

Nike nodded. "You, Gwendolyn Frost. For thousands of years, the women of your family have served me, acting as my Champions, helping me keep the order of things, helping me keep the world balanced between good and evil, between victory and defeat."

I remembered what Daphne had said about Champions, how they were people chosen by the gods. To help other people.

To be heroes.

I thought of the images that I'd just seen of all the women and all the battles over the years. I was a part of that? It didn't seem possible. It just didn't seem *right,* much less *real.* Sure, my Grandma Frost was the strongest person I knew, and my mom had been the same way before she'd died. But me? Not so much. I couldn't even make any friends at Mythos, and I wasn't some great warrior like the other kids were.

"Why me?" I asked. "I'm not like the other kids here. I'm nobody."

I winced as I repeated what Jasmine had said to me moments ago in the library, the real library. Or wait, maybe this was the real library now? My head *definitely* hurt.

"You're not nobody," Nike said in a sharp tone. "You are Gwendolyn Frost, and you are my Champion."

Eyes wide, I stared at her, wondering what I'd done to make her angry. After a moment, the goddess's face softened once more.

"When everyone else ignored Jasmine's death, you were the only one who cared, Gwendolyn," she said in a serious tone, as if that was something of great importance.

"But I didn't *do* anything," I protested. "Not really. Nothing important anyway. I just kind of fumbled around and followed people and used my Gypsy gift to pick up vibes. It wasn't anything that anyone else couldn't have done."

"No," Nike agreed. "But you at least cared enough to try. That was something. Just like when you told your mother how that other girl was being abused."

"You saw that, too?" I whispered.

She nodded. "I see many things, but most of all, I see the strength and the goodness in your heart. But I can't make you do anything you don't want to, Gwendolyn. This has to be your choice."

I stood there, thinking about things. I didn't believe I was Champion material at all. But who was I to argue with a goddess? Especially the goddess of victory? But I wasn't just going to go into this blindly either.

"What happens if I say no?" I asked. "In the library right now?"

"You mean to the Spartan boy?" Nike asked.

"Why, he'll die, of course," Vic, the sword snapped, staring at me with his one eye. "If the prowler doesn't kill him, the Valkyrie surely will. What do you think will happen?"

Grief filled me, and my knees trembled. *Logan.* I

lurched over to one of the library tables and leaned on it for support.

"That won't be your fault, Gwendolyn," Nike said. "The Spartan boy made his own choice to come into the library. It was what was always going to happen to him."

What was always going to happen to him? What did that mean? That it had all been fated or something from the very beginning? I wondered if the goddess knew that this was what was always going to happen to me, too, but I didn't ask.

Now that I knew Logan would die, my choice had been made for me. Yeah, I was still totally pissed at him for—for everything. But he'd come after me tonight, had followed me to the library for whatever reason. I couldn't ignore that or the feelings I had for him. I just . . . couldn't.

"All right," I said. "I'll be your Champion, Nike."

A smile spread across the goddess's beautiful face, and her wings twitched behind her back. "Then hold out your hands, Gwendolyn Frost, and accept all the gifts that I can give to you."

I did as she asked. Nike placed Vic, the sword, into my hands. The weapon stared up at me with his one eye.

"All right then," he said in a slightly more satisfied tone. "Can we get on with killing things then?"

"Um, I don't actually know how to kill things," I said.

"She doesn't even know how to kill things proper-like? What kind of girl have you given me to, goddess?" Vic protested, fixing his eye on Nike once more.

Nike let out a laugh. "Vic is a little bloodthirsty. You'll get used to it."

I kind of doubted that.

Nike stared at me another moment, then did a most curious thing. She leaned over and kissed me on the cheek.

Immediately I felt a cold power flow through me, as though my blood had turned to ice. I braced myself, waiting for the flashes to kick in, although I had no idea what I would see by touching a freaking *goddess*. But the icy sensation vanished, and I didn't get any vibes off her. Still, I felt different, like something inside me had shifted into a new place, like a switch had been turned on. I exhaled, and my breath frosted in the air in front of me, even though I didn't feel cold anymore.

Nike reached out and put her hands over mine. I stared up into her eyes—eyes that were neither purple nor gray but instead the soft color of twilight. And I felt that power in her gaze envelop me again. A cold, hard power, but one that was not unpleasant.

"Now, go," Nike said. "Save the Spartan boy."

I looked up at her. "But how am I supposed to do that? I don't even know how to fight—"

The goddess smiled at me and stepped back, her body suddenly shimmering and melting the way that twilight always did as it gave way to true night—or the approaching dawn.

"Wait!" I said. "Tell me what I'm supposed to do—"

But Nike had already vanished, taking her wisdom along with her.

With a gasp, I snapped back to reality. I stood in the same spot I had before, right in front of the glass case that had held the sword—the sword that I was still holding in my hand.

"Can we get on with killing things then?" Vic repeated in a slightly petulant tone, and I noticed that he had a really cool British accent. "It's been so long since I've tasted blood. I'm famished."

I blanched and not just because it was totally *freaky* how the sword's mouth moved underneath my palm. "You actually *like* the taste of blood—"

A sharp whistling sound behind me made me throw myself to the side. A sword slammed down onto The Case, cleaving it in two and sending glass and bits of wood everywhere. I scrambled to my feet to find Jasmine already turning toward me, her sword held high once more.

Jasmine smirked at the weapon in my hand. "That little toothpick won't save you, Gypsy."

"Toothpick?" Vic muttered in an indignant voice. "Did she just call me a bleeding toothpick? Kill her! Kill her now!"

"If you've got any tips on how to do that, I would be more than happy to listen to them," I snapped, raising Vic up in response. "Because I totally suck at this sort of stuff in gym class."

"Oh, fantastic," Vic muttered. "Just bloody fantastic. The goddess has given me to a bleeding *pacifist*—"

I would have pointed out that I wasn't a pacifist, just totally uncoordinated, but Jasmine came at me again, her sword moving in a silver blur. Block, block, block. That was all that I could do to keep her frenzied attacks from cutting into me. Still, the Valkyrie was a lot stronger than I was, and every one of her blows felt like somebody was hitting me with a sledgehammer. The sheer force of them jarred my whole body, making it hard for me to just keep standing upright.

I desperately tried to remember all the things that I was supposed to have learned in those mock fights in gym class. Tried to swing my sword and move my feet the way that I remembered Coach Ajax showing us how to do.

But try as I might, I couldn't touch Jasmine. I couldn't even nick her with my sword. I was doing pretty good just to keep her from killing me. I'd seen enough fights in gym to realize that unless I did something drastic, Jasmine was going to ram her blade through my heart very, very soon.

I stared into her face, watching her eyes, trying to guess what she was going to do next, how she was going to come at me next. Her once-blue eyes were still completely red, just like the prowler's were. If anything, the color had darkened since she'd started attacking me, and it looked like blood had filled the sockets where her eyes were supposed to be. Jasmine's pink lips were drawn back into a snarl, but there was a vague blankness in her face, the same sort of blankness that was in Morgan's features. It was like part of Jasmine wasn't even here anymore, like someone or something outside her body had taken control of her and was fueling her, feeding her power just so she could kill me.

I was willing to bet that something was the Bowl of Tears.

Jasmine swung at me again, and I stepped back out of reach. She slipped on a book that had fallen off the shelves while we'd been fighting, and I used the chance to leap over her and run back to the center of the library.

"What are you doing?" Vic said. "Why are you retreating? The fight's back that way!"

"Shut up, Vic!" I said over the noise of the blood roaring in my ears and my bare feet slapping against the cold marble floor. "Unless you want to go back into that case for another decade or two."

Vic shut up.

I skidded to a halt in front of Morgan, who was still lying on the table staring up at nothing. By this point, the blood in the Bowl of Tears had bubbled up to the surface, looking like a crimson volcano about to erupt. Whatever was going to happen next, it wasn't going to be good. I couldn't beat Jasmine, but I could destroy that . . . that . . . that evil *thing*.

"Here goes nothing," I muttered, and raised Vic up over my head with both hands.

Jasmine skidded around the corner of the bookcase, her sword still clutched in her hand. She froze when she saw what I was about to do.

"No!" Jasmine screamed. "Don't!"

Too late. I slammed the sword down as hard as I could onto the Bowl of Tears. The second the sword touched the Bowl, a scream filled the library, sounding so loud and high and full of pain that it seemed to tear the very air itself into pieces. Crimson light erupted from the Bowl, burning so bright that I had to look away from it.

After that, I wasn't really sure what happened. The light kept burning, the voice kept screaming, and a blast of heat hit me, so hot that it felt like it would sear all the skin from my body. But for some reason, the sword in my hands stayed as cold as ice. I tightened my grip on Vic and brought the blade up, as if it would protect me from the intense light and heat.

Somehow, it did.

As soon as I brought up the sword, the light and heat lessened, as though the weapon had turned into some kind of shield or something. I backed up a few steps and forced myself to open my eyes, to look at what was happening.

A swirling crimson cloud of . . . of . . . of *magic* hung in the library in front of me, centered over the Bowl of Tears. The cloud arced up, as if it was trying to escape, but I could see that the end of it was like a tornado, swirling around faster and faster and eating everything above it. Like a cartoon genie being forced back into its bottle, whether it wanted to go or not.

Just before the last of the magic cloud got sucked down into the Bowl of Tears, an enormous pair of red eyes popped open and swirled around in the middle of it. The eyes fixed on me, narrowing to angry slits, and a blast of emotion hit me—one of absolute rage and hate and evil. I cried out and staggered back from the force of it. The eyes stared at me another second before they and the rest of the magic cloud disappeared into the Bowl.

I shivered, because I knew, I just *knew,* that those eyes had been real. That they'd belonged to someone who'd seen me. Who hated me. Who wanted me *dead* more than anything else.

Loki, a voice whispered in the back of my mind. The evil god might be trapped in a prison realm, but somehow, Loki had been able to peer into the library tonight—and I'd felt just how much he wanted to destroy me. I shivered again.

The magic cloud vanished. So did the crimson light. The screams, the noise, the magic, everything. It was all gone, and the library was still and quiet once more.

Then, the Bowl of Tears slipped off of Morgan's chest, fell to the marble floor, and shattered into a thousand pieces.

Chapter 23

The remains of the Bowl of Tears turned black, shriveled up, and started evaporating, just the way that the Nemean prowler outside the library had when Logan had killed it—

Logan.

I turned around, but I didn't see the Spartan anywhere in the library. What I did see was Jasmine coming at me once more, her sword still clutched in her hands.

"You've ruined everything!" she screamed. "My revenge, my sacrifice to Loki, everything!"

The Valkyrie kept coming at me, and I backed up. Only this time, my foot was the one that slipped on a fallen book. I hit the floor hard, and Vic, the sword, fell from my hand and skittered across the cold marble.

"Can't believe she bloody dropped me *again*...," I heard him mutter.

On my hands and knees, I scrambled after the weapon, but it just kept sliding farther and farther away from me. Finally, it stopped, and I saw Vic glaring at me in disapproval.

I'd just reached for the sword when two black stiletto boots planted themselves in front of me. Uh-oh. I looked up to find Jasmine standing over me.

"Time to die, Gypsy," she muttered, and raised her sword high, ready to bring it down on my head and kill me for good this time—

A spear flew through the air and punched all the way through the middle of Jasmine's chest. The Valkyrie's mouth opened in a perfect O, and surprise flashed in her eyes. Her sword slipped from her fingers, and she stumbled back against the table where Morgan was lying. Jasmine stared at me, her beautiful face full of pain and disbelief, and she crumpled to the library floor. Dead. This time, I knew that the slick crimson blood rapidly pooling under her body was real.

It was awful.

"Now *that's* what I'm talking about," Vic crowed in a chipper voice.

"Shut up, Vic," I whispered.

I picked up the sword, got to my feet, and turned around.

Logan Quinn stood behind me.

Deep ugly red lines slashed down his cheek from where the Nemean prowler had clawed him, and his black tuxedo jacket and white shirt hung in tatters on his body. More claw marks covered his chest, and I could see blood dripping out of the wounds. The Spartan's metal shield was still strapped to his arm, although it had been torn into two separate pieces by the prowler. Still, despite his injuries, pride filled Logan's ice blue eyes, warming them.

In that moment, he was the most beautiful thing I'd ever seen.

I ran over to him and held out my arms. I wanted to hug him, kiss him, touch him—and then I remembered that I couldn't. That my Gypsy gift, my psychometry, wouldn't let me. Not without flashing on him. Not without seeing what had just happened between him and the prowler. Not without me learning all of Logan's secrets. And I didn't want to do that. Not now, not like this.

I stood there a moment, my arms outstretched. Then, I slowly dropped them to my sides.

"Are you okay?" I whispered. "Where's the prowler?"

"Dead. Its body is back in the stacks. It didn't evaporate since it was the real deal this time and not just an illusion." Logan put his fingers up to the bloody wounds on his face and winced. "Well, since I'm alive and Jasmine and the prowler aren't, I'd say that qualifies as okay. You?"

I shrugged. There was no way to tell him all the crazy things that had happened in the library tonight and all the things that I was feeling, especially when I stared into his eyes.

"Thank you," I said in a quiet voice. "I don't know how you found me or why, but thank you. Jasmine and her prowler would have killed me, if it hadn't been for you."

He gave me a crooked smile that made my heart speed up. "I couldn't let you just walk out of the dance all pissed off, now could I?"

"But . . . but why come after me at all?" I asked, my eyes never leaving his.

Logan stared at me. After a moment, he drew in a breath. "Because I—"

"What is going on in here?" a sharp voice called out.

Startled, I raised my sword up even as my head snapped around to the double doors at the back of the library. To my surprise, they were open once more and three people crowded into the doorway—Professor Metis, Coach Ajax, and Nickamedes. I spotted Daphne and Carson lurking behind them, trying to see what was going on inside.

Nickamedes stepped into the library and walked toward me, his face even paler than usual and his mouth wide open in shock. The librarian had a right to be stunned. It looked like a bomb had gone off in here. Thousands of books littered the marble floor, dozens of shelves had been knocked over, tables and chairs had been upended and sliced to ribbons by the Nemean prowler—and that was just the damage I could see from where I was standing.

And then, there was the biggie—Jasmine Ashton slumped against one of the tables, her sightless eyes staring up at the ceiling, Logan's spear through her chest, her blood coating the floor around her. Right above her, Morgan McDougall was still stretched out on top of the table, like some comatose fairy princess waiting for her handsome prince to come and wake her up with a kiss.

I winced. This was so not going to be fun.

Sure enough, Nickamedes rounded on me and stabbed his finger in my direction. "What have you done to my library, Gwendolyn?"

There was a lot of explaining to do after that. A *lot* of explaining. I told Professor Metis and the others about everything that I'd found out about Jasmine's plot to use the Bowl of Tears to control Morgan. How Jasmine had wanted to get revenge on her slutty best friend for sleeping with Samson. How Jasmine had claimed that she and her whole family were Reapers who served Loki.

I didn't tell them about seeing Nike, though, and that the goddess had told me that I was her Champion. I still wasn't sure how I felt about all that—or if it had even been real to start with and not something that I'd just imagined.

Sometime in the middle of it all, Morgan woke up from whatever kind of zombie trance Jasmine had put her in. The Valkyrie blinked, sat up, looked at all of us, and demanded to know what was going on—and exactly who had stolen her homecoming tiara, ruined her designer dress, and scratched up her face. Coach Ajax took her aside and tried to explain things to her. The Valkyrie still looked confused, though. Just like I felt.

While everyone was busy with Morgan, I showed Professor Metis the sword I'd grabbed out of The Case in the back of the library. The one that Nike had given back to me during my dream, vision, or whatever that had been. Sometime during the commotion, Vic had closed his eye, and he wouldn't open it back up or talk no matter what I did or said or how I pleaded with him to show Metis that he was in fact kind of alive.

"It's okay, Gwen," Professor Metis said, staring at the sword with a strange look on her face. "I believe you about the sword."

I glared down at the spot where Vic's closed eye was. "So what do you want to do about it? Do you want to take it and stick it back in one of the artifact cases?"

Metis shook her head. "No, I think you should hang on to the sword, Gwen. At least for now. We've got a lot to do tonight, and it would just get lost in the mess anyway. We'll talk about it later, okay?"

I shrugged. I supposed I could hang on to Vic. Even if the fact that the sword could look at and talk to me was kind of bizarre.

"I think you were very brave tonight, Gwen," Metis said, her green eyes soft and kind in her face. "Trying to help Morgan. Your mother would be very proud of you."

I frowned, wondering once again at the familiar tone in Metis's voice when she'd talked about my mom. But then I thought of how I'd seen my mom's face when I'd first picked up the sword, of how she had seemed to smile at me. Emotion clogged my throat, and I just nodded. I thought my mom would be proud of me, too. And that made me happier than anything else had in a long time.

Metis smiled at me, then walked over to Ajax and the still-stunned Nickamedes. The three of them huddled together, talking about who they needed to call, how long it would take to clean up the mess in the library, and what to do with Jasmine's body—the real one—this time. I wondered if they would put it in cold storage in the morgue, like Jasmine had claimed they'd done to her other body, the illusion she'd created to fool us all.

Thirty minutes later, I stood off to one side and watched while a couple of men dressed in dark coveralls loaded Jasmine into a black body bag and zipped it shut. Despite the fact that she'd tried to kill me, I still felt sorry for the Valkyrie.

Her best friend had betrayed her, and her boyfriend had cheated on her. She'd faked her own death to make them feel guilty about what they'd done, but it had backfired, and she'd realized just how little they really cared about her. Just how little everyone had cared about her. So Jasmine had decided to make her best friend pay for everything, especially her hurt feelings.

Jasmine Ashton had been the richest, most beautiful and popular girl in our class, and she'd had everything that she could possibly want—except real friends.

Speaking of friends, I was pretty sure that I had at least a couple now, although my feelings for Logan had zoomed way past the friendship point and had turned into something else completely. The Spartan stood a few feet away, talking to Daphne and Carson about everything that had happened.

Professor Metis was over there, too, looking at Logan's injuries. She took his hands in hers and stared into the Spartan's eyes. After a few seconds, a golden glow enveloped Logan. As I watched, the ugly cuts on his face slowly closed shut like they'd never even been there to start with. So did the deeper, bloodier ones on his chest. Metis had told me about her magic and how she could heal people. It looked like Logan would be just fine in a few minutes.

But I didn't feel like joining them yet. Somebody should stay with Jasmine just a little while longer.

A minute later, Daphne said something in a soft voice to the others and walked over to me. The Valkyrie stood beside me, a blank expression on her face as we watched one of the men start scrubbing Jasmine's blood off the marble floor.

"I'm sorry," I said. "I know she was your friend."

Daphne shrugged. "Maybe. Maybe not. I don't think that I ever really knew Jasmine. I never would have thought that she could have done any of this."

I wondered if anyone here at Mythos had known what Jasmine was really like—or if they would even care that she was dead for real this time.

"It's not your fault, you know," Daphne said in a low voice. "Jasmine made her own choices, just like she always did. She wanted revenge on Morgan, and she decided to go all Reaper on everyone to get it. You and Logan were only defending yourselves. That's the way things are here at Mythos. People come, people go, and some people die."

"Maybe," I replied. "But Morgan and Samson broke her heart and then lied to her about everything. They thought it was funny, like a game or something, sneaking around behind Jasmine's back. So I still feel sorry for her, you know?"

"Yeah," Daphne said. "I know."

We didn't say anything for a few minutes.

"Well," Daphne said. "The homecoming dance is still going strong, but Carson, Logan, and I are going to head over to Carson's dorm. He has some Dionysian wine that his dad shipped him in special from Napa."

I raised an eyebrow. "The band geek has liquor?"

Daphne smiled. "Who knew? Seems like there's a lot of things about Carson that I don't know. But now, I get to find out, thanks to you. So you want to come with or what?"

"Sure," I said. "Just give me a minute."

Daphne nodded, and she went back over to Carson and Logan. Metis had finished healing Logan, and the three students said their good-byes to the professor, headed toward the double doors, and walked out of the library. Metis watched them a few seconds before going back over to Ajax, who was still trying to console Nickamedes about the huge mess in the library.

No one saw me slip to the back of the library where the sword case had been. I looked at the remains of the glass and wood before slowly raising up my head.

And there she was on the second-floor balcony, the

one filled with the statues of all the gods and goddesses. Nike's statue stood right above the smashed antiques case, as if she'd been watching over it—and me—this whole time. Maybe she had. The thought comforted me the same way that hugging Grandma Frost always did.

Nike looked the same as she had when I'd seen her. A long, loose gown flowing around her body, wings arching up over her back, a cold, terrible sort of beauty filling her face. I don't know why I'd never noticed her standing up there before. Maybe because I hadn't been looking. Maybe because I hadn't been ready.

"Ahem," a voice coughed.

I looked down at the sword in my hand. I'd completely forgotten that I'd been holding on to the weapon this whole time. It was weird, but it felt almost like a natural extension of my arm now. A part of myself, even.

Vic had opened his twilight-colored eye again and was studying me intently. Well, as intently as he could with only the one eye.

"You did okay tonight, for a bloody rookie," the sword said, his mouth moving under my hand and tickling my palm. "Although you really should get your Spartan friend to show you a few things. Because he has the potential to be a *real* warrior."

"Later, Vic," I said. "Much, much later."

He seemed to nod. "Well then, by your leave, I think I'll take a little nap. All this excitement has worn me out. I'm not as young as I used to be, you know."

"Of course not," I said in a kind voice. "You take your nap, Vic. We can talk about everything else later."

I'd scarcely finished saying the words before the eye snapped shut again. I might have only imagined it, but it felt like the part of the hilt that was Vic's mouth curved into a soft smile.

I was about to lower the sword and leave the library when something shimmered on the blade itself, above Vic's face and the rest of the hilt. I held the sword up to the light, turning it this way and that, so I could see what had caught my eye.

It was the symbols that I'd seen before on the blade, the faint letters that I hadn't quite been able to make out. Now, they glowed with a cold, silver fire, and, for the first time, I could clearly read the words that had been carved into the sword's blade—*Victory Always.*

Of course. Nike was the Greek goddess of victory, and this was her sword.

And now, it was mine, given to me by the goddess herself to help me be her Champion.

I only hoped that I was worthy of Vic and the strange, unwavering faith that Nike seemed to have in me.

Chapter 24

What happened at the Library of Antiquities the night of the homecoming dance was the talk of Mythos Academy for the next week.

But not in the way that I expected.

Even though she didn't seem to remember anything, Morgan McDougall still managed to take credit for everything, from thwarting Jasmine to destroying the Bowl of Tears to killing the Nemean prowler. It was like Logan and I hadn't even been there and she'd saved everyone at the academy from a fate worse than death.

Not all of the kids believed her, though, and wild rumors spread as fast as people could text them. Everything from how a group of Reapers had planted a magic bomb on campus to drunk kids performing a crazy ritual to Jasmine coming back from the dead and destroying the library because she was pissed that she hadn't been crowned homecoming queen before she'd been murdered. The last one was a little truer than anyone knew.

I kept my head down through the whole mess. Something told me that the fewer people who knew that I'd been involved in what had happened, the better. I still remembered the glowing red eyes that had been swirling around in the cloud of magic when I'd destroyed the Bowl of Tears. How the eyes had been fixed on me and exactly how full of hate, rage, and anger they'd been. I remembered what Jasmine had said about being a Reaper and how there were other Reapers at the academy, other kids and profs who served Loki, who wanted to free him from his prison and return the god to the mortal realm so he could bring about another Chaos War—something that Nike had told me I was somehow supposed to help her with.

Despite my unease, life returned to normal. I went to my classes and worked my assigned shifts at the library. Actually, I worked double shifts, because Nickamedes had more or less decided that I alone was responsible for the destruction of his precious library, so he was making me help him clean it from top to bottom as punishment. If I thought that Nickamedes hadn't liked me before, he absolutely *hated* me now. So yeah, my world was pretty much back to normal.

I'd called Grandma Frost the night that everything had gone down at the library and told her what had happened. She'd immediately offered to come to the academy to comfort me, but I'd told her that I was okay. The truth was that I'd needed some time to myself to think about things—a lot of things. Finally, a couple of days later, I managed to get away from Nickamedes long enough to sneak off campus and go see her.

"You knew all along, didn't you?" I asked Grandma Frost as we sat in the kitchen eating the sticky, sinfully sweet chocolate fudge that she'd just made. "That we come from a long line of warrior chicks who serve a kick-ass goddess."

"Warrior chicks? Is that what the kids are calling it these days?" Grandma Frost smiled and reached for another piece of fudge, her bright scarves fluttering with the motion. She'd just been doing a reading for a client, so she was dressed in her usual Gypsy clothes.

I rolled my eyes. "Come on, you know what I mean."

"Of course I know. That's what makes us Gypsies, Gwen."

I frowned. "How does being warrior chicks make us Gypsies? You never told me that before."

Grandma Frost stared at me, a serious look on her face. "Gwen, why do you think that we can do the things that we can do? Why do you think that I can see the future or that you can touch objects and know everything about them? Where do you think that power comes from?"

I opened my mouth, but no answer came to me. I shrugged.

"We can do those things and more because Nike has gifted us with that power. Back when our very first ancestor served Nike, the goddess rewarded her by giving her the gift of seeing the future. Over the years and generations, that psychic gift has taken on many different forms, like your mother's ability to sense the truth and your psychometry."

"But I thought we were Gypsies," I said. "Not warriors."

" 'Gypsy' is just another word for those who are gifted by the gods," Grandma said. "Who have special powers and abilities like we do. We're just as strong in our magic and just as much warriors as all the Valkyries, Amazons, and other kids you go to school with."

So Daphne had been right after all. I was a warrior, just with a different kind of magic.

I thought for a minute about what my grandma had said. "Okay, so Nike gave us our powers. I guess I can understand that. But there are tons of other gods and goddesses out there. I mean, you should see all the statues of them in the library. So . . . are there more people out there like us? More Gypsies? More people Nike has gifted?"

"Yes and no." Grandma Frost stared at me. "There are more Gypsies out there, but each family is gifted by a single god or goddess, which means that we are the only ones gifted by Nike, just like there is only one family that has been gifted by Athena and Ares and Odin and so on."

"Have you ever met any of the other Gypsies?" I asked.

"Yes," Grandma Frost said in a dark tone. "But not all of them are like us."

"What do you mean?"

She stared at me with her violet eyes. "Not all of them are good, Gwen. Some of them are lazy or indifferent or use their powers to gain wealth and power. And some of them are Reapers."

"Reapers? Like Jasmine?"

Grandma Frost nodded. "Just like Jasmine—and worse."

So there were other people, other kids, running around just like me who had powers? And some of them were Reapers of Chaos? I shivered at the thought.

"So why didn't you tell me any of this before?" I asked. "About where our gifts come from and Reapers and Gypsies and why I got shipped off to Mythos in the first place? It would have made things . . . easier for me. Simpler. At least, then I would have understood. I would have given the academy a chance. I would have believed in all the magic to start with."

I hesitated, thinking about something else that had been on my mind lately. "Did you and Mom ever . . . go to Mythos? Were you students there, too?"

Grandma gave me a sad smile. "We did. And that's why we decided that you shouldn't have to."

"What do you mean?"

She sighed. "We're part of a dangerous world, pumpkin. Gypsies, Reapers, Loki. We're all tangled together like a ball of string. You can't have one without all the others. But your mom and I wanted better for you. We wanted you to have a normal life. We wanted you to grow up slowly, naturally, without always worrying about Reapers trying to kill you."

I thought of Daphne and Carson and Logan and all the other kids at school. About how all the violence and gods and magic seemed normal to them—and about how Carson had told me that they'd all lost somebody to the Reapers. Suddenly I was grateful for what my mom and grandma had done, for protecting me as long as they had.

"But then, I picked up Paige's hairbrush and had my magical freak-out," I said. "Is that why Professor Metis came here?"

"Partly." Shadows darkened Grandma Frost's violet eyes, and she didn't say anything for a moment. "Metis thought that it was time for you to go to Mythos, for you to learn where your power really came from and how to better control it as it grows. And I'm not as young as I used to be, Gwen. I wanted you to go to the academy, too, so you'd be safe. At least, as safe as you can be there."

"But what about Nike?" I asked. "Did you and Mom serve as her Champions, too?"

Grandma nodded. "We did. Nike comes to us all and asks us to serve her when she thinks that we are ready."

"So why didn't you tell me about that either?"

"Because it was your decision to make, Gwen. Just like your mom and I made it before you. Just like your own daughter might make it someday." She sighed. "So many of the kids at Mythos are expected to be great warriors from birth. Your mom and I didn't want to put that kind of pressure on you. We wanted you to make your own choices because you wanted to, not because you felt you had to uphold some great family legacy. Besides, being a Champion is as good as having a target painted on your back. Reapers kill warriors, sure, but they'll do anything—*anything*—to take down a Champion."

My stomach twisted at her words. "Why is that?"

"Because Champions always have the strongest magic, the best fighting skills, the bravest hearts. That's why they're picked to be Champions in the first place—because they can do the most good. That makes them the biggest threats to Loki and his Reapers. We just wanted to protect you as long as we could, pumpkin." Grandma paused. "And we also didn't want you to grow up to be as spoiled as some of the kids are."

I frowned. "What do you mean?"

She shrugged. "It's hard living in a world where you know Reapers want nothing more than to kill you and your children. So most warrior parents indulge their kids and give them whatever they want—cars, clothes, jewelry—just in case they're not around to see their kids grow up. I'm not saying that it's wrong or it's right, but it's not how your mom wanted to raise you. She wanted you to know the value of money—and life, too. Most especially life."

That must be why the professors at Mythos let the kids get away with so many things, too—smoking, drinking, hooking up—because the profs knew that we could all be killed by Reapers on any given day and they thought that the students should live it up in the mean-time. But Grandma's words raised another question in my mind.

"So do we have money, then? I mean...a lot of money? Like the other kids' parents do? And if we do, then why do I have to work in the Library of Antiquities?"

Grandma shrugged again. "Not as much money as some, but enough. More than enough. Your working in the library was actually Professor Metis's idea. She thought interacting with all the other students there would help you adjust to the academy. Of course, it didn't quite work out that way."

No, it hadn't. I pushed the plate of chocolate fudge away. My head was spinning with too much informa-tion for me to enjoy them right now. I still couldn't quite believe everything that Grandma had told me, every-thing that I'd learned the past few days, all the secrets that had finally been revealed to me. Knowing that I was in danger now because I'd agreed to be Nike's Champion didn't exactly put me in a great mood. But that was the thing about secrets—they were almost never good.

Grandma Frost didn't say a word. Instead, she reached over and put her hand on top of mine. As al-ways, I felt the soft, warm blanket of her love wrap around me. And I knew that no matter what happened, no matter how crazy things got, Grandma Frost would always love me just as much as I loved her. Just as much as I'd loved my mom.

I thought about how I'd seen my mom, Grace, when I'd first picked up Vic, the sword. Of how I was now part of the same thing that she had been. Of how my mom had smiled at me like she approved of what I was doing. The idea, whether it was true or not, made me miss her a little less, made the ache of her loss and my guilt over her death a little easier to bear. Maybe this was one secret that I could live with after all.

"But enough talk about Gypsies and gods and everything else," Grandma said, a light, teasing tone creeping into her voice. "Metis told me about seeing you at the homecoming dance with a very cute Spartan boy, the same Spartan boy who helped you that night in the library. You've been holding out on me, Gwen. Now, I want to know all about him."

I still had more things to figure out, more things that I wanted to ask her about my mom and the academy and being Nike's Champion. But all that could wait. Right now, I just wanted to enjoy this moment with my grandma.

"You want to know about Logan Quinn?" I asked, arching my eyebrow.

"Every little detail," Grandma quipped. "Now spill, as you kids say."

I just laughed and shook my head. We stayed there in the kitchen, eating and talking, the rest of the afternoon.

Chapter 25

The next day, Professor Metis called me into her office. The last time that I'd been in here had been the day that I'd come to Mythos Academy at the start of the fall semester, and I'd been too angry and pissed at her and everyone else to really notice things.

Old, thick myth-history books lined the shelves in the bookcases that covered two of the walls, while a couple of clay pots of sunflowers and violets sat on the windowsill. Above them on either side of the window were various plaques, showing all of the professor's degrees and awards. There were *tons* of those. Metis's desk was piled high with papers and pens and stuff, along with a tiny marble statue that perched in the left-hand corner. It looked like a smaller version of the one of Athena, the Greek goddess of wisdom, that stood in the Library of Antiquities, but I wasn't sure.

But the weirdest things were the weapons. A whole rack of them stood in the corner. A couple of swords, a staff, some daggers, even a crossbow and the bolts for it. With her silver glasses and quiet, scholarly vibe, Metis had never struck me as being a warrior. Not like Coach Ajax, anyway, who was all ripped, muscled, and totally Hulked out.

Professor Metis was staring out the window at the quad when I came inside. I shut the door behind me and stood there, waiting until she noticed me. After a moment, she turned around and smiled at me.

"Hello, Gwen. Sit down, please. There are some things that we need to talk about."

Yeah, I'd figured as much, since, you know, I'd been involved in the death of a student, the destruction of the library, and a whole bunch of other Bad, Bad Things. So I did as she asked and took the seat in front of her desk.

Professor Metis sat down as well. Her green eyes flicked to one of the framed photos on the desk, but since it was turned around the other way, I couldn't see who was in it. Her husband or kids, I supposed. Maybe a boyfriend or a pet.

"How are you today, Gwendolyn?"

I shrugged. "Fine, more or less."

And I really was. Yeah, I'd seen and done some bad stuff in the past few days, and I'd learned so many things about myself, my Gypsy gift, and why I was here at Mythos that it kind of blew my mind. And maybe I was still totally freaked out that a goddess had chosen me to be her Champion. But at least I had some answers now, and I'd learned more than one secret about myself. I thought I was handling it all okay.

"Well, I wanted to say that I was most pleased by the

report that you turned in yesterday," Metis said. "The one about Nike. You're getting an A on it."

I sat up a little straighter in my chair. After everything that had happened, writing the report had been easy. I'd actually been paying more attention in myth-history class, too. At night, when I had time, I'd started reading everything that I could get my hands on at the library about Nike, Loki, and the Chaos War. There were so many books with so many conflicting stories that it was hard to know what was real and what wasn't. But it had always been that way for me here at Mythos Academy, the school of myths, magic, and warrior whiz kids.

"Thanks," I said. "It was easy for me to write. I, uh, had a lot of experience to draw on with it after everything that happened in the library."

"Yes," Professor Metis said in a quiet voice. "I supposed that you did."

Metis reached up, took off her silver glasses, and stared at me. For the first time, I noticed how pretty she was, with her black hair, bronze skin, and green eyes. She was also younger than I'd thought, about my mom's age before she'd died—in her early forties.

"We need to talk about what happened in the library," Metis said. "Because while your actions were very brave and noble, they've also put you in a great deal of danger."

"Danger?" I asked. "What kind of danger?"

"You mentioned that Jasmine told you about her family, about how they're all Reapers who serve Loki. I have reason to believe that Jasmine told them what she was doing, that she was planning to use the Bowl to sacrifice Morgan," Metis said. "Her parents and her older brother have gone into hiding, along with the rest of her family. Aunts, uncles, cousins, everyone. They've all gone underground. The members of the Pantheon can't find them anywhere."

"Wait a minute. It sounds like you were going to . . . arrest them or something."

"Or something," Metis agreed, a grim note creeping into her voice. "I don't know how, maybe from another student, but Jasmine's family found out that you were there that night. The Ashtons aren't the kind of people to let their daughter's death slide. They might come after you."

"But I didn't *kill* her," I protested. "Logan did, and only to save me. As for everything else, I didn't really *do* much of anything that night. All I did was run around and be afraid and try not to get killed."

"You did a little more than that, Gwen. You destroyed the Bowl of Tears, one of the Thirteen Artifacts, one that many Reapers, many of Loki's followers, desperately wanted to get their hands on. And you stopped Jasmine from sacrificing Morgan, a sacrifice that would have increased Loki's power and possibly further weakened his prison. That makes you a target for all of the Reapers and their revenge."

I stuck my hands deeper into the pockets on my purple hoodie and shivered. I knew her words were true.

Before at Mythos, I'd been nobody, just like Jasmine had said. That Gypsy girl who saw things. But now, I was that Gypsy girl, the one with secrets of her own.

"Normally, this wouldn't be a huge problem, as that's what students here at Mythos are trained for—how to use their magic, how to fight, and especially how to defend themselves against Reapers," Metis said. "But you've only been at Mythos a few months, and you haven't had any of the training the other students have been exposed to their whole lives. That's why I let you keep that sword from the library, because you're going to learn how to use it. As soon as possible. May I see it please? The sword?"

I reached down and picked up Vic from where I'd put him on the floor when I'd first come into the office. Since that night in the library, I'd been carrying the sword around with me everywhere I went, just like all the other kids did with their weapons of choice. But Vic never opened his eye or talked to anyone but me. Truth be told, he still creeped me out a little bit. So yeah, now I believed in gods and goddesses and Chaos and stuff. But a talking sword was still a little much for me to handle.

I passed Vic over to Metis, who drew the sword out of the black leather scabbard that Coach Ajax had given me for him. I held my breath, wondering if Vic would open his eye and glare at the professor for interrupting his nap. That's what he always did to me when I tried to talk to him when he didn't want me to. Vic was kind of a pain that way, always wanting to do things on his schedule instead of mine.

"It's a beautiful sword," Metis said, admiring the silver blade. "One that is certainly fit for Nike's Champion."

It took a second for her words to sink in. "How did you—" I bit my lip.

Metis smiled. "How did I know that Nike picked you to be her Champion?"

She'd totally busted me. Because seeing Nike and all the things that the goddess had said to me was something that I hadn't told anyone else about, besides Grandma Frost.

Metis slid Vic back into his scabbard and handed him to me. Then, she walked over to the rack of weapons against the wall and pulled a staff from the top slot. The professor brought the weapon over to me so I could see it. The staff was made out of a thick polished golden wood. It was completely smooth and plain, although I could see that some sort of writing had been carved down the front of it.

"Every Champion is given a special weapon by her god or goddess to help her in her various battles," Metis said. "And Champions can always recognize other Champions."

"How? How can you tell if someone is a Champion?"

The professor shrugged. "Most of the time, it's just a feeling you get; you just know someone is a Champion.

We're all sort of . . . drawn to each other. Like magnets continually attracting and repelling each other. Especially those on opposite sites, those who serve opposing gods. For example, it wouldn't surprise me if you one day encountered Loki's Champion, since you serve Nike. The two gods have been fighting for centuries now—and so have their Champions."

Loki had a Champion? Just like Nike did? I hadn't forgotten about seeing the evil god's red, red eyes that night in the Library of Antiquities. That hate-filled stare had haunted my nightmares ever since, even though I knew Loki was locked up where he couldn't hurt me. I doubted the same could be said about his Champion, though.

Determined to think about something else, I stared at the letters on Metis's staff. "What does your weapon say? And why can't I read them?"

Metis smiled. "Only a Champion can see the runes, the message, on her weapon. Mine says: 'In wisdom, there is great strength.' "

Wisdom? My eyes flicked back to the statue on the edge of Metis's desk. Athena was the Greek goddess of wisdom, which meant that Metis had to be her Champion. Daphne had told me that the professor was a Champion, but I hadn't really believed her. I *so* needed to start believing Daphne more.

"But if you're a Champion, why are you here at the academy?" I asked. "Why aren't you out fighting Reapers or something?"

Metis put the staff on the rack with the rest of the

weapons, walked back to her desk, and sat down. "Because my job as a Champion is to be here and watch over the students. To teach them wisdom and everything that they need to know to fight Reapers. And now, I'm here to teach you, Gwen."

She hesitated. "Just the way Grace would have wanted me to."

For a moment, I was stunned. Just . . . *stunned.* Then, my brain kicked back into gear. "Grace? My—my *mom?* What do you know about her? Why would she want you to teach me how to be a Champion?" The questions spilled out of my mouth one after another.

"Your mother and I were friends," Metis said. "Best friends, actually. Back when we went to Mythos."

Professor Metis put her silver glasses back on and picked up a picture frame from the corner of her desk, the one that she'd looked at a few minutes ago. She turned it out so that I could see it. Two people stood in the photo, two girls with their arms slung around each other and wide grins on their faces. One of them was a younger version of Metis, taken when she was about my age.

The other girl in the photo was my mom.

Brown hair, violet eyes, pale skin, wonderful smile. Grace Frost had been beautiful even back then. My mom had hated having her picture taken, so I didn't have many photos of her, especially when she was young. But this one—I knew that this one was something special.

"Can I—can I touch it?" I whispered. "Please?"

Metis slipped the photo out of the frame and held it out to me. Hand trembling, I reached for it. My fingers latched onto the soft, slick edge, and I closed my eyes and let the memories sweep me away.

So many images flickered through my mind, all of my mom and Metis. Laughing, talking, walking across campus together, eating lunch in the dining hall, practicing in the gym, and doing all the other things that Mythos students did. There were other images, other feelings, associated with the photo, too. The complete faith they'd had in each other, the trust between them, all the whispered secrets and heartaches they'd shared. But through it all, Metis and my mom had loved each other— like sisters. That was the emotion I felt the most—love. It was . . . nice to know that someone had cared about my mom just as much as I did. That someone else missed her just as fiercely as I did.

I opened my eyes and swiped away a couple of tears.

"You can keep it, if you want," Metis said in a low voice. "I have another copy."

I nodded, not trusting myself to speak just yet. Instead, I carefully ran my fingers over the photo, feeling the emotions ripple out of it and into me.

We didn't speak for the better part of a minute, but finally Metis cleared her throat.

"Anyway," Professor Metis said. "Your mother and I were friends. She saved my life more times than I can remember, and I plan on doing the same for you, Gwen. To help with that, I've rearranged your schedule a bit.

Now, in addition to your regular gym class, you're also going to be getting private lessons every day from your combat tutor to bring you up to speed on how to use your sword."

Combat tutor? I wasn't sure that I liked the sound of that.

Metis looked toward the frosted glass door. "Come in now, please."

A second later, the knob turned, the door opened, and Logan Quinn stepped inside the office.

"I believe that you and Mr. Quinn already know each other," Metis said. "He seemed to be the most logical choice to be your tutor, given what happened in the library."

I hadn't really talked to Logan since that night. Afterward, he'd gone over to Carson's dorm with Daphne and me, but he hadn't hung out with us, instead saying he was tired and was going back to his own room. I'd looked for him ever since, but I never seemed to spot him in the halls or out on the quad, and he never glanced my way in gym class or came into the library while I was working.

I smiled at Logan, thinking that maybe this wouldn't be so bad after all, but he only gave me an icy stare with his eyes. I frowned. What was that all about? I'd thought we were at least friends now, maybe even something more. I'd certainly hoped so, anyway.

"Logan will work with you every morning before classes start," Metis repeated. "You're to learn every single thing that you can from him, Gwen. Because this is not a joke, and the danger that you are in is very, very real. Do you understand?"

I shivered and nodded. Then, another thought occurred to me. "Um, what about . . ."

I gestured at Vic. It might be kind of hard to learn how to fight with a sword that was alive. And what would I tell Logan about what Vic was and who had given him to me?

Metis looked at the sword, then me. "It's your sword, Gwen. You'll learn how to use it. I'm sure it will behave for you, as my staff does for me. As for everything else, I'll leave that up to you."

Her staff must be a whole lot different from Vic, because I couldn't imagine Vic ever obeying me. But at least she was going to let me tell Logan about the weapon and everything else in my own time, in my own way.

"I think that covers things for now," Professor Metis said. "It's getting late. Go on and enjoy the rest of your day, and remember, you have another essay due next week."

"Yes, Professor," I said.

"Logan, Coach Ajax talked to you about this," Metis said. "You are to work Gwen as hard as you need to in order to train her fast, understand?"

"Yes, ma'am," he said.

"Good. The two of you can go now."

Professor Metis grabbed a stack of papers and started shuffling through them. I slipped the photo of my mom that Metis had given me into my messenger bag, careful not to wrinkle it. Then, Logan and I left her office and walked outside the English-history building. It was after six now, and the quad was deserted except for a few students coming in and out of the dining hall and the Library of Antiquities. Twilight crept across the grass and trees, bathing them in soft shades of purple and gray.

The two of us stood at the edge of the quad, not quite looking at each other. *Awkward.*

"So," I finally said. "You're my combat tutor now?"

Logan nodded.

"Did Metis ask you? Or did she make you?"

I asked because I wanted to know, no, because I *needed* some kind of clue as to how Logan felt about me. Something that would tell me whether he was interested in me or had just been forced into all of this.

"No," Logan said in a quiet voice. "She didn't make me. She, Coach Ajax, and Nickamedes asked me, and I told them yes."

"Why?"

For the first time, Logan looked at me, his mouth curving up into a small, sexy grin. "Somebody's got to watch out for you, Gypsy girl. Trouble seems to follow you wherever you go. We both know that you can't even walk around campus without running into people—literally."

His smile melted some of the ice in his eyes, and for a moment I felt like things had gone back to the way they were before the homecoming dance. That we were back to the teasing sort of flirting that had been going on between us. So I screwed up my courage and did something that I'd been thinking about ever since that night in the library.

"Well, maybe you'd like to talk about it some more. Over . . . coffee or . . . whatever."

Yeah, I was totally asking him out, and he knew it.

But he didn't like it, because Logan immediately stiffened. The warmth in his blue eyes snuffed out, and his mouth tightened. He took a step back and shook his head.

"That's not a good idea, Gwen."

Uh-oh. He'd used my name, which meant he was serious. My heart squeezed in on itself.

"Why not? I . . . like you. A lot. And it seems like you might . . . like me, too?" I winced. The words hadn't sounded so *needy*, so freaking *desperate,* in my head.

For a second, Logan's face softened. "I do like you, Gwen. A lot. I think there's something really special about you."

His features hardened once more. "But there are things that—that you just don't know about me. About Spartans and what we are. Things that you don't want to know. Especially about me. I'm not the guy you think I am. I'm not some sort of hero. Not at all."

Logan got that look in his eyes, that wild, hurt, desperate sort of look that Paige Forrest had had right before I'd picked up her hairbrush. Whatever secrets the Spartan had, they were biggies.

And all that I had to do to find out what they were was reach out and touch him.

Logan was the first boy I'd liked in, well, forever. And he was standing here telling me that, yes, he liked me, too, but that we couldn't even go have coffee together. Much less do anything else. I wanted to know what he was hiding from me, what secret he thought was so terrible that I wouldn't want to be with him.

And I wanted to know right *now*.

It would be so very easy to use my Gypsy gift, my psychometry, on Logan. To grab his hand and see all of his secrets. The temptation to do it was so *strong*.

But then, I thought about Jasmine Ashton and how the Valkyrie had used her powers, her magic, to get what she'd wanted—revenge on her best friend. I remembered what Grandma Frost had told me about the other people like us, other Gypsies. About how some of them used their powers for selfish things. About how some of them were evil.

Slowly, I curled my hands into fists. No. I wouldn't be like that. I wouldn't do that. Not to Logan. Not to someone I cared about. I wouldn't use my gift, the one that Nike had given my family, to force him to reveal his secrets. I was smarter than that now. I was better than that now. I was better than Jasmine and all the other Reapers like her, who only used their powers to hurt others.

So I just stared at him, my feelings for him so obvious in my violet eyes. But Logan just looked away.

"Logan!" a voice called out. "There you are!"

A girl walked across the quad toward us—the same girl Logan had taken to the homecoming dance. The one who'd been pissed that he'd been dancing with me. Daphne had told me that her name was Savannah Warren and that she was an Amazon who lived in Valhalla Hall. I'd asked around and figured out it was her room and her window that Logan had jumped out of the day I'd run into him outside the dorm after I'd swiped Jasmine's laptop.

Savannah gave me a dirty look and slid past me to get to him. Logan put his arm around her. He turned his head, and she stood on her tiptoes and kissed him. Logan pulled Savannah even closer, and she wrapped her arms around his neck. My fisted hands clenched together that much tighter. If the Amazon stuck her tongue any farther down Logan's throat, she was going to poke his brain out of the back of his skull. If there was even anything in there to start with.

After a minute of sucking face, the two of them broke apart. Logan smiled down at her, although his eyes were still cold in his face. Savannah turned and smirked at me, and I felt my heart ice over. So this was how it was going to be. Logan Quinn, man-whore of Mythos Academy, was back in full force, and I was just that Gypsy girl to him again.

"Are you ready, babe?" Savannah asked, putting her head on Logan's shoulder and peering up at him through her long, perfect eyelashes.

"Sure. Let's go," Logan said. "The Gypsy and I were done here anyway."

And then, he turned and walked away with her. He never even looked back at me.

I stood there, feeling like my heart had just been broken without it ever having really been offered up for sacrifice in the first place.

Chapter 26

Later that night, Daphne came over to my dorm room with a pizza in one hand and a six-pack of soda in the other as part of our plans for a serious study session and a total gossip fest. I'd been responsible for dessert, of course, and Grandma Frost had loaded me up with chocolate, peanut butter, and pumpkin fudge when I'd seen her yesterday.

Daphne and I spread the food out on the floor and sat down in front of the TV, which I turned to the latest *Project Runway* marathon, per Daphne's request. While the Valkyrie stared at the fashions on the flickering screen, I opened the pizza box and stopped cold.

"What is *this?*" I asked.

What was inside the box didn't look like a pizza to me. Oh, there was a crust and some mozzarella cheese under there somewhere, but the whole top of the pizza was covered with some sort of exotic meat, a suspicious spicy-smelling white sauce, and steamed vegetables, cut into fancy shapes, of course. My eyes narrowed. Was that wilted spinach? Yucko.

"I got it at the dining hall," Daphne said, digging into the steaming pie and grabbing a slice. "It's a grilled lamb Florentine pizza. It's the latest thing on the menu."

"Whatever happened to plain old cheese and pepperoni? Or ham and pineapple?"

Daphne rolled her eyes. "Pepperoni? That is *so* boring and *so* over." Her black eyes flicked to my clothes. "Just like all those hoodies that you wear. We seriously have to go shopping, Gwen. You totally need some new threads."

I might not have been friends with the Valkyrie long, but I was starting to learn her moods—and that there was no point in arguing with her about my hoodies. So I sighed, grabbed a slice of pizza, and bit into it. Okay, so it was actually kind of good, spinach and all, but I wasn't going to tell Daphne that. At least, not yet.

"So," Daphne said, cracking open a soda with her fingernails and causing pink sparks of magic to fill the air. "I ran into Morgan at the dining hall when I went to get the pizza."

"And how was that?"

Daphne hadn't really had much to do with Morgan and the other Valkyries since she'd gone to the homecoming dance with Carson. We'd been hanging out a lot, though, and were slowly becoming real friends. I liked a lot of things about Daphne. She was cool and funny and a complete nerd when it came to talking about computer stuff. She wasn't at all like the spoiled, selfish Valkyrie princess I'd thought she was that day when I'd first confronted her in the girls' bathroom.

Daphne shrugged. "About what I'd expected. Morgan tried to get me to sit with her and the others. They wanted to know all about my *big date* with Carson. But I knew that if I told Morgan anything, she'd make fun of me behind my back just like Jasmine did."

"I'm sorry."

Daphne shrugged again. "Don't be. I told Morgan exactly what I thought of her and what a ho-bag she was for sleeping with Samson behind Jasmine's back. And then, I gave the other girls all the e-mails that I pulled off Jasmine's laptop, all the ones that Morgan and Jasmine had swapped back and forth, talking about everyone."

I almost choked on my pizza. "You didn't!"

Daphne gave me a wicked grin. "I did. You should have seen their faces. They were all so pissed that they started yelling at Morgan right in the middle of the dining hall. They were all still screaming at her when I left to come over here."

It wasn't the bloody, gruesome revenge that Jasmine had wanted, but I supposed it was something. Maybe now at least the other girls would know what Morgan was really like and they could steer clear of her.

"What about you?" Daphne asked. "Did you meet with Metis like you were supposed to? What did she say?"

I wasn't quite ready to tell Daphne about the goddess Nike picking me to be her Champion, so I glossed over that part. But I told Daphne everything else, including the fact that Metis thought I might be in danger from Jasmine's family since they were all Reapers.

"I've met Jasmine's family," Daphne said. "Metis is right to be worried. Her brother is especially freaky. I always thought he was wound a little too tight, no matter how cute he was."

"Metis didn't tell me that," I said. "But she rearranged my schedule. Now I get to have private lessons with a combat tutor every morning before classes start. Metis wants me to learn how to actually use my sword."

I gestured at Vic, who was in his scabbard and hanging on the wall right next to my Wonder Woman poster.

"Combat tutor?" Daphne asked. "Metis assigned you a tutor? Who?"

"Logan Quinn."

Daphne's black eyes gleamed. "Really? That's *very* interesting."

"It's not going to be like that at all," I said, a bitter tone creeping into my voice. "Logan told me so himself. He pretty much gave me the *I-like-you-but-we-can't-go-out-for-some-stupid-reason* speech. And then, he stuck his tongue down Savannah Warren's throat right in front of me on the quad."

Daphne winced in sympathy.

I hadn't told Daphne how I felt about Logan, but I

was pretty sure that the Valkyrie had guessed. It was probably as obvious to her as her feelings for Carson had been to me.

"I'm sorry, Gwen," she said.

I just shrugged.

We ate in silence for a few minutes, before Daphne steered the conversation back to a safer subject—Carson and how wonderful she thought that he was.

"Did I tell you that he wrote a song for me?" Daphne said in a dreamy tone. "It goes something like this. . . ."

Despite my other problems, I found myself getting caught up in Daphne's story, and soon we were laughing and giggling like we'd been BFFs forever. Once again, that sense of normalcy, of peace, crept over me. Gossiping with a friend over pizza. I couldn't think of a better way to spend the night.

Sure, there was still a lot of stuff going on. A goddess had given me a sword and declared me to be her Champion, and Jasmine's family and the rest of the Reaper bad guys wanted to do some pretty nasty things to me. I'd just told the boy I liked that I actually, well, *liked* him, and before going off with another girl he'd told me that we couldn't be together

My eyes went to my mom's photo, which was on my desk right under Vic's spot on the wall. I planned to get a frame for the picture of her and Metis and put it there as well. Maybe it was my imagination, but it seemed like my mom was always smiling right at me whenever I looked at her picture now. Like she could see me from wherever she was or something. Maybe she could.

Mythos Academy was a place of magic after all, where legends were real and anything could happen.

And I'd finally figured out something else, too. That the people you loved never really died, not as long as you kept your memories of them alive, not as long as they lived on in your heart. And my mom would always be in mine.

Daphne snapped her fingers in front of my eyes. "Earth to Gwen!"

"What? What did you say?"

She gestured at the pizza box in between us. One single slice lay inside. "I asked you if you wanted the last piece of pizza."

I looked at her, then at my mom's picture again and Vic and the rest of my cozy little dorm room. Finally, my eyes landed on the small statue of Nike that I'd bought from the campus bookstore. The winged figure of the goddess of victory sat on my desk, right next to my mom's photo.

As I stared at the statue, Nike's eyes suddenly snapped open, just like Vic's had done to me that first night in the library. They were the same color as Vic's eye, the same color as the goddess's eyes had been when I'd seen her, the same color as my eyes. A beautiful mix of purple and gray that always made me think of twilight.

As I watched, mouth hanging open, one of the eyes slowly lowered and went back up again. Was she . . . winking at me? I blinked, and the figure's eyes were closed just like they had been before.

But for once, the sight didn't freak me out. Instead, I felt like I'd earned the goddess's approval, like I'd achieved some sort of . . . peace or something. Some sort of victory. At least for tonight.

"Gwen?" Daphne asked again. "Are you okay?"

"Tell you what," I said, looking at my friend. "Why don't we split the last piece?"

Daphne smiled. "Works for me."

"Me too."

So we did.

BEYOND THE STORY

A Clash of Inspirations

I blame *Clash of the Titans* for this book. When I was a kid, it seemed like every time we had a movie day at school we would watch one of two films—*The Princess Bride* (inconceivable!) or, you guessed it, *Clash of the Titans* (the old Harry Hamlin version, not the new one with Sam Worthington).

Ideas for books don't always come to me overnight. Sometimes, it seems like they are years in the making. I think this is the case with *Touch of Frost* and the Mythos Academy series. It all started with movie day. I remember thinking how cool the movie made mythology seem. But more than that, I thought it was interesting how all these gods, goddesses, humans, and monsters interacted with each other.

Over the years, I read various mythology-based works, including *The Iliad* and *The Odyssey,* among others. Mostly, I read these stories for class assignments, but I enjoyed them all the same. Well, most of them, anyway. Some are better than others. But it always amazed me just how many different stories and different versions of those stories were out there.

And my interest in mythology didn't stop there. I read more stories and watched more movies and more TV shows.

Many years later, I watched my first episode of *Xena: Warrior Princess*. I was immediately hooked. Here were fun (and admittedly campy) stories about gods, goddesses, and the ultimate kick-ass warrior chick who could hold her own against all of them. How cool was that?

And then came the movie *300*, which was just a loud, brash, bloody, violent, visual spectacle. I enjoyed the entertaining story about warriors bravely battling on even in the face of impossible odds.

Somewhere along the way, in the back of my mind, I thought that it would be cool to someday write my own mythology-based story and put my own spin on things with my own characters, magic, and more.

I don't remember the exact day that the lightbulb went off inside my head. I had been thinking about writing a young adult book for a while, but I was struggling to come up with a concept. Then I thought what if I had a smart, plucky, slightly snarky heroine and put her in a world full of ancient warriors and magic that she didn't really believe in? What if there was an evil god who was trying to take over the world? What if my heroine was the key to stopping this evil god? What if she was stronger and more of a warrior than she ever thought she could be?

The idea just snowballed from there until it finally became *Touch of Frost* and the basis for the Mythos Academy series—magic, myth, and monsters. I hope that everyone has as much fun reading the book as I did writing it—and that the gods don't take too much offense at my reimagining of them. Happy reading!

Gwen's Class Schedule

First period: English lit. I love books—really, I do—but would it kill the professor to let us read some freaking comic books or graphic novels every once in a while? Seriously, they're so much more fun than all this so-called classic literature that I'm stuck reading all the time.

Second period: Calculus. I'm good at calculus, but I totally do not see the point of it. All those x's and y's are all hypothetical anyway, right?

Third period: Geography and world politics. The geography is interesting, but the world politics part is a total snooze. Besides, everyone knows that politicians lie.

Lunch break: A miserable hour where I get to eat by myself in the back of the dining hall while everyone else hangs out with their friends. Oh, goodie.

Fourth period: Chemistry. Meh. I'm totally ambivalent about chemistry.

Fifth period: Gym, aka weapons training. I hate gym class. Hate it, hate it, *hate it*. Why can't I just be book smart? I have a 4.0 GPA. Why do I have to be coordinated, too? That's just too much to ask.

Sixth period: Myth-history. Professor Metis is pretty cool, but it cracks me up that she and the other kids actually *believe* all this stuff about gods, goddesses, mythological monsters, and Reapers of Chaos. It's not history, and it's certainly not real. Uh, is it?

After-school detour: Yeah, I'll admit it. I sneak off campus every chance I get, hop on a bus, and go see my Grandma Frost, who lives close to the academy. What are the Powers That Were at the academy going to do— expel me?

After-school job: I have to hustle from my Grandma Frost's house back to the academy so I can work at the Library of Antiquities a few days a week. Boring. But the worst part is Nickamedes, who actually thinks that all the dusty pieces of junk in the glass cases are real artifacts—that they actually have *magic* attached to them. Whatever, dude. I think you've been stuck in the library a little too long. Although there's this sword that I just can't seem to stay away from. . . .

Gwen's First Report on Select Gods and Goddesses for Professor Metis's Myth-History Class Dated October 1

So I'm supposed to write this report on some of the various gods and goddesses we'll be learning about during the semester. Note that I am writing this in protest, Professor Metis, as you know that I don't really believe in all this magic mumbo jumbo. But since I want to keep my perfect 4.0 GPA intact, here goes:

Nike: the Greek goddess of victory. Nike was responsible for leading the other members of the Pantheon—the good magic guys—to victory over Loki and his Reapers of Chaos way back in the day. Since Nike is the embodiment of victory, she can never be defeated, not even by a superbad guy like Loki. Never losing? Ever? Sounds like a pretty cool gig to me.

Athena: the Greek goddess of wisdom. She and Nike are rumored to be pretty tight. I can see why, since victory and wisdom usually go hand in hand.

Loki: the Norse god of chaos. Loki started out as a simple trickster, but over time his power-hungry nature got the best of him and he started planning to take over the world. He would have succeeded, too, if not for Nike and the other members of the Pantheon banding together to lay the smackdown on him and his evil followers, the

Reapers of Chaos. The other gods have imprisoned Loki twice now, but he doesn't seem to me like the kind of guy who's ever going to give up. . . .

Sigyn: the Norse goddess of . . . well, I'm not sure exactly what she's the goddess of. Some of my myth-history books say she's the goddess of devotion. Kind of a lame thing to be a goddess of, if you ask me. Anyway, Loki's wife loved him so much that when the other gods imprisoned him the first time around she held a bowl—the Bowl of Tears—up over his head in order to stop snake venom from dripping onto his handsome face. Kind of dumb, if you ask me, staying with a guy who's basically a comic book supervillain. Sigyn *so* needs to move on.

Addendum to First Report
Added at Request of Student
Dated October 30

Ignore previous report. Well, at least the snarky comments. Okay, okay, ignore pretty much the whole report. And I, uh, take back what I said before about none of the gods and goddesses being real. I've got a talking magic sword named Vic that says otherwise.

Plus, it's kind of hard not to believe in gods and goddesses after you've come face-to-face with one—especially Nike, the Greek goddess of victory, who's the ultimate kick-ass warrior chick.

And you learn that Nike's the reason that you have

magic in the first place. That the goddess gifted your first ancestor with magic way back in the day.

And you learn that pretty much every girl in your whole family since then has served Nike in some way over the years.

And most especially when Nike picks you to be her new Champion. Seriously, me, a freaking *Champion*. I don't really think that I'm Champion material at all, but Nike seems to think otherwise for whatever reason. The goddess has plans for me. Big plans. I'm just not quite sure what they are—or how much danger they'll put me in. . . .

Read on for a peek at the
magic, myths, and monsters
Gwen will face in

KISS OF FROST,

coming in December.

Chapter 1

Logan Quinn was trying to kill me.

The Spartan relentlessly pursued me, cutting me off every single time I tried to duck around him and run away.

Swipe-swipe-swipe.

Logan swung his sword at me over and over again, the shining silver blade inching a little closer to my throat every single time. His muscles rippled underneath his tight long-sleeved T-shirt as he smoothly moved from one attack position to the next. A smile tugged up his lips, and his ice blue eyes practically glowed with the thrill of battle.

I did not glow with the thrill of battle. Cringe, yes. Glow, no.

Clang-clang-clang.

I brought up my own sword, trying to fend off Logan before he separated my head from my shoulders. Three times, I parried his blows, wincing whenever his sword hit mine, but the last time I wasn't quite quick enough. Logan stepped forward, the edge of his sword a whisper away from kissing my throat before I could do much more than blink and wonder how it had gotten there to start with.

And Logan didn't stop there. He snapped his free wrist to one side and knocked my weapon out of my hand, sending it flying across the gym. My sword somersaulted several times in the air before landing point down in one of the thick mats that covered the gym floor.

"Dead again, Gypsy girl," Logan said in a soft voice. "That makes twelve kills in a row now."

I sighed. "I know. Believe me, I know. And I'm not any happier about it than you are."

Logan nodded, dropped the sword from my throat, and stepped back. Then, he turned and looked over his shoulder at two other Spartan guys who were sprawled across the bleachers, alternately texting on their phones and watching us with bored disinterest.

"Time?" Logan asked.

Kenzie Tanaka hit a button on his phone. "Forty-five seconds. Up from thirty-five seconds the time before."

"Gwen's lasting a little longer at least," Oliver Hector chimed in. "Must be the Wonder Woman T-shirt finally adding to her awesome fighting skills."

My face flushed at his snide tone. Okay, so *maybe* I had worn my favorite long-sleeved superhero shirt this morning in hopes that it might bring me a little luck, which I seriously needed when it came to any kind of fight. But he didn't have to mock me about it, especially not in front of the others.

Oliver grinned and smirked at me. I crossed my arms over my chest and gave him a dirty look.

I didn't know what Oliver's deal was, but he always seemed to go out of his way to annoy me. Maybe he thought he was being charming or something. Some guys at Mythos Academy were like that—they thought being total jerks was supercool. Whatever. I had zero interest in the Spartan that way. Oh, Oliver was cute enough with his dirty blond hair, forest green eyes, tan skin, and lazy grin. So was Kenzie, with his glossy black hair and eyes. Not to mention the obvious muscles the two of them had and the lean strength that was so evident in their bodies. The only problem was that the two Spartans weren't Logan Quinn.

Logan was the one I was interested in—even if he had already broken my heart back in the fall.

Thinking about my stupid, hopeless, unreturned feelings for Logan soured my already grumpy mood, and I stalked across the mats toward my sword.

The gym at Mythos Academy was about five times the size of a regular one, with a ceiling that soared several hundred feet above my head. In some ways, it was completely normal. Bright banners proclaiming various academy championships in fencing, archery, swimming, and other froufrou sports dangled from the rafters, while wooden bleachers jutted out from two of the walls. Mats covered the floor, hiding the squeaky parquet basketball court from sight.

And then there were the weapons.

Racks and racks of them were stacked against another wall, going up so high there was a ladder attached to one side to get to the weapons on the top rows. Swords, daggers, staffs, spears, bows, quivers full of curved, wicked-looking arrows. All of them razor sharp and ready to be picked up and used by the students, most of whom took exceptional pride in showing off their prowess with the sharp, pointed edges.

The weapons were one of the ways in which Mythos Academy was anything *but* normal.

I reached my sword, which was still wobbling back and forth, reminding me of my old piano teacher's metronome slowly ticking from side to side. I reached down, but before I could tug the sword out of the mat a round silver bulge on the hilt snapped open—revealing a narrowed, angry eye.

"Another bloody defeat," Vic muttered, his displeasure giving even more bite to his British accent. "Gwen Frost, you couldn't kill a Reaper to save your bloody life."

I narrowed my own eyes and glared at Vic, hoping he would get the message to *shut up already* before Logan and the others heard him. I didn't want to advertise the fact that I had a talking sword. I didn't want to advertise a lot of things about myself. Not at Mythos.

For his part, Vic glared right back at me, his eye a curious color that was somewhere between purple and gray. Vic wasn't alive, not exactly, but I'd come to think of him as that way. Vic was a simple enough sword—a long blade made out of silver metal. But what made the sword seem, well, human to me was the fact that the hilt was shaped like half of a man's face—like there was a real person trapped there inside the metal who was trying to get out. A slash of a mouth, a groove of a nose, a round bulge of an eye, the curve of an ear. All that added up to Vic, whatever or whoever he really was.

Well, that and his bloodthirsty attitude. Vic wanted to kill things—Reapers, specifically. *Until we're both bathed in their blood and hungry for more!* he'd crowed to me on more than one occasion when I was alone in my dorm room practicing with him.

Please. The only things I could kill with ease were bugs. And even then only the tiny ones. The big ones crunched too much and made me feel all icked out and guilty. Doing the same to Reapers of Chaos, some seriously bad guys, was *totally* out of the question. Not unless I got doused in radioactive goo and developed superpowers or something, like Karma Girl, one of my favorite superheroines.

"What are you going to do when a real Reaper attacks you?" Vic demanded. "Run away and hope he doesn't chase after you?"

Actually, that sounded like an excellent plan to me, but I knew Vic wouldn't see it that way. Neither would Logan, Kenzie, or Oliver, since the guys were all Spartans, descended from a long line of magical mythological warriors. Killing things was as natural as breathing to them. It was what they'd been trained to do since birth, along with the other kids at the academy.

For the most part, the guys at Mythos were either Vikings or Romans, while the girls were Valkyries or Amazons. But tons of other ancient warrior types attended the academy, everyone from Samurais and Ninjas to Celts and Persians to the Spartans in front of me.

Killing was definitely *not* natural to me, but I'd been thrust into this twisted world back at the beginning of the school year. That's when I'd first started attending Mythos, after a serious freak-out with my Gypsy magic back at my old public high school. Now, the academy with all its warrior whiz kids, scary Reaper bad guys, mythological monsters, and an angry, vengeful god was a place that I just couldn't escape—no matter how much I would have liked to.

Especially since there was a goddess counting on me to do something about all the Bad, Bad Things out there in the world—and the ones hidden here on campus, too.

"Shut up, Vic," I growled, tugging the sword free of the mat.

I felt Vic's mouth move underneath my palm like he was going to backtalk me some more, but then he let out a loud *harrumph* and his eye snapped shut. I sighed again. Now he was in one of his *moods,* which meant I was going to have to cajole him to open his eye and speak to me again later in the day. Maybe I'd turn on the TV in my dorm room and see if there was some kind of action-adventure movie on. Watching the bad guys get theirs always seemed to bring Vic out of one of his funks, and the bloodier the movie was the better he liked it.

"Who are you talking to, Gwen?"

Oliver Hector's voice sounded right beside me, and I had to clamp my lips together to keep from shrieking in surprise. I hadn't heard the Spartan sneak up on me.

"Nobody."

He gave me a look that said he thought I was a complete freak, then shook his head. "Come on. Logan wants you to practice shooting targets next."

I looked around, but Logan had disappeared while I'd been talking to Vic. So had Kenzie Tanaka. They'd probably gone to get an energy drink out of one of the vending machines outside the gym, leaving me alone with Oliver. Great.

Even grumpier than before, I stalked behind Oliver over to the other side of the gym, where an archery target had been set up. The Spartan headed for one of the weapons racks, while I kept going toward the bleachers.

The four of us had dumped our bags on the bleachers when we'd first come into the gym at seven this morning. I'd only been going to Mythos a few months, and I hadn't had the lifelong warrior training that the other students had. Now, I was struggling to catch up, which meant schlepping over to the gym every single morning for an hour's worth of work with Logan and his friends before my regular classes started.

Out of all the kids at the academy, the Spartans were the best warriors, and Professor Metis had thought they could whip me into shape in no time flat. It wasn't working out that way, though. I just wasn't warrior material, no matter what some people—goddess included—thought.

I slid Vic into his black leather scabbard and laid him flat on one of the bleachers so he wouldn't fall off. I'd already dropped the sword enough times this morning. Then, I reached into my gray messenger bag for a mirror and brush so I could pull my hair back into a tighter, neater ponytail, since it had come undone while I'd been sparring with Logan.

I squinted at my reflection in the smooth glass. Wavy brown hair, winter white skin dotted here and there with a few freckles, and eyes that were a strange shade of purple. *Violet eyes are smiling eyes,* my mom had always said. I thought of how easily Logan had kicked my ass while we'd been training. Nope, I wasn't smiling about anything this morning.

When I was done fixing my hair, I put the mirror and brush back into my bag and threw it onto the bleachers. In the process, my bag hit Oliver's and knocked his to the floor, because I was just that kind of total uncoordinated klutz. And of course, the top of his bag popped open and all kinds of stuff spilled out, tumbling over the mats. Pens, pencils, books, his iPod, a laptop, some silver throwing daggers.

Sighing, I got down on my knees and started scooping everything back into the bag, careful to use the edge of my sleeve and not actually touch anything with my bare fingers. I had no desire to see into the inner workings of Oliver Hector's mind, but that's what would happen if I wasn't careful.

I managed to get everything back into the bag except for a thick red notebook. A couple of the metal rings had been bent out of shape, and they snagged on the fabric every time I tried to slide the notebook back into the bag where it belonged. I just didn't have a long enough sleeve to bend all the metal down, and I couldn't get a good grip with the soft cotton anyway. Exasperated, I took hold of the metal with my sleeve so I wouldn't scrape my skin, then grabbed the bottom of the notebook with my bare hand.

The images hit me the second my fingers touched the red cover.

A picture of Oliver popped into my head, one of the Spartan leaning over the desk in his dorm room and writing in the notebook. One by one, the images flashed by, giving me a condensed high-def version of Oliver alternately doodling, drawing, and scribbling furiously in the notebook. After a few seconds, the feelings kicked in and I started experiencing Oliver's emotions, too. All the things he'd felt when he'd been writing in his notebook. The dull boredom of doing class assignments, the annoyed frustration of trying to understand some of the complicated homework, and then, surprisingly, a soft, dreamy fizz that warmed my whole body—

"What are you doing? That's mine," Oliver snapped in a harsh voice.

I shook off the images and feelings and looked up.

The Spartan stood over me, his features tight and pinched.

"Sorry," I snapped back. "I didn't think a guy like you would be so protective of his notebook. What's in here that's so supersecret? A list of everyone you've slept with? Let me guess. You don't want me to know who you've been hooking up with. You want to tell everyone yourself because that's what all the guys at Mythos do— brag about their stupid conquests, right?"

Oliver's face actually paled at my words. Seriously. He just went white with shock. For a second, I wondered why, but then I realized he must have heard about my psychometry—about my magic.

I wasn't a warrior like the other kids at Mythos, not exactly, but I wasn't completely without skills either. I was a Gypsy, a person gifted with magic by one of the gods. In my case, that magic was psychometry, or the ability to touch an object and immediately know, see, and feel its history.

My Gypsy gift, my psychometry, was actually cooler—and a little scarier—than it sounded. Not only could I see who had once worn a bracelet or read a book, no matter how long ago it had been, but I also could feel that person's emotions. Everything she'd been thinking, feeling, and experiencing when she'd been wearing that bracelet or reading that book. Sometimes, everything she'd ever felt, seen, or done over a whole lifetime, if her attachment to the object was strong enough. I could tell if a person had been happy or sad, good or bad, smart or dumb, or a thousand other things.

My magic let me know people's secrets—let me see and feel all the things they kept hidden from others and even from themselves sometimes. All their conflicting emotions, all the sly things they'd done, all the things they only dreamed about doing in the deepest, blackest parts of their hearts.

Maybe it was dark and twisted of me, but I liked knowing other people's secrets. I liked the power that the knowledge gave me, especially since I didn't have any of the wicked cool fighting skills the other kids at Mythos did. Knowing other people's secrets was sort of an obsession of mine—one that had almost led to me getting killed a few weeks ago.

It was also the reason I held on to Oliver's notebook now. I'd totally expected the boredom and the frustration I'd sensed. Those were both emotions I'd felt many times before when I'd touched other kids' notebooks, computers, pens, and all the other ordinary everyday objects they used to help them do their schoolwork.

But that warm, soft, fizzy feeling? Not so much. I knew what it was, though—love. Or at least like—*serious* like. Oliver Hector had a major, major crush on someone, enough to write about that person in his notebook, and I wanted to know who it was.